Renewing His Hope

Wings of Faith Series Book 1: An Inspirational Love Story

Barbara Jane Oliver

Synergistic Connections, LLC

Paperback ISBN: 978-1-968938-00-0

E-Book ISBN: 978-1-968938-01-7

Beta Reader: Kate Marie at Beta Reader Bookings, LLC

Proofreading: Brandy Patton at WordWiser Ink Editing Lab

Book Cover: Miblart Book Cover Design

First Edition 2025

Visit the **Author's Website** at https://barbarajaneoliver.com/

Published by Synergistic Connections, LLC

Also By Barbara Jane Oliver

<u>WINGS OF FAITH SERIES</u>

- Before the Blessing: A Bristol Heights Novella (Colton & Nicole): Download FREE When You Subscribe to My Newsletter

- Renewing His Hope Book 1: Daniel & Samantha: Available Now

- Soaring in Faith Book 2: Aaron & Meghan: Available 23 February 2026

- Running with Grace Book 3: Brandon & Grace: Available 25 May 2026

<u>BRISTOL HEIGHTS SANCTUARY SERIES</u>

- Sanctuary in His Arms Book 1: Joshua & Simone: TBA

- Sanctuary of Truth Book 2: TBA

Dedication

I dedicate this book to my Lord and Savior, Jesus Christ. Thank You for giving me life, breath, and your everlasting love. You are always with me, walking beside me and guiding me through all the pathways of my life. I am eternally grateful. It's all for Your Glory! Amen!

Inspirational Scripture for Wings of Faith Series of Books

Isaiah 40:31: But those who hope in the Lord will renew their strength. They will soar on wings like eagles; they will run and not grow weary, they will walk and not be faint.

Acknowledgements

I WOULD LIKE TO express my heartfelt gratitude to my husband, Ronald. I appreciate your unwavering support, strength, and love. Thank you for consistently being present in my life. I hold you in the highest regard. Furthermore, I extend my appreciation to my daughter, Erica, for enlightening me on the existence of living miracles. You genuinely fill me with cheer! Additionally, I wish to thank my parents, Mom and Dad, as well as my brother, Willie Jr. There are no greater cheerleaders in this world than you. I cherish each of you deeply!

To Page and Michele, my Mastermind sisters! Thank you for showing up faithfully every Monday on Zoom, for cheering me on, and for sharing your wisdom so generously. Your encouragement, honesty, and support have been such a gift on this author journey. I'm deeply grateful to walk this path with you both.

I extend my sincerest gratitude to Beta Reader Bookings, LLC for your insightful and thoughtful feedback on this narrative. Additionally, I express my appreciation to WordWiser Ink Copy Editing Lab for your meticulous attention and dedication to clarity. Both of you have offered candid reflections, and your diligence in detail has significantly enhanced the quality of this book.

Contents

Renewing His Hope

Wings of Faith Series Book 1: An Inspirational Love Story

Barbara Jane Oliver

Synergistic Connections, LLC

Prologue

The scent of damp earth filled Daniel's lungs as he stood alone by Teresa's grave. The cemetery had emptied an hour ago, mourners drifting away with whispered condolences he barely registered. Only his sister's hand on his shoulder penetrated the fog of his grief.

"Daniel, I'm so sorry," Miranda said, her voice breaking. "I'll miss Teresa so much. Please let me know if there's anything I can do."

"Thank you, Mandy." The words scraped his throat raw. "I appreciate you being here for her. For us." The word *'us'* nearly broke him. There was no *'us'* anymore.

Now, with Miranda gone, Daniel stared at the fresh mound of soil covering the woman who had been his wife for eight precious years. His fingers curled around the funeral program, creasing the image of Teresa's smiling face. Only weeks earlier, they had envisioned their future home and family. Now, she was gone, taken by an aneurysm no one had detected.

All this had happened during the time he was teaching his tenth-grade English class. He had come home to find her peaceful but still, as if she were napping. The doctors said it had been quick. A small comfort that felt like no comfort at all.

The wind rustled through the maple trees, sending a shower of red and gold leaves spiraling down around him. October had been Teresa's favorite month. *"See how everything changes?"* she would marvel, her eyes shining. *"God's showing off for us."*

The memory sent a surge of rage through Daniel's chest. He tilted his face toward the heavy clouds gathering overhead.

"Why?" The word came out in a strangled whisper at first, but it swelled, cracking in his throat as he tilted his face toward the heavens. "Why did You take her from me?"

A gusty wind swept through the graveyard, rattling the leafless branches, offering no solace. There was only the profound emptiness surrounding him.

His fingers curled into fists, his nails biting into his palms. "You promised to watch over us! You swore You would protect us!" His voice rose, raw and jagged, each word splintering inside him like glass. "And this is what You do?"

Silence.

The kind that wasn't just quiet. It was an absence, a void where God was supposed to be.

"I trusted You," he whispered. His knees buckled, the damp earth seeping through his slacks as he collapsed beside the headstone. "I believed every promise about working all things for good.

But what good can come from this? You're supposed to be a loving Father. What kind of father abandons his children?"

A drop of rain landed on the back of Daniel's hand, followed by another. He should have taken it as a sign and as some reminder of God's presence. But to Daniel, it felt like a mockery.

He pressed a trembling hand against Teresa's name, tracing each carved letter with the reverence of a prayer he no longer believed in. "If this is Your idea of love, then I want no part of it."

The first rain began to fall in earnest as Daniel pushed himself to his feet. His body felt foreign, stiff, and awkward as he walked toward his car. Each step took him further from Teresa and the faith they had shared. Behind him, raindrops darkened the soil of her grave, each one like a tear from the heaven that he no longer believed in.

Chapter 1

Two Years Later

"Sam, can you discharge the patient in room 12? The paperwork's done. They just need their discharge instructions," Dr. Brandon Lawson said as he approached.

Samantha looked up from the computer where she had been documenting a patient's assessment. At thirty-five, she had a decade of emergency medicine experience under her belt, and took pride in staying sharp under pressure.

"No problem at all, Dr. Lawson," she replied brightly. "I will be there in two minutes."

Dr. Lawson smiled in return, nodding his head in acknowledgment. He had worked for seven years at Lakeside Community Hospital's emergency department, developing a reputation for providing effective and empathetic care. Samantha appreciated how he treated everyone with kindness, knowing that such traits were essential for anyone pursuing a vocation in healthcare.

Samantha Kelly had found her calling in the ER, thriving in the unpredictable rhythm of emergency medicine. She had started in the medical and surgical areas before transitioning to the ER, where the fast pace and critical care felt like home.

After gaining valuable experience caring for patients admitted to inpatient treatment, Samantha sought to expand her skills into another area of nursing. With the help of her nurse manager, she transferred to the emergency department. It was an immediate fit, and the transition was seamless.

At the nursing station, Samantha grabbed the chart for room 12. Eight-year-old Timothy Morgan had taken a nasty fall while playing tag, leaving him with a deep knee gash. His mother, Constance, had rushed him in, panicked by the bleeding.

Timothy was an active, spirited young boy. He preferred running and frolicking outside with his friends more than he enjoyed playing indoors.

Hours prior, while playing tag with the neighborhood children, Timothy slipped and fell, causing a deep, alarming cut on his knee that bled extensively. Unable to stop the bleeding, his mother rushed her son to the hospital for care.

Fortunately, Timothy's injury did not require stitches. After Dr. Lawson assessed him and determined that cleaning the wound and providing pain relief were sufficient, Samantha took the necessary steps to prepare for his treatment with efficiency and gentleness.

Before stepping inside, she whispered, "Lord, please give me the right words to comfort this child." These quiet prayers had always kept her grounded.

Samantha worked quickly. Whenever the cleaning solution stung, she distracted Timothy with questions about his favorite superhero.

"You're doing great, Timothy," she encouraged when he winced, but didn't pull away. "You're much braver than some adults I've treated."

His mother, who had been holding his hand throughout the procedure, gave Samantha a grateful look. The unspoken communication between them needed no words.

After receiving permission from his mother, Samantha delighted the young boy by presenting him with a colorful sticker. When Timothy saw that the sticker was in the image of his favorite superhero, he broke into a wide smile.

With Samantha's help, he proudly placed his Superman sticker on his shirt, right over his heart. Samantha and Mrs. Morgan stifled amusement at the sight, knowing that Timothy would likely wear it for the rest of the day and show it off to all his friends as a badge of honor.

Finally, with everything prepared, Samantha walked across the exam room and gently pulled back the curtain. Timothy and Mrs. Morgan immediately looked toward her.

"Can I go home now, Ms. Kelly?" Timothy bounced on the exam table. "I feel better! I promise to be extra careful next time...and I won't fall!"

Samantha exchanged a glance with Mrs. Morgan before kneeling at eye level with the little boy. She made sure she had Timothy's complete attention before responding.

"Yes, Timothy, you are all patched up and ready to go home. But first, I'm going to go over your pain medication and the treatment for your wound with you and your mom." Samantha knew she wasn't only providing medical care. She was also instilling confidence and hope in a young patient eager to return to his adventures.

Timothy took a long gulp of air, preparing to speak, but Samantha raised her finger, signaling she wasn't finished explaining. "You need to listen carefully," she continued, her tone firm yet warm. "That way, both you and your mother can make sure your healing process goes smoothly."

Samantha kept her expression composed and open. In her experience, engaging children of his age to be active participants in their care often instilled a sense of responsibility and control over what could be a daunting situation.

Timothy nodded solemnly. "I'll do everything you tell me to do, Ms. Kelly. And Mom will do it too, right?" He peered at his mother, his face lit with eager anticipation. It was a look children embody when they seek the love and approval of their parents.

Mrs. Morgan replied with a gentle smile and a soft voice. "Yes, Timothy. You and I will follow Dr. Lawson's and Ms. Kelly's instructions so your knee will get all better." She adoringly stroked the top of her son's head.

Samantha loved seeing when it was time for patients and families to go home. She found joy in observing the mother-son relationship and was grateful to be a small part of their lives.

"Just remember to change the bandages and call us if you have any concerns," she reassured Mrs. Morgan, using clear and straightforward instructions.

Mrs. Morgan listened attentively, expressing gratitude as she met Samantha's gaze. "Thank you so much for your help." Appreciation filled her voice. Reinvigorated, Timothy hopped down from the examination table and gave Samantha a tight hug around her waist.

"Thank you for taking good care of me, Ms. Kelly," he exclaimed in a way that only eight-year-old boys can. "And I really appreciate the sticker you gave me. It's awesome!"

"You're welcome, Timothy," Samantha graciously responded. This time, she gave a joyful smile without hesitation. "All I want is for you to get better and stay safe."

"I will," Timothy replied, already striding toward the emergency room exit doors. "Bye, Ms. Kelly!" he called over his shoulder.

Samantha laughed, warmth spreading through her chest. "Goodbye, Mrs. Morgan and Timothy! Take care and enjoy the sticker!"

Beaming, Timothy held his mother's hand as they walked away. A sense of purpose filled Samantha as she straightened her scrubs. This was where she belonged. Serving, healing, and striving to make a difference.

Chapter 2

"DON'T FORGET THAT YOUR five-paragraph essay on *The Scarlet Letter*'s moral themes is due on Monday!" Daniel Forrester called over the ringing of the school bell.

At forty, Daniel barely noticed the scrape of chairs and the rustle of backpacks anymore. The noise was routine, a familiar background to his otherwise empty evenings.

November sunlight streamed through the windows, warming the polished floor. Outside, maple trees burned red and gold against the sky. Once, Daniel would have pointed them out to his students as inspiration for their poetry assignments. Now, he barely registered the beauty beyond noting the changing season.

As the teenagers streamed toward the door, their minds already shifting to their next class, Daniel stood at his desk, a pillar of calm amid the organized chaos. Teaching these bright young minds about classical literature had become more than a job. It was the one area of his life that still made sense, the only place where purpose hadn't abandoned him.

"Mr. Forrester!" Patrick Mills, a spirited fifteen-year-old with an engaging personality, leaned over the desk, his trademark grin in place. "Any chance we can push the essay to next Friday? It might boost your chances of winning Teacher of the Year when voting comes around in the spring."

Two years ago, Daniel might have laughed and shared the moment with Teresa over dinner. Now, only a faint smile appeared. In the wake of his wife's death, teaching had become both an anchor and an escape. Only then did the burden of sorrow lighten, however momentarily.

"While I appreciate you stepping up as the advocate for your classmates," Daniel replied, his tone measured but kind as he adjusted the stacks of papers on his desk, "I must inform you that the deadline remains unchanged."

Patrick nodded good-naturedly, his disappointment evident but not crushing. "I felt it was my duty to my peers in AP English to give it a try."

As he turned to leave, Daniel caught the slight droop in the boy's shoulders. Something in that small gesture of defeat stirred Daniel's empathy, breaking through the protective numbness he had cultivated.

"Patrick," Daniel called, surprising himself. The student turned back, eyebrows raised in question. "Your analysis of Dimmesdale's character last week was excellent. It'll be interesting to see how you develop those ideas in your essay."

Patrick's face brightened, a genuine smile replacing his earlier calculated charm. "Really? Thanks, Mr. Forrester! I've been thinking about his public versus private identity and how that relates to social media today."

"That's exactly the kind of comparison I'm looking for," Daniel encouraged, a professional satisfaction warming him. It was a pale echo of the joy teaching once brought him, but real, nonetheless.

As Patrick hurried out to join his friends, Daniel sank into his chair, suddenly aware of the energy it took to engage with his students' enthusiasm. Every morning, he put on this persona of a competent teacher and attentive mentor. Yet, beneath this exterior, the emptiness yawned wider. By the day's end, the effort of maintaining this facade left him drained.

He reached for the stack of grammar quizzes, wincing at the twinge in his shoulders. Coach Michaels had asked him to help with football practice tomorrow, and his body was already protesting after yesterday's drills with the defensive line. But the routine of coaching, like teaching, kept him tethered to some semblance of normalcy. The physical exhaustion sometimes helped him sleep, though nothing seemed to quiet his restless mind entirely.

As the hallway buzzed with laughter, Daniel's gaze fell on the day's whiteboard quote: *We dream in our waking moments, and walk in our sleep.* Nathaniel Hawthorne's words now seemed to mock him. Hadn't he been doing just that? Sleepwalking through his life since Teresa?

The final bell rang. Daniel packed his bag, the weight of the day settling over him. There was a time when Teresa would surprise him with coffee, sitting in his classroom while he graded papers. Sometimes, she would bring cookies for his students, who adored her almost as much as he did.

Now, the quiet wasn't peaceful. It was just an absence of sounds and a silence that stretched all the way home.

In the teacher's lounge, he poured a cup of stale coffee from the pot that had likely been sitting there since morning. The harsh fluorescent lighting emphasized the room's dated decor. There were motivational posters that were faded from years of exposure, vinyl chairs with small tears patched by duct tape, and a refrigerator that hummed loudly enough to occasionally interrupt conversations. Despite its shabbiness, the lounge was a sanctuary for the faculty, a place where they could shed the professional veneer required in front of their students.

Daniel barely registered the bitter taste of the brew as he took a sip. Miss Ashworth, a mathematics teacher with a perpetually neat bun and colorful scarves, waved from across the room where she sat with a group of other faculty members. Their animated conversation paused as they noticed him.

"Daniel, we're heading to The Sweet Tea Tavern. Would you like to join us?" Her invitation was warm and genuine.

He mustered a polite smile, already shaking his head before she finished speaking. "Thanks, but I've got papers to grade."

Though valid, it was the same excuse he had used countless times. The stack of essays in his bag would indeed consume his evening. In the first months after Teresa's death, his colleagues had persisted, constantly inviting him to gatherings and check-in coffee dates. Gradually, they learned to accept his refusals with understanding nods and kind smiles, their concern evident but respectfully contained.

Only Stanley Michaels, the head football coach and his closest friend at the school, continued to push past Daniel's carefully constructed walls. As if summoned by the thought, Stanley appeared in the doorway, his broad frame filling the space. Even in his late forties, Stanley maintained the athletic build of his college football days, though his dark hair had begun to gray at the temples.

"There you are." Stanley crossed to the coffee machine. "Are we still on for practice tomorrow?"

Daniel nodded, relieved by the straightforward question that required no emotional excavation. "Of course. The team's looking good for Friday's game."

Stanley studied him for a moment, concern etching lines around his eyes. Daniel braced himself for another well-intentioned attempt to draw him out of his self-imposed isolation.

"Daniel, some of us are grabbing a bite at The Sweet Tea Tavern. Why don't you—"

"I appreciate it," Daniel cut him off gently. "But, like I already told the others, I need to get home." The thought of forced small talk and sympathetic glances across a table made his chest tighten.

Stanley's expression softened. "One of these days, I'll wear you down, my friend." He clapped Daniel on the shoulder, his grip firm and reassuring. "Get some rest. Those boys are going to run us ragged tomorrow."

Daniel managed a genuine smile this time. Stanley had been there through the darkest days, sitting silently beside him when words failed, never pushing too hard but never giving up either. There was a steadiness to the man that Daniel had come to rely on, even if he couldn't reciprocate the friendship as he once had.

As Daniel walked to his car, autumn leaves crunched beneath his feet, a sound that had once delighted him. The early November afternoon held that perfect crispness that he and Teresa used to cherish. They would take long walks on days like this, hand in hand, watching the world transform into a canvas of reds and golds. Teresa would collect the most vibrant leaves, pressing them between the pages of her Bible—small treasures that marked the seasons of their life together.

"Beautiful day, isn't it, Mr. Forrester?" Mrs. Jennings, the school librarian, called from the adjacent parking space as she loaded books into her trunk. Her silver hair gleamed in the sunlight, and her kind eyes crinkled at the corners.

"Yes, it is," he replied automatically, even though he hadn't really noticed until she mentioned it. The realization brought a pang of shame. How many beautiful days had he missed while lost in the fog of grief?

Once inside his car, Daniel sat for a moment, hands resting on the steering wheel. He should be grateful. He had a job he loved, students who respected him, and colleagues who cared. So why did gratitude feel so far beyond his reach? Why did each day feel like an uphill climb, as if the summit never got any closer?

A church flyer tucked into his sun visor caught his eye. It was an announcement for the fall festival at New Hope Baptist Church, where he and Teresa had been active members. Miranda, his sister, had left it on his windshield last Sunday. It was another gentle attempt to draw him back to the community that had once been central to his life. The bold **EVERYONE WELCOME** seemed to emphasize his absence, a reminder of another part of himself he had left behind.

Daniel tucked the flyer into the glove compartment without reading it. There had been a time when he found solace in the church, and his faith had sustained him through life's challenges. But now, prayers felt like empty words echoing in a void. Where was God when Teresa collapsed that day? Where was the divine comfort that was supposed to ease this unbearable ache?

The drive home was a blur of familiar streets and automatic turns. Daniel pulled into his driveway, staring at the house that once held so much promise. The two-story Colonial with its wide front porch and blue shutters had been Teresa's dream home. They had chosen it together, planning for a future filled with children's laughter and decades of memories. Now, it stood as a monument to all they had lost—all *he* had lost.

Now, he dreaded the quiet that awaited him inside. Every evening followed the same pattern. Grade papers, eat something that required minimal preparation, maybe watch the news, and finally, when exhaustion overcame restlessness, attempt to sleep. The nights were the hardest. He lay in the dark, too aware of the empty space beside him as memories flooded back just as sleep began to claim him.

Daniel grabbed his briefcase and headed inside, pausing to collect the mail that included bills, advertisements, and a handwritten letter from his mother. He tucked the note into his pocket, knowing it would contain loving words of encouragement he wasn't ready to read. His parents' unwavering faith had once been his foundation. Now, it felt like a language he no longer spoke or understood.

Once inside, he moved through the evening routine with mechanical precision. Papers were spread across the dining table, and his red pen was ready to mark thoughtful comments and suggestions on his student's schoolwork. A microwaved dinner was eaten without tasting, and the television's murmur provided background noise, filling the silence that threatened to swallow him whole.

Night pressed against the windows as Daniel stood before the bookshelf, his gaze locked on Teresa's photo.

Her smile hadn't changed. It was still full of light and untouched by the weight of time.

He reached out, fingertips grazing the cool glass. "I miss you," he whispered. The words felt small against the silence.

Daniel turned away, unable to bear the intensity of his grief. Night had fully settled, and with it came a familiar restlessness. He used to find peace in prayer and quiet moments of reflection. Now, he longed only for sleep and those brief hours of oblivion before dawn broke and he had to face another day without her.

Tomorrow, he would return to Greater Pines High School. He would teach his students about Hawthorne and Emerson. He would help Coach Michaels prepare the team for Friday's game. He would smile, nod, and answer questions, moving through the day like a man walking underwater, with everything slightly distorted —the sounds muffled, and his movements requiring extraordinary effort.

But tonight, in the solitude of his home, Daniel Forrester allowed himself to acknowledge the truth he had hidden from everyone else. He was a man who once found meaning in faith, hope, and love, but now, he felt only emptiness where his heart should be.

Chapter 3

Samantha drove down Brookside's tree-lined streets, mentally ticking through her endless to-do list. With each item she marked off, new errands sprouted in their place, multiplying like stubborn weeds in an untended garden.

The late autumn air carried an unexpected warmth for November, and she rolled down her window to let the breeze tug at the loose strands of her hair. Brookside, situated about 100 miles southwest of Atlanta, had been her home since her father's death. She had been thirteen when she and her mother relocated here, their lives forever altered.

The substantial life insurance policy had provided financial security, but money couldn't fill the void left by her father's absence. It could never replace his empty chair at the dinner table, the silence where his booming laugh used to fill their home, or the way she missed him saying, *"good night, princess,"* as part of their evening ritual. These were the real losses that no amount of funding could ever replace.

Her mother, Irene Kelly, desperate to escape the frenetic pace of city life, had hoped Brookside's tranquility would heal their wounded hearts. She envisioned a fresh start where the change of scenery might help them adapt to their new reality.

For Samantha, adjusting to these seismic shifts had been overwhelming. Adolescence, with its already tumultuous emotions, tangled miserably with her grief. Starting eighth grade at a different school had left her feeling adrift and battered by the winds of change and loss.

Each day had brought new challenges, all compounded by the ache of losing her father. Yet even amid turmoil, Samantha recognized a quiet thread of gratitude. Her parents had instilled in her a deep-seated faith in Christ Jesus, who was a guiding light through her dark times.

With biblical teachings woven into the fabric of her being, Samantha consistently turned to the Lord whenever uncertainty loomed. In times when despair threatened to consume her, she found reassurance in knowing she had a divine Protector and Provider. This sacred connection enabled her to cast her fears and heartaches upon Him, ensuring she never experienced abandonment, even in her loneliest moments.

"Lord, thank You for seeing me through that time," she whispered. Samantha had developed a habit of talking to God throughout her day. These were not performative prayers with flowery language, but honest conversations as natural as breathing.

Tragedy struck again during Samantha's junior year at Brookside State University. She could still hear Patricia Harris, her mother's close friend, on the phone: *Come quickly! Your mother has collapsed at the grocery store!*

Samantha had raced to the ER, but by the time she arrived, her mother was gone. The loss hollowed her out, leaving an emptiness she couldn't begin to understand. In that heartbreaking moment, her world shattered.

Suddenly, Samantha faced a life completely alone at twenty-one. She had to plan a funeral and also decide whether to continue her nursing studies, which were set to resume mere weeks after burying her mother. The weight of sorrow had left her spirit utterly defeated and lost in a fog of grief and uncertainty.

Samantha discovered her mother's Bible while going through her belongings. Its pages were creased, and the margins filled with handwritten prayers.

She traced her mother's notes, absorbing the faith that had carried them both. *Lord, help me hold on to this.*

With renewed purpose, Samantha returned to the university, her heart brimming with motivation. Each day became a testament to her hard work and dedication. Her faithfulness paid off as she excelled in her classes, earning high praise from her professors, who recognized her commitment and tenacity.

On graduation day, Samantha imagined her parents were in the audience, their faces beaming with pride as she walked across the stage to receive her nursing degree. Those bittersweet memories became sacred treasures she held close to her heart.

But presently, the carefree days of college were behind her, replaced by an ever-growing, mountain-sized to-do list. That morning's rushed breakfast of toast and orange juice left her stomach growling in protest. She needed real food.

She patted her stomach and chuckled. "Okay, okay, I got the message. It's time to take a break and feed both of us."

Glancing at her watch, she saw it was 1:20 p.m. She could still make it to Heavenly Delights Diner, a cozy little spot known for serving breakfast and lunch until two o'clock. She pictured indulging in her favorite panini sandwich, perfectly toasted with melted cheese, fresh vegetables, and Willow's *"crafted by angels"* secret sauce. She could also grab a fresh salad for dinner later.

Although Thanksgiving was a few weeks away, today bore all the hallmarks of a beautiful spring day. Each breath of fresh air filled her with a sense of renewal. She reveled in this time of year, eagerly expectant of the changes that the seasons would bring.

After ten minutes of cruising the paved streets, Samantha finally parked in front of Heavenly Delights, its pastel-colored façade inviting her inside. She gathered her purse from the passenger seat, stepped out of the car, and locked the doors. As she approached the entrance, the enticing aromas of freshly brewed coffee, spicy cinnamon, and baked bread enveloped her, beckoning her to come inside.

The moment she crossed the threshold, comfort filled her. Behind the counter stood Willow, the diner's vibrant proprietor. The warmth of her smile was like sunshine on a cold day.

"Sam! I was wondering when you'd show up," she called, her voice full of welcome. "How have you been?"

Willow Barnes, no more than a few years older than Samantha, had a remarkable knack for making everyone who walked through the diner's doors feel like family. Their friendship blossomed over many visits. One afternoon, Samantha wandered in after a grueling hospital shift, craving a much-needed pick-me-up. Willow suggested an exquisite caramel-vanilla latte, topped with a cloud of hazelnut-flavored whipped cream that had bewitched Samantha from that first sip.

Since then, she had become a regular. The friendship she developed with Willow transcended the boundaries of casual acquaintances. Shared laughter, heartfelt conversations, and a mutual appreciation for good food and friendship solidified their bond.

Samantha's eyes lit up. "Oh, that panini is going to make my day so much better!" she declared. Willow's laughter chimed gently as she reacted to her friend's dramatic enthusiasm.

"I can't believe I've been out all day and completely forgot to eat. My stomach certainly let me know it was time for a break!" They exchanged knowing smiles that shared an understanding of life's little challenges.

"Not a problem! I'll whip you up a grilled eggplant and smoked mozzarella cheese panini right away, exactly the way you love it! Are you going to eat it here at the diner, or should I wrap it up for you to enjoy later?" Willow's voice brimmed with warmth as she sauntered to the sizzling grill in her homestyle kitchen.

The kitchen, adorned with colorful spices and the scent of fresh ingredients, was a second home to Willow. The enticing smell of melting cheese hung in the air as she quickly and skillfully prepared the sandwich.

"Do you mind if I sit here and enjoy my lunch? I'm starving! I might inhale it to get it into my system faster." Samantha's eyes were wide with hunger as she glanced longingly at her sizzling panini coming to life. She leaned into her best pleading expression, hoping to evoke sympathy. "Oh, and I was also hoping you could make me your famous chicken and pecan salad to take home. That would be perfect for my dinner tonight!"

Willow let out a hearty laugh. "You're quite the character! Of course, you can eat at the counter. I'll be closing the doors in about ten minutes, so you're welcome to stay while Anna and I finish cleaning up and closing everything down. Honestly, I'm glad to have the company." There was genuine affection in Willow's voice, which made Samantha feel at ease.

At that hour, only a handful of patrons lingered, leisurely finishing their meals. Since the quaint establishment served breakfast and lunch, Willow hired a few extra employees to support her through mealtime rushes. She had sent the other staff home and worked with her newest hire, Anna Parks, to close the diner.

Samantha settled into her frequent spot at the counter, her stomach rumbling in anticipation. When the panini finally arrived, she inhaled the mouthwatering scent that wafted up—smoky, rich, and filled with the promise of tantalizing flavor. Without hesitating, she grasped the sandwich and took her first bite. The delicious combination of textures and tastes sent delight rushing through her.

She lifted her eyes to Willow with gratitude. "Thank you so much for this. I think you just saved my life!" Willow laughed heartily as Samantha relished every bite. She returned to attend to the remaining customers as they satisfied themselves with their meals.

"So," Willow said, returning to wipe the counter beside Samantha. "I haven't seen Olivia lately. How is she doing at the veterinary clinic?"

Samantha smiled at the mention of her closest friend. "She's doing great. They just promoted her to head veterinary technician last month, and she's been working extra shifts to get settled into the role. The animals adore her. There's this three-legged Labrador that won't let anyone else take his blood samples."

"That sounds exactly like our Olivia. She always had a way with souls who can't speak for themselves, whether they're furry or feathered."

Samantha nodded. Five years ago, when her world had crumbled after discovering her ex-boyfriend's devastating betrayal, it had been Olivia who helped her gather the fragments of her broken heart. Their connection, forged through shared faith and understanding, had been a lifeline during those dark days.

Willow continued, her voice dropping conspiratorially. "The other day, I had a gentleman in here who couldn't stop talking about the *angel of a nurse* who helped his mother in the ER last week. From his description, I'm pretty sure he was talking about you."

Heat rushed to Samantha's cheeks. "I was just doing my job."

"That's what makes you special, Sam. Your *just doing my job'* is most people's above and beyond." Willow's eyes softened with genuine affection. "You deserve someone who recognizes that... someone who'll nurture your spirit the way you nurture others."

The eight years of singleness since her break-up with Paul had taught Samantha much about herself and what she truly needed in a relationship. The painful lesson of being unequally yoked had been seared into her heart, making her cautious about opening herself to romantic possibilities again.

Her work at the hospital, friendships with Olivia and Willow, and her faith community had filled her life with purpose and connection. If God intended to bring someone special into her life, she trusted His timing would be perfect.

"If it's meant to be, the Lord will make it happen," Samantha said, echoing the wisdom her mother had often shared. "Until then, I'm grateful for the blessings I already have, including this extraordinary sandwich and good friends like you and Olivia."

Half an hour later, Samantha left the diner feeling full and satisfied. She clutched her purse in one hand while the other held the takeout container. The coveted salad Willow had prepared was securely sealed inside.

With a smile of contentment playing on her lips, Samantha unlocked her car door and slid into the seat, ready to embark on the next leg of her day. Renewed with energy and determination, she steered her vehicle down the street toward her upcoming errands, confident she could conquer any task.

Chapter 4

Samantha hurried through patient charts as her fingers moved instinctively over the keyboard. The antiseptic scent of the ER barely registered anymore, but today, the beeping monitors and overhead pages seemed more grating than usual.

"Are you heading out, Sam?" Dr. Lawson leaned against the nurses' station, exhaustion etched into his face.

Samantha nodded, clicking save. "Yes. I just finished my last chart. That shift was brutal."

"I can't believe we had three cardiac arrests," Brandon shook his head. "And that burn case with the little boy... "

"But he's stable," Samantha reminded him with a tired smile. "And seeing his parents' relief when you told them he'd be okay... that's what makes it all worthwhile."

Brandon exhaled, rubbing his neck. "True. You always find the bright side, huh?"

Samantha didn't miss the hint of wistfulness in his tone. Over the years, they shared several conversations about her beliefs, but Brandon remained firmly skeptical. She said a quick, silent prayer for him, as she often did for her colleagues.

"It gets me through the hard days," she replied, gathering her belongings. "Speaking of which, I just found out I've got tomorrow off. Melissa needed to swap shifts."

"Lucky you. Any big plans for your surprise day off?"

"Actually... I'm making my mom's pasta sauce," Samantha said. "It's been years."

Brandon nodded. "Sounds like a good plan. Try and get some rest, Sam."

Walking to her car, she could almost hear her father's laugh and smell the basil and oregano simmering in her mother's sauce. Some memories never faded.

"I miss you both so much," she whispered, sliding into her car.

Samantha allowed herself exactly thirty seconds to sit with the grief before taking a deep breath and turning the key in the ignition. Her therapist had suggested this technique years ago. The rumble of her sedan's engine provided a comforting rhythm as she pulled out of the hospital parking lot.

The sky blushed pink and gold as Samantha drove toward Grocery Haven Super Market, humming along to the worship song on the radio. After today's shift, the reminder of God's presence was a comfort.

She mentally checked her list. She needed San Marzano tomatoes, fresh basil, and her mother's favorite olive oil. This sauce had to be perfect.

When her phone chimed with a text notification from Olivia, she waited until she was stopped at a red light to glance at it.

Still on for breakfast and studying at Heavenly Delights on Friday? Need to talk about the church retreat planning.

Samantha smiled. Her weekly Bible study breakfasts with Olivia were an anchor in her sometimes chaotic schedule. She texted back when the light turned green.

Absolutely! Can't wait. Need my Willow fix too!

Pulling into the Grocery Haven parking lot, Samantha found herself searching for a specific spot—third row, about midway down—where she always tried to park. Her mother had been superstitious about parking spots, claiming that finding *"your spot"* open was a sign of good luck for the day. Samantha was skeptical of luck, yet the belief lingered, a subtle tribute to her mother.

Today, her spot was taken. She shrugged it off and found another space, gathering her reusable bags from the passenger seat. As she entered the store, the cool air and bright fluorescent lighting greeted her, along with the familiar layout she had navigated countless times before.

Her canvas tote swung against her hip as she moved through the evening crowd, methodically filling her basket with items from her mental list. She lingered in the produce section, carefully selecting tomatoes for her salad as her mother had taught, checking for weight and firmness. Her mother's voice echoed in her memory:

A good tomato feels like it's full of life, Sam. Heavy for its size, with a little give when you press gently.

The memory brought both comfort and a fresh pang of loneliness. Most of her friends from nursing school had married and started families. Even Olivia had been dating a veterinarian from her clinic for the past few months. Meanwhile, Samantha's last relationship had ended disastrously with her ex-boyfriend's betrayal, leaving wounds that had taken years to heal.

"Lord," she prayed quietly as she bagged her carefully selected tomatoes. "I know Your timing is perfect. If marriage is in Your plan for me, I trust You'll bring the right person at the right time. And if not, I know Your path for me is still good."

The prayer calmed her, as it always did. Her bond with God had been her rock since childhood, especially after losing her parents and then weathering infidelity in her previous relationship. Where human relationships had sometimes failed her, her faith remained steadfast.

As she reached the pasta aisle, an inexplicable nudge made her turn down the refrigerated section instead.

That's when she saw him. A tall man, standing frozen in front of the display, staring so hard at the shelves she half-expected them to crack.

His lost expression tugged at her heart. As a nurse, she recognized that look. Patients and their families frequently wore it when confronted with overwhelming situations. Despite her natural reserve with strangers, especially men, Samantha was drawn forward.

"Excuse me. You look like a deer caught in the headlights. Do you need some help?"

The man turned toward her, and Samantha felt an unexpected flutter of awareness at the intensity in his dark eyes. Beneath the initial irritation that flashed across his face, she glimpsed a human fragility that aligned with her own experiences—vulnerability, perhaps even a hint of grief.

"I was wondering," she tentatively suggested, her nursing instincts taking over. "When I saw you standing here, you reminded me of some of the patients in the hospital where I work. They know they're there for a valid reason, but that doesn't stop them from wanting to escape before seeing a doctor."

When he didn't respond, heat crept into her cheeks. Perhaps she had overstepped.

She hesitated. "Sorry... I didn't mean to overstep. Good luck finding what you need."

As she turned away, his voice stopped her.

"Wait. I wasn't trying to be rude. I'm just a little... distracted."

Samantha turned back, surprised by the half-smile tugging at his otherwise serious face.

"I would appreciate your help if you're still willing to offer it," he added, his eyes searching hers with a plea that was hard to resist.

Their gazes connected, and everything else seemed to stand still. He stood an impressive six feet, two inches, towering over her five-foot-six frame. But instead of feeling intimidated, Samantha felt strangely at ease.

"I could really use a hand," he continued, gesturing vaguely at the shelves. "I'm usually quite capable when it comes to grocery shopping, but not today. I'm trying to be a good brother to my sister. She's asked me to bring her a specific item from here that I've never bought before."

His eyes darted around the aisle, and a sheepish chuckle escaped him. "Honestly, I think all the options are making me a bit dizzy," he confessed, a wry smile softening his worried expression. "I just want to make sure I get it right for her."

Samantha's professional demeanor softened, melting into a moment of candid openness. There was an undeniable charm in watching this tall, handsome man. He seemed determined to fulfill his sister's request and navigate the grocery aisles, though it clearly pushed him out of his comfort zone.

"What are you looking for?"

He handed her his phone. "Smoked salmon salad. There are so many options, and I have no idea which one she meant."

Samantha glanced at the text message, then at the refrigerated display. Sure enough, there were at least six different types of smoked salmon salad, varying in spice levels and ingredients.

"Let me guess... she didn't specify which kind?" Samantha asked with a sympathetic smile.

"Exactly." He ran a hand through his short locs. "And now I'm overthinking it."

Samantha laughed, the sound bubbling up naturally. "I think I have a solution," she said, pointing to the display. "Why don't you choose the one you think tastes good? That way, if she doesn't like it, at least you'll be able to enjoy it."

His face brightened at the simple suggestion. "That's... brilliant. Why didn't I think of that?"

Their eyes met again. This time, his smile reached his eyes, crinkling the corners and revealing a warmth that hadn't been there before. A wave of long-forgotten excitement fluttered in Samantha's chest. It was a sensation she hadn't felt in years, at least not since before her ex-boyfriend's betrayal.

Stop it, she scolded herself. *You don't even know this man.*

But as he reached for a container of spicy smoked salmon salad, his arm brushing against hers, she couldn't deny the spark of connection between them.

"Thank you." He placed the container in his cart. "I'm Daniel, by the way. Daniel Forrester."

He extended his hand, and Samantha noticed he wasn't wearing a wedding ring. The observation caught her off guard. Why had she even looked?

"You know, you did that all wrong. That was *not* the way you were supposed to say it."

His hand froze mid-air, as if he was shocked into silence.

"What you were supposed to say was, 'My name is Forrester... Daniel Forrester.' That's the way James Bond does it in the movies." She mimicked a British accent, her eyes dancing with mischief.

"Anyway, my name is Samantha... Samantha Kelly," she replied, placing her hand in his. "But you can call me Sam."

His handshake was warm and friendly. "Thank you for saving me from a slow death from my own indecision, Sam."

The sound of her name, as he spoke it, sent another tiny tremor through her. Pulling her hand back, Samantha was surprised by her reaction to the stranger.

"I'm glad I could help." She adjusted her tote bag. "I should probably get back to my shopping. I hope your sister enjoys the salad."

Although Daniel nodded, she saw a fleeting look of disappointment on his face. "Of course. Thank you again."

Samantha turned to leave but then paused. She glanced back over her shoulder.

"If you need help finding anything else, I'll be in the produce section," she offered, surprising herself with the invitation.

His smile widened. "I'll keep that in mind."

Samantha continued her shopping, but her thoughts kept drifting back to Daniel. It had been so long since she felt that immediate connection with someone. After her ex, she had thrown herself into her work and her faith, convinced that romance wasn't in God's plan for her.

Lord, what was that? she prayed silently as she examined the basil, checking for wilted leaves. *I'm not even looking to meet someone.*

As if in answer, a verse from Proverbs floated through her mind: *Trust in the Lord with all your heart and lean not on your own understanding; in all your ways submit to him, and he will make your paths straight.*

Samantha placed the basil in her basket, a small smile playing on her lips. Whatever that interaction had been, whether the start of a promising connection or just a brief encounter, she would trust God's plan. After all, He had never failed her before, even in her lowest moments.

As she made her way to the checkout line, she scanned the store, hoping for another glimpse of the mysterious Daniel Forrester. But he seemed to have vanished.

"That's probably for the best," she murmured to herself as she placed her groceries on the conveyor belt.

Still, as she drove home with her carefully selected ingredients, Samantha couldn't help wondering if their paths might cross again. The unexpected flutter in her chest returned at the thought, and she found herself humming along to the radio once more. This time, it was to a love song she hadn't paid attention to in years.

Chapter 5

Daniel scowled at the fluorescent lights glaring down from Grocery Haven's high ceilings. The Friday night crowd jostled around him, only adding to his irritation.

He had planned to spend the evening grading essays and unwinding with a book and a cup of tea, not wandering aimlessly through the supermarket.

Daniel tightened his grip on his phone, recalling his sister's last-minute request. Her husband was stuck at work late, leaving her scrambling for dinner. His brother-in-law, Noah, worked for a major real estate brokerage firm, and erratic hours often meant that personal plans had to be rearranged at a moment's notice.

As part of his job, he was required to be available whenever it suited prospective home buyers, which sometimes left Miranda improvising dinners or making last-minute arrangements.

Unable to say no to his little sister's pleading, Daniel found himself adrift in the supermarket's chaotic aisles, surrounded by cereal boxes and frozen foods.

Finding smoked salmon salad shouldn't have been this hard. Shoppers breezed past, grabbing items while he stood frozen, scanning shelves in vain.

"Why does this place seem like a maze?" he muttered, gripping the shopping cart handle to rein in his fraying patience.

His jaw clenched as he scanned the refrigerated section for the third time, his exasperation mounting. He had never been this unproductive during a grocery run, but tonight, he was out of his element, as if navigating a labyrinth that twisted and turned at every corner.

Daniel paused, gathering himself, but it was to no avail. He reminded himself that tomorrow, he needed to help Stanley fine-tune the athletes for their highly anticipated game scheduled for Friday night.

The team's recent victory against their longstanding rivals had electrified the players, generating excitement and energy he was eager to harness. Daniel enjoyed these moments with the squad, remembering his own high school football days. The camaraderie of the teammates brought to mind simpler times when friendships made everything effortless.

For all the inconvenience, Daniel didn't object to doing this favor for Miranda. He was grateful she lived in the same town, which allowed him to be there for her when she needed his support and vice versa.

He pushed through the narrow aisles, aware of the market's chaos. He concentrated on finding a container of smoked salmon salad, which Miranda insisted she was craving. Her passing comment about wanting that particular dish spurred him to provide it for her, despite its being just one meal.

He glanced to his left and right. Unlike him, the other customers appeared resolute and on task. Their determination shone through in their brisk, confident strides as they maneuvered their full carts, reaching for items with familiarity and ease.

Grocery shopping was typically not a chore for Daniel, yet tonight it was an uphill battle. Overwhelmed by the chatter and hustle surrounding him, he incurred an uncharacteristic sense of disorientation. He was like a fish out of water, struggling to find its place. Annoyance simmered, and he struggled to contain his growing irritation at his failure to locate the elusive salad. The eruption of his frustration was inevitable.

He was ready to give up and tell his sister to order takeout when a lilting voice broke through his frustration.

"Excuse me. You look like a deer caught in the headlights. Do you need some help?"

Daniel turned, caught off guard. The woman before him wore royal blue scrubs that hugged her curves in a way that was both professional and effortlessly flattering. Her dark brown hair, half-pinned up, framed a face full of warmth.

But it was her eyes, golden brown, intelligent, and kind, that truly held him captive.

For an inexplicable moment, the constant weight he carried since Teresa's death seemed to lift slightly, like a momentary reprieve from gravity.

"I was wondering," she ventured gently. "When I saw you standing here, you reminded me of some of the patients in the hospital where I work. They know they're there for a valid reason, but that doesn't stop them from wanting to escape before seeing a doctor."

Her analogy struck him as oddly perceptive. He did want to escape. Not just from this store but from the endless cycle of grief and anger that had defined his existence for the past two years. He fumbled for words, aware that his silence might come across as rudeness. He had spent so long avoiding meaningful interactions with strangers that his social skills were rusty and inadequate.

When she apologized and stepped away, Daniel realized he had put his foot in his mouth without speaking. The feeling of a kindred spirit made him want to rectify the situation and not let this brief connection slip away.

"I would appreciate your help if you're still willing to offer it," he added, surprised by his own openness.

Their gazes locked, and for a moment, the bustling supermarket faded into background noise. He noticed the gentle curve of her cheeks and the fullness of her lips as they moved into a smile. There was a quiet confidence in her stance that spoke of someone comfortable in her own skin. Daniel couldn't remember the last time he had been so immediately drawn to someone, and the realization thrilled and unsettled him.

After introducing themselves, Samantha led the way to the refrigerated display case, and Daniel found himself noticing details he had no business observing. The confident sway of her hips, the effortless grace with which she moved through the crowded aisles, the way her royal blue scrubs hugged her curves—it was distracting in a way he hadn't felt in years.

He told himself it was a simple observation, nothing more. But when she gestured toward the selection of salads, he caught the delicate movement of her wrist and her long, graceful fingers. There was something steadying about her presence, as if she thrived in moments of decision-making.

He forced himself to focus on the words coming out of her mouth, but the problem was, he liked the way she spoke. Her voice had a warmth that settled inside him, unfamiliar but strangely welcome.

This is nothing, he told himself. *Just a conversation with a kind stranger.*

Her solution to his dilemma was brilliantly simple. Choose a salmon salad that he would enjoy himself, creating a win-win situation regardless of his sister's preference. The clarity of her thinking cut through his indecision, and Daniel found himself selecting a container of spicy smoked salmon salad with newfound decisiveness.

"I'm glad I could help," she said. "I should probably get back to my shopping. I hope your sister enjoys the salad."

Daniel nodded, feeling an unexpected wave of disappointment. "Of course. Thank you again."

As Samantha turned to leave, she paused and glanced back over her shoulder, giving him a view of her profile that momentarily stole his breath. The gentle slope of her neck and the way the light caught her golden-brown skin made it appear to glow from within.

"If you need help finding anything else, I'll be in the produce section," she offered with a smile that reached her tawny eyes, transforming her already beautiful face into radiance.

His own smile widened in response. "I'll keep that in mind."

As she strolled away, Daniel remained rooted to the spot, watching her retreating figure. His eyes were mesmerized by the gentle sway of her hips, and the confident set of her shoulders. All of it held his attention far longer than it should have. Her presence lingered, making the store seem dimmer in her absence. He replayed their spirited exchange like a favorite song stuck on repeat.

Daniel remembered how her eyes crinkled when she laughed, and how her clever James Bond joke had transformed his frustration into amusement. Her voice had a gentle authority and a determination that spoke of someone accustomed to helping others through difficult moments.

With effort, he suppressed the smile that threatened to overtake his face and headed toward the checkout. He had responsibilities waiting. He had essays to grade, football practice to help with tomorrow, and a meeting with Principal Jeremy Watkins on Monday about class curriculum changes. This was the life he had carefully constructed since Teresa's passing, leaving little room for new connections, no matter how intriguing or attractive.

Yet as he drove toward Miranda's house, Samantha Kelly's image persisted in his mind. He couldn't stop thinking about her voluptuous form, her radiant skin tone, and the mesmerizing golden-brown eyes that seemed to pierce his carefully constructed walls. At each traffic light, he recalled the subtle floral scent that surrounded her when she leaned close to examine the salmon salad options, the musical quality of her laugh, and the brush of her hand against his as she pointed out her recommendation.

"Focus," he muttered, gripping the steering wheel tighter. Tomorrow would be busy enough without daydreaming about a chance encounter with a kind, beautiful stranger. He needed to deliver Miranda's salad, then return to his empty house where stacks of ungraded papers awaited his attention.

His fingers tapped a restless beat against the wheel. The whisper of temptation to circle back to the produce section had been strong, but he resisted. For two years, he had avoided anything resembling attraction, unwilling to betray Teresa's memory or risk the pain of loss again. He had learned the hard way that God's promises of protection meant nothing—that faith was a hollow comfort when faced with devastating grief.

Yet, for the first time in two years, *focusing'* on his routine felt insufficient. A change happened during that short interaction with Samantha. He had built walls around his heart, but a crack appeared, revealing a missing piece of light. The discovery filled him with a mixture of terror and exhilaration.

Daniel reached for the radio, turning up the volume to drown out his thoughts. But even the pounding bass couldn't silence the quiet voice inside that whispered: *What if she's not just a chance encounter? What if there's a reason your paths crossed tonight?*

He shook his head, dismissing the thought. He had given up believing in divine timing or heavenly intervention long ago. Still, as he pulled into Miranda's driveway, he couldn't help but wonder if he might see the beautiful Samantha Kelly again, and what it might mean if he did.

Chapter 6

The autumn air stung Daniel's cheeks as he paced the sidelines. Leaves scattered across the field, but his focus stayed on the players clashing in drills. Beside him, Coach Stanley Michaels watched with a critical eye as both men evaluated the strengths and weaknesses of the team in real time.

The thump of colliding helmets was punctuated by the thuds of bodies hitting the turf with a force that echoed the spirit of competition. Grunts of exertion mingled with shouts, forming a familiar symphony that stirred a forgotten sense of camaraderie within Daniel. His voice joined Stanley's as they called out instructions, their commands slicing through the controlled chaos of practice.

"Thompson! Watch your left side!" Daniel barked. "You're leaving yourself vulnerable!"

"Miller, tighten that formation!" Stanley added. "Hanson, give him some support!"

The players adjusted their stances and drove forward again, sweat glistening on their faces. Their determination was evident in every play.

Daniel felt a surge of pride watching these young men push themselves. Their efforts were pure, untarnished by the complexities and disappointments of adult life. For a moment, he envied the simplicity and uncomplicated joy of being part of a team working toward a common goal.

"Jenkins, that's the hustle I've been looking for!" Daniel shouted as a lanky sophomore successfully intercepted a pass. The boy's face lit up with a grin that could have powered the stadium lights.

After two hours of practice, Stanley blew the whistle. The players jogged over, some dropping to their knees. Their helmets were pushed back as they waited for feedback.

Stanley paced before them, the crunch of damp grass under his cleats interrupting the attentive silence that had fallen over the teenagers. He delivered his final notes, his words a mixture of praise and constructive criticism. The players, eager for affirmation, sprang to their feet and thrust their arms toward the circle's center.

"On three, we say, 'Go Team!'" Stanley boomed, his voice carrying across the empty bleachers. "One! Two! Three!"

"GO TEAM!" Their collective shouts vibrated in the autumn air, binding them together in a moment of unity. Laughter and friendly jabs followed as the athletes retrieved their gear and thundered toward the locker room. Lively chatter floated across the field, with conversations about weekend plans, upcoming movies, and pending homework assignments.

As they left, Daniel flashed back to his high school years. In those days, the rules were clear, and his future spread before him like an open road.

But his thoughts weren't on lesson plans or the adjourned football practice. They were on Samantha.

"You okay, Daniel?" Stanley asked as he fell into step beside him. "You seemed somewhere else today. Is everything all right?"

The question shouldn't have surprised him. After three years of them coaching together, Stanley had developed an uncanny ability to read his moods. Feeling tension in his neck, Daniel massaged the area with his hand.

"I'm fine, Stanley. At least, I think I am." He was uncertain how to explain the strange effect a brief interaction with a stranger had on him. "I met someone last night while I was at the grocery store." His shoes scuffed against the grass-streaked turf, leaving green stains on the worn leather. "She helped me find something, and we talked for a few minutes, that's all."

Stanley waited, letting the silence stretch.

"She was... kind. Beautiful," Daniel admitted, shaking his head. "And I can't stop thinking about her. It feels wrong... like I'm somehow betraying Teresa."

He exhaled sharply, rubbing his jaw. But no matter how hard he tried, Samantha's smile wouldn't leave him.

"It was just a five-minute conversation about salmon salad, for heaven's sake," Daniel muttered, more to himself than to Stanley. "Why can't I shake it?"

Stopping abruptly, Stanley turned to Daniel, his face serious and questioning. "Let me make sure I understand," he began kindly. "You met an attractive, compassionate woman who showed kindness toward you. You had a pleasant conversation that brightened your day. And now you're beating yourself up for having a natural reaction to that connection?"

Heat flooded Daniel's cheeks, rising to his ears with embarrassment. Laid out like that, it sounded ridiculous. But the guilt continued to churn in his stomach.

"Teresa meant everything to me." His voice was barely audible above the distant sounds of traffic. "We had eight incredible years together, and it wasn't nearly enough. Sometimes, I still reach for her when I first wake up, forgetting that she's not beside me anymore."

A cloud passed overhead, momentarily dimming the sunshine. In that brief shadow, Daniel could almost feel Teresa's presence. He recalled the gentle weight of her hand in his and the scent of her perfume. Even the sound of her laugh, which used to make his heart skip a beat, seemed to echo in his memory.

Stanley stepped closer, compassion softening his features. The lines around his eyes deepened as he regarded Daniel. "Listen, experiencing attraction or even companionship won't diminish what you had with Teresa. Having feelings for another woman doesn't betray her memory."

"Doesn't it?" Daniel's fingers tightened on his collar, his knuckles going taut. Behind his closed eyelids, memories of Teresa's laugh warred with the stranger's gentle smile. "It feels like I'm trying to replace her."

"Daniel," Stanley answered firmly, his voice resonating with conviction. "No one could ever replace Teresa. She was unique, and so was your love for her. Being open to new connections doesn't erase your past. It simply means you're allowing your heart to grow. It's telling you it may be time to take a step toward healing."

Daniel stared at his friend in surprise. "I can't, Stanley." The words were gravel in his throat. "The pain of losing Teresa nearly destroyed me. I won't risk that again. I just can't."

A flock of birds took flight from a nearby tree, their wings beating a steady rhythm against the sky. Daniel watched their soaring flight, envying their freedom and ability to rise above the earth and all its complications.

"Ultimately, the choice is yours," Stanley stated patiently. "But think about this. Maybe this encounter is a sign that you're beginning to feel ready, or at least ready to consider the possibility of letting someone new into your life. Not today, and perhaps not tomorrow, but maybe someday."

Daniel sighed and extended his hand, grateful beyond words for his friend's wisdom. Their handshake was an unspoken affirmation of their brotherly bond. "Thank you, Stanley. Thanks for listening and understanding where I'm coming from." He drew a shaky breath. "But right now, I need to focus on what matters. And that's teaching, coaching, and guarding what's left of my heart."

They walked back toward the school in companionable silence, their shoes leaving twin trails in the morning dew. Behind them, the sun climbed higher in the sky, burning off the last wisps of fog from the field.

As they approached the building, Daniel glanced at the empty field, and Teresa's voice echoed in his mind: *It's okay to smile, and to feel something again.* She would have wanted that for him.

Maybe Stanley was right. Maybe this wasn't a betrayal but another step forward. The thought unsettled him as he stepped into the familiar halls of Greater Pines High School.

Chapter 7

Samantha pulled into a parking space at Heavenly Delights. The scent of warm pastries curled through the air. The crisp November breeze carried a hint of fallen leaves and a quiet nudge that Thanksgiving was approaching.

Her stomach clenched in protest, the toast and orange juice from that morning long forgotten. After twelve hours on her feet, a meal and a moment of peace were all she wanted.

"Just a quick bite," she murmured to herself. "And then it's time to go home."

The bell jingled as Samantha stepped inside, and the warmth replaced the autumn chill. A few familiar faces looked up, nodding in greeting.

Mrs. Johnson raised her coffee cup in a silent hello, while Quincy Carter's laughter rumbled from his usual corner booth. This was her church family and her diner family. This place was home.

"Sam!" Willow called, stepping from behind the counter. "It's so good to see you. It feels like it's been ages."

"I know." Samantha sighed as she slid onto her usual stool at the counter. "The flu hit our staff hard. I've been drowning in extra shifts."

Unbuttoning her coat, she relaxed as the diner's familiar comfort enveloped her, melting away the tension.

Willow arched a brow. "You're working yourself to the bone. When was the last time you ate a real meal?"

Heat crept into Samantha's cheeks. "Well... "

"That's what I thought," Willow huffed. "I'm fixing you a caramel-vanilla latte and a proper meal. And no arguments."

"Yes, ma'am." Samantha laughed, the sound releasing some of the tension she had been carrying.

As Willow worked, Samantha took in the familiar space. Heavenly Delights wasn't just a diner. It was a refuge, a place where food and friendship restored more than just hunger.

The espresso machine hissed, filling the air with the rich aroma of caramel and vanilla. As Samantha exhaled, the strain of the day finally began to loosen its grip.

"Rough day?" Anna asked, pausing beside her with a tray of dirty dishes balanced expertly on one hand. Anna had started working at the diner just a few months ago but had quickly become a part of the Heavenly Delights family.

"It was just the usual emergency room chaos. But there was this little boy today... he came in with a nasty cut on his arm. He was so brave and didn't cry once while I cleaned it up. It reminded me of why I became a nurse in the first place."

Anna smiled. "You're good with kids. Have you ever thought about switching to pediatrics?"

"Sometimes," Samantha admitted. "But there's something about the ER. I like never knowing what's coming through those doors next and being able to help people on what might be the worst day of their lives."

"Here you go, one signature latte." Willow placed the steaming mug before her. The whipped cream formed perfect peaks and was dusted with just the right amount of cinnamon.

"You're an angel. I don't know what I'd do without you." Samantha wrapped her hands around the warm ceramic.

"You would probably waste away on frozen dinners," Willow teased, her eyes twinkling. "I heard a rumor, though, that may change soon."

Samantha paused mid-sip. "And what rumor is that?"

Willow leaned against the counter, lowering her voice conspiratorially. "So... is there any reason you've been smiling at that latte like it's more than just coffee? Or should I say, is there any person responsible for that dreamy look you've been wearing?"

The question caught Samantha off guard, and she nearly choked on her drink. "What? No, I—"

"Oh, honey, your face says it all." Willow grinned. "Anna told me she saw you with a rather handsome gentleman at the grocery store last week. She said he was tall with an athletic build and neat locs. Does that ring any bells?"

Samantha felt warmth blooming across her cheeks, and it had nothing to do with the hot beverage. "That was... his name is Daniel."

"Daniel," Willow repeated, nodding approvingly. "And?"

"And nothing," Samantha protested, though her quickened pulse betrayed her. "He was lost in the store, looking for something for his sister. I helped him find it. That's all."

"Uh-huh," Willow said, clearly unconvinced. "And you want me to believe that's the reason why you're blushing like a schoolgirl?"

Despite her embarrassment, Samantha couldn't help the smile tugging at her lips. "Well, there was something about him," she admitted softly. "I can't explain it. We talked for maybe ten minutes, but... "

"But he made quite an impression," Willow finished for her.

"Yes." Samantha traced the rim of her mug, gathering her thoughts. "It felt... significant somehow. Like—"

"Like God nudged you to notice him?" Willow suggested.

Samantha met her friend's understanding gaze. "Exactly. How did you know?"

"That's how I felt when I met James." A shadow of old grief passed over Willow's face at the mention of her late husband. "Sometimes, the Lord brings people into our lives at just the right moment."

The diner's bell jangled as a group of teenagers burst through the door, their laughter and chatter filling the space. Willow straightened. "Duty calls. But this conversation isn't over." She pointed a mock-stern finger at Samantha. "I want details when I get back."

Left alone with her thoughts, Samantha's mind drifted, unbidden, to Daniel. She shouldn't be thinking about him, not like this.

But she couldn't forget the way his eyes had flickered with something raw, something barely concealed beneath his careful composure. She was intimately familiar with that depth of emotion. For years, she had seen that same grief mirrored in herself.

And yet, it wasn't just his sadness that unsettled her. It was the way he looked at her, the weight of his gaze. There was also an awareness that passed between them in the stolen moments of silence. She had spent so long guarding her heart, convinced that attraction alone was never enough.

So why did she feel something more? Something like... possibility?

Her hand drifted to the cross pendant at her throat, and memories of her mother flooded back. She smiled as she thought of the quiet mornings they had spent reading scriptures together at the kitchen table, her mother's worn Bible open between them. She would always say: *Remember, Sam, God's timing is perfect, even when it doesn't make sense to us."*

The clatter of plates pulled her from her reverie as Willow returned with a steaming plate of herb-crusted chicken, roasted vegetables, and wild rice.

"I didn't order this," Samantha protested weakly.

"Consider it medicine," Willow insisted. "Doctor's orders. Or in this case, cook's orders."

The first bite melted in her mouth, and Samantha realized just how hungry she had been. "This is incredible," she managed between mouthfuls.

"Someone needs to take care of you while you're busy taking care of everyone else." Satisfaction was evident in her voice. "Now, back to this Daniel fellow... "

Samantha laughed, shaking her head. "There's nothing to tell. Really."

"But you'd like there to be," Willow observed shrewdly.

"I don't know." Samantha set her fork down. "After what happened with Paul... " She swallowed hard, the bitter taste of that betrayal still fresh despite the years that had passed.

Willow's expression softened. "Not all men are like him, Sam."

"I know that in my head," Samantha sighed. "But my heart... it's harder to convince."

"And that's perfectly understandable. But at some point, you have to ask yourself if you're protecting your heart, or are you just building walls around it?"

Samantha fell silent, contemplating the truth of her words. She had been so careful since her ex-boyfriend, Paul, guarding herself against potential hurt. But in doing so, had she been shutting out God's blessings too?

"Besides," Willow continued, her tone gentler. "This doesn't have to be a romance novel with love at first sight and fireworks. It could just be a new friendship. You know... someone to occasionally have coffee and conversation with."

Samantha nodded, feeling some of her tension ease. "You're right. I'm probably overthinking this whole thing. I'll probably never see him again."

"Or, you might walk in here tomorrow and find him sitting right there, at that table by the window," Willow countered with a knowing smile.

"The odds of that happening—" Samantha began, but Willow cut her off with a light laugh.

"The odds don't matter when God's involved, honey." She tapped the cross pendant on Samantha's necklace. "The Lord specializes in divine appointments."

"But what if—," Samantha hesitated, voicing the fear lurking in her mind since that encounter at the grocery store. "What if he's not the man I think he is? What if I'm just seeing what I want to see?"

Willow's voice was steady with the wisdom of experience. "That's why we pray for discernment. And that's why we take things one step at a time. You don't have to figure out your entire future with this man after one meeting in the grocery store."

As Samantha finished her meal, the conversation shifted to other topics such as the latest hospital gossip, upcoming church events, and Willow's plans to expand the diner's menu. By the time Samantha was ready to leave, the weight of her long day had lifted considerably.

At the door, she turned back to hug Willow. "Thank you. For the food and the perspective."

Willow returned the embrace. "Anytime, dear heart. And Sam? Be open to what God's doing. Sometimes His greatest blessings come in unexpected packages."

Driving home, Samantha replayed Willow's words in her mind. Perhaps she had been too quick to dismiss the possibility of re-opening her heart. After all, God had healed her from the pain of losing both parents and from Paul's betrayal. Maybe it was time to trust Him with this aspect of her life, too.

She stopped at a red light, and her thoughts turned to Daniel, a man she barely knew yet couldn't forget. Samantha offered a silent prayer.

Lord, if it's Your will, let our paths cross again. And if not, help me to be content with the life You've given me.

The light turned green, and Samantha drove on, a curious mix of hope and peace settling in her heart. Yet beneath that peace, a flicker of apprehension remained. Opening her heart yet again meant risking pain. She asked herself the question. Was she truly ready for that?

Chapter 8

Eight years earlier, Samantha meandered through the bustling halls of Atlanta's Lenox Mall, escaping the demands of her nursing duties for a rare moment of respite. The scent of pretzels mingled with the buzz of shoppers flitting from store to store. Sunlight streamed through the expansive skylights, turning the marble floors into rivers of liquid gold. After she had spent hours scouring racks for the perfect additions to her wardrobe, her hunger gnawed, temporarily stopping her excursion.

The food court's offerings blurred together until a small West African restaurant caught her eye. The sign proclaiming, *Home of the Best Creamy Peanut and Chicken Soup*, piqued her interest. Excited, she approached the counter to place her order. Minutes later, she settled at a sunlit table, inhaling the aromatic steam rising from her bowl.

That first spoonful was an exquisite experience. The soup transported her to the deliciousness of after-church Sunday dinners.

Samantha was back in her mom's kitchen, where similar earthy spices and savory scents had once danced in harmony under her mother's loving orchestration. Comfortably lost in memories and the flavors of her meal, she barely noticed someone clearing their throat beside her table.

Samantha looked up into warm brown eyes and a confident smile. A tall, sharply dressed man balanced a tray in one hand, the other pressed to his chest in apology.

"Forgive me for interrupting," he said, his voice smooth. "But I couldn't help noticing that you're enjoying one of my favorite dishes." He leaned in slightly. "And I thought, perhaps, a woman with such excellent taste might allow me to join her for lunch."

Samantha's eyebrows rose. "Uh-huh. Well, as far as pickup lines go, I'd say you get a solid B-plus. But tell me... does this usually work for you?"

He grinned. "You're the first woman I've ever tried this on." He gestured to her tray. "So, how's my success rate so far? You'll have to tell me the answer."

Something about his confidence intrigued her. "What's your name?"

"Paul Winston," he said easily.

She paused, then smiled. "Well, Paul, I think I'd enjoy some company."

Relief brightened his features as he settled into the chair across from her. Their conversation flowed. Samantha shared stories about her work as an ER nurse in Brookside, while Paul detailed his position at the World of Coca-Cola Museum in downtown Atlanta. His eyes brightened as he described his much-loved city—the dynamic Children's Museum, the sprawling Georgia Aquarium, and the iconic Olympic Park—all of which came alive with his colorful descriptions.

"You should come and explore them for yourself," he suggested. "I'd love to be your tour guide and show you all the best exhibits."

They exchanged numbers, though Samantha doubted anything would develop from it. Two hours of travel lay between their cities. Yet, to her surprise, her phone flickered to life the next night with his name flashing brightly across the screen.

Their first call stretched into a marathon conversation that went on for ages. Paul's laughter warmed her evening as they shared hopes and dreams. A current ignited between them, forging a connection and defying the miles separating them.

Over the following months, their romance blossomed. Samantha's heart quickened with each passing mile marker as she drove to Atlanta, anticipation building with every mile.

When Paul ventured to Brookside on weekends, he would arrive bearing little surprises. Once, it was a box of her favorite tea from a specialty shop in Atlanta. Another time, it was a beautifully crafted devotional journal he had noticed her admiring in a local bookstore. These small tokens were meaningful gestures that made her feel special and understood.

After three years, Samantha began imagining a future painted in permanent strokes. She lingered at the jewelry store windows and pictured a sparkling ring on her finger. Her computer browser history became a trove of Atlanta hospital job listings, each click an exploration of possibilities. Every time she prayed, she thanked God for bringing a man into her life who harmonized ideally with her plans.

One Saturday, with love and optimism in her chest, Samantha decided to surprise Paul with a lovingly prepared home-cooked meal. Exchanging apartment keys months ago had been, what she thought, a gesture full of meaning. She hummed gospel tunes while chopping vegetables in his kitchen, the aromas of simmering sauce and sautéed onions filling the space with domestic promise.

The key turned in the lock, snapping her from her cooking reverie. Butterflies danced in her stomach as she imagined Paul's delighted reaction to this impromptu meal. But instead of his usual cheerful greeting, she heard feminine giggling filtering through the doorway, followed by the wet sound of kissing.

The wooden spoon clattered from her numb fingers as Paul stumbled through his door. His lips were locked with a stranger's, and his hands roamed her body with intimate familiarity. The reality of his betrayal destroyed her expectations, leaving her amazed in disbelief.

Time crystallized, transforming with the cold precision of ice. The couple froze when they spotted her. But then, Paul's expression morphed from shock into a mask of cold fury. Instead of the remorse she desperately hoped for, he attacked with defensive retorts.

"How dare you show up in my apartment unannounced!" he snapped, the accusation slicing her deeply. "You're trying to trap me, aren't you? Don't you understand that as a man, I need my freedom?" His words were a cold slap, dismissing her pain and confusion. Samantha's world caved in, leaving her to grapple with the harsh reality of Paul's betrayal and the erosion of her self-worth.

The walls she had painstakingly constructed around their future crumbled, one jagged brick at a time. His accusations reigned as hail in a storm. A tremor ran through her hands as she hastily gathered her belongings—items that once stood as symbols of a shared history, now reminders of love turned toxic.

He followed as she fled to her car, insisting she was overreacting. His nonchalant revelation that he dated other women throughout their relationship shattered her remaining trust. The words, *I didn't think you'd mind,* pierced her soul. That was the final hammer blow, sealing the coffin of her aspirations, dreams of marriage, romance, and a life meant to be built on faith and devotion.

The drive to Brookside passed in a fog thicker than her tears. Samantha barely registered the sounds of the world around her as she pulled into a gas station. Her hands shook uncontrollably while she filled a Styrofoam cup with bitter coffee, which she knew she wouldn't taste. Streetlights blurred into streaks of color outside her car window as she navigated home on autopilot.

She carried her mother's wisdom: *Baby girl, guard your heart with all diligence, for everything you do flows from it.*

Though comforting in childhood, those words now were a daunting admonition.

Her apartment's silence crushed her when she finally stumbled inside. She collapsed onto her bed, instinctively burying her face into pillows, which offered no solace against her gut-wrenching sobs. Each cry ripped from a place deeper than her chest. There was an aching void from where she had once stored her dreams of building a God-centered life with someone who genuinely prized her.

Time lost all meaning as the hours passed. Exhaustion eventually dragged Samantha into a fitful sleep. But peace eluded her. Fractured dreams invaded her, filled with haunting images of Paul in another woman's arms, displaying carefree abandon as he shattered her hopes and shared vision.

In the days that followed, his calls and texts bombarded her phone:

Baby, I'm sorry.

I've ended things with her.

Give me another chance.

We can be exclusive now, I promise.

Each message twisted the knife, plunging it deeper until she mustered the strength to block his number.

Alone in her apartment, humiliation and anger warred fiercely inside her. Shame washed over her, flooding her with the force of a dark tide. She had ignored that still, small voice of caution that urged her to tread carefully. Anger surged through her veins at her own naivete for compromising the values lovingly instilled by her parents during countless Sunday services and evenings spent in Bible study.

The haunting words of First Corinthians 6:19-20 resonated within her:

Do you not know that your bodies are temples of the Holy Spirit, who is in you, whom you have received from God? You are not your own; you were bought at a price. Therefore, honor God with your bodies.

She had given Paul both her heart and her body. Marriage, a covenant relationship blessed in faith, was the intended destination for those precious gifts. Kneeling beside her bed, Samantha cried out her regrets in a torrent of tears and soft-spoken pleas for mercy. She realized she needed more than healing. She needed to rediscover her identity in Christ and reaffirm that her worth wasn't dependent on any man's affection. Jesus's profound sacrifice for her soul established her significance.

The path ahead looked long and lonely. As the sunrise colored her room in soft pinks and golds, a calm settled over Samantha. She couldn't change the past, but she could consciously choose the direction of her future. With God's help, she would rebuild her life on a faith-based foundation, safeguarding her heart and body for a love that would honor her and her Lord, Jesus Christ.

Samantha had drifted away from attending church since she met Paul. The weekends when she wasn't working had become a sacred time for them—a chance to share future plans, dreams, and fleeting moments together. In the corners of her mind, she rationalized her absence from church, convincing herself that God would surely want her to be happy. After all, a committed relationship, she told herself, must be part of God's plan.

In retrospect, Samantha could trace how subtly she had drifted from her once fervent faith. Weekends that were once sacred times filled with worship had slowly changed into time for personal pursuits. They had become occasions devoted entirely to Paul, an enticing but ultimately hollow substitute.

Samantha rationalized missing church services by telling herself God would understand her choices. After all, didn't the pursuit of love align with His divine plan? Yet, notwithstanding her justifications, a persistent, still voice within her soul had never quieted and was a constant reminder of her inner conflict.

The Holy Spirit's gentle nudges surfaced during moments of quiet introspection. The Spirit's urging brushed against her ear during hurried morning prayers when Paul's kisses often tested her boundaries. And the Spirit's voice called out to Samantha's soul in the silent void of Sunday mornings spent in places far removed from the comforting sanctity of God's house.

Yet, each time, she chose to push that divine wisdom aside, opting instead to chase her heart's risky desires. As a result, the peace that had once flooded her life dried up, leaving drought and turmoil in its wake.

During her descent to rock bottom, she discovered the foundations vital for true rebuilding. Barely a week after discovering Paul's betrayal, she slipped into the far pew of her beloved church, Cottonwood Faith Community Center. Tears streamed down her cheeks as the choir sang *Great Is Thy Faithfulness* in perfect harmony. The hymn had invariably been a source of comfort during her darkest hours. Each note was a homecoming, reminding her of the love and grace she had recklessly forsaken.

After the service, she sought out her pastor and told him her story. His face creased with compassion as she recounted the events that brought her to that moment.

"The Lord hasn't forgotten you, daughter," Pastor Scott Wilson gently reassured her. "In fact, I have a certain someone you need to meet."

That *'someone'* was Olivia Stewart, a spirited young veterinary technician. Her journey from the shadow of heartbreak to the light of healing aligned with Samantha's own path.

They planned their initial coffee date as a casual catch-up. But it effortlessly morphed into a lengthy discussion that lasted for hours as they recounted their testimonies, exchanged scriptures, and shed tears over their shared experiences of loss and renewal.

Olivia's presence and support bolstered Samantha during the aftermath of her heartbreak. Her prayers and wise counsel helped steer Samantha back toward a solid ground of faith.

"Always remember who you are in Christ," Olivia gently reminded her. "No earthly man can love you the way Jesus does." These words resonated within Samantha, gradually becoming a mantra that fueled her revitalization.

Slowly, with the gradual brightness of dawn breaking after the longest midnight, Samantha's spirit revived. Wednesday evening Bible study became her refuge, offering solace in the company of fellow believers. And Sunday worship saturated the empty places she had tried to fill with Paul's fleeting affections. Samantha's church family surrounded her with a love that asked nothing in return, showing her what the essence of authentic Christian companionship meant. Her life was transforming, and Samantha embraced it.

As time passed, the frequency of she and Olivia's late-night phone calls gradually diminished, marking Samantha's increased strength and independence. However, her bond with Olivia blossomed into an irreplaceable connection. She was a true sister in Christ who could celebrate her triumphs and, when necessary, speak truth into her life with love and compassion.

They continued to meet regularly, and their conversations flowed between the trials of their daily lives and the uplifting joys of their spiritual growth. The depth of Olivia's influence on Samantha's life was striking, catalyzing her ongoing personal transformation. This journey of rediscovery and resilience stood as a poignant testament to the transformative power of genuine Christian fellowship.

The memories faded as Samantha placed her mother's Bible on her nightstand. A week had passed since her late-afternoon meal at Heavenly Delights. It had been seven days of grueling double shifts as more of her colleagues fell victim to the stubborn flu strain sweeping through the hospital. She barely had time to eat, let alone visit her favorite diner.

But tomorrow morning promised the relief of a rare day off after the punishing schedule. She smiled at Olivia's text confirming their breakfast plans:

8 a.m. at Heavenly Delights. Bible study + gossip session. Don't be late!

Exhaustion pulled at her limbs as she slipped under the covers, but her mind remained stubbornly active, replaying her conversation with Willow and, inevitably, circling back to thoughts of Daniel. Had that brief encounter at the grocery store meant anything to him? Or had she imagined the connection between them?

Sleep finally claimed her, her dreams a peaceful respite from the hospital's constant demands.

The next morning, Samantha pushed open the door of Heavenly Delights, the bell announcing her arrival. The usual breakfast rush had subsided, leaving the diner in that perfect lull between the early birds and the lunch crowd. Sunlight streamed through the windows, warming the cozy space.

"There she is!" Willow exclaimed, abandoning her task at the coffee machine to hurry around the counter. She pulled Samantha into a quick, flour-dusted hug. "I was beginning to think you'd found another favorite diner."

Samantha laughed, returning the embrace. "Never! I've just been drowning in work. The hospital's been short-staffed for days."

"Well, I'm glad you finally have a morning off," Willow said, returning to her post. "Your usual?"

"Yes, please. And I'll have whatever pastry just came out of the oven. It smells divine."

"Blueberry scones," Willow confirmed with a wink. "And you're just in time. They're still warm."

Samantha settled into her favorite spot at the counter, savoring the rare moment of calm. Her gaze drifted to the door, expecting Olivia to burst through any minute with her characteristic energy and warmth.

"I saw Olivia yesterday," Willow mentioned as she placed a steaming latte before Samantha. "She said she'd be meeting you here this morning."

"Yes, we've been trying to coordinate our schedules for weeks." Samantha wrapped her hands around the warm mug, inhaling the rich aroma of caramel and vanilla. "Between my hospital shifts and her emergency calls at the veterinary clinic, it's been nearly impossible."

The bell above the door jingled, and Samantha turned expectantly. But it wasn't Olivia who stepped through the doorway.

Her breath caught as her gaze collided with familiar dark-brown eyes that had haunted her thoughts for days.

Daniel Forrester stood just inside the diner's entrance, his expression shifting from surprise to unmistakable pleasure as their eyes met across the room.

Chapter 9

THE BELL ABOVE HEAVENLY Delights jingled as Daniel entered, shaking off the November chill. After a tough morning assisting Coach Michaels with football drills, his muscles ached, and his stomach protested against another hastily prepared breakfast.

The warm scent of cinnamon, coffee, and fresh bread enveloped him, stirring memories of Sunday brunches with Teresa. She had loved discovering new cafés, her enthusiasm contagious. The grief that usually followed felt fainter today, like an old photograph, edges softening with time.

The diner hummed with quiet conversation, punctuated by the clink of silverware and the occasional burst of laughter. Daniel paused at the entrance, scanning for an empty table, when his gaze fell on a familiar face.

Samantha Kelly sat at the counter, cradling a steaming mug. Gone were the royal blue scrubs. Today, a cream sweater softened her features, its warmth complementing her rich complexion.

Dark waves spilled over her shoulders, unbound, as though she had finally exhaled after a long day.

Daniel hesitated, his heart suddenly racing. Their meeting at the grocery store had replayed in his mind countless times over the past weeks, despite his attempts to push it away. Stanley's words echoed in his thoughts: *Maybe this encounter is a sign that you're beginning to feel ready.*

Samantha turned, and their eyes met. Surprise flickered across her face, and then something warmer. The jolt in his chest caught him off guard.

"Daniel." Samantha's voice lifted in surprise, warmth threading through it.

He hesitated, then stepped forward. "Sam." Her name felt familiar, easier on his tongue than he expected. "I didn't expect to see you here."

"I didn't expect to see you, either," she replied with a small laugh. "To tell you the truth, I'm pretty much a regular here. Willow makes the best caramel-vanilla latte in town."

As if on cue, Willow popped up behind the counter, wiping flour from her hands. "Well, well, look who Sam brought in," she teased, eyeing Daniel with open curiosity.

"Yes, this is Daniel Forrester," Samantha said. "We met at the grocery store a couple of weeks ago. Daniel, this is Willow Barnes, owner of this slice of heaven and maker of the life-changing lattes."

Daniel extended his hand. "Nice to meet you. Any friend of Sam's... "

"Must have excellent taste," Willow finished with a warm smile, shaking his hand. "Can I get you something to drink while you decide on food? Coffee? Or maybe tea?"

"Coffee would be great. Black, please."

Willow nodded and turned to prepare his drink, but not before giving Samantha a meaningful look that Daniel couldn't quite interpret.

"Would you like to join me?" Samantha gestured to the empty stool beside her. "That is, unless you're meeting someone?"

"No, I'm alone," Daniel said, settling onto the stool. "I just needed something to eat after helping with football practice this morning."

"Are you a coach?" Samantha's head tilted, her eyes alight with curiosity.

"No, just an assistant." Daniel scratched the back of his neck. "Stanley Michaels runs the team. I pitch in whenever I can, mainly to keep my students from slacking off in the English class that I teach."

"That's wonderful," Samantha said, her smile genuine. "I bet the students appreciate having you there on the field with them."

Daniel shrugged, unexpectedly warmed by her interest. "They tolerate me. Especially when I run drills that leave them gasping for breath."

Her laughter was musical, sending a pleasant sensation through him. "I can picture it. The stern English teacher who quotes Shakespeare while making them run laps."

"'Once more unto the breach, dear friends,'" Daniel quoted with mock severity, surprising himself with the ease of their banter.

"'Or close up the wall with our English dead,'" Samantha finished, her eyes twinkling.

Daniel raised his eyebrows, impressed. "Henry V. Not many people can continue that quote."

"My father loved Shakespeare." A wistful note entered her voice. "He was an English professor at Spelman College. He used to read the plays aloud, doing all the different voices. I inherited his collection of leather-bound volumes after he passed."

"I'm so sorry about your father," Daniel said quietly, recognizing the subtle shift in her expression. She had the look of someone who carried grief as a familiar companion.

"Thank you. It was a long time ago, when I was thirteen." A shadow crossed her face before she brightened again. "So, did your sister enjoy that salmon salad?"

The abrupt change of subject told Daniel she wasn't ready to share any more details about her loss, and he respected the boundary. "She did. I delivered it and received the appropriate sisterly gratitude, which in Mandy's case, meant she immediately asked when I could bring over some of her favorite ice cream."

Samantha laughed again, the sound washing over him like warm sunshine. "That sounds about right. Siblings have a talent for extending one favor into an ongoing service."

"Do you have any siblings?" he asked, eager to learn more about her.

"No, I was an only child. But I've seen enough family dynamics in action to recognize the pattern."

Willow returned with Daniel's coffee and two plates bearing enormous cinnamon rolls drizzled with white icing, steam rising from their centers.

"I didn't order—" Daniel began.

"On the house," Willow interrupted with a wink. "First-time customers get the full Heavenly Delights experience."

"She's not kidding about the *'heavenly'* part." Samantha gestured to the pastry. "These cinnamon rolls have been known to induce religious experiences."

Daniel picked up his fork and cut into the warm roll. The aroma of cinnamon and butter wafted up, making his mouth water. He took a bite and couldn't suppress a groan of appreciation as the flavors melded on his tongue.

"See... I told you," Samantha said, a triumphant gleam in her eyes.

"That is... " Daniel took another bite, searching for adequate words. "Wow. I may need to rethink my Saturday routine."

"Willow has that effect on people. I wandered in here after a rough shift at the hospital about three years ago, and I've been a loyal customer ever since."

Daniel realized Samantha's presence made it easier for him to breathe. The constant weight of grief seemed lighter, enabling him to simply enjoy the moment. The coffee was excellent, and the pastry was decadent. What he appreciated most was the comfortable conversation with someone who didn't look at him with the mixture of pity and concern he had grown accustomed to seeing.

"Speaking of the hospital, how long have you been working there?"

"Almost ten years now," Samantha replied. "I started out on the medical-surgical floor, but after a couple of years, I transferred to the emergency department. I love the variety. You never know what's going to come through those doors."

"It must be challenging," Daniel remarked, genuinely curious. "You deal with people who are in some sort of crisis every day."

Samantha considered this, her expression softening. "You're right. It can be hard seeing people at their most vulnerable. But there's something sacred about being able to help during those moments." She paused, her fingers absently touching the small cross pendant at her throat. "But I believe it's where God called me to be."

The mention of God sent a familiar uneasiness through Daniel. Once, he would have understood that sentiment completely. Now, it reminded him of the vast distance between the faith he once had, and the emptiness that had replaced it.

If Samantha noticed his discomfort, she didn't comment on it. Instead, she glanced at her watch and sighed. "I'm supposed to meet my friend Olivia for our weekly Bible study, but she just texted to say she's running late from an emergency at the veterinary clinic where she works."

"You're a woman of routine," Daniel observed, pushing aside his instinctive recoil at the mention of Bible study. "Coffee, cinnamon rolls, and scripture."

"I need the structure. It keeps me grounded. And the company's nice too."

Their eyes met again, and Daniel was reluctant to end their conversation. "I've enjoyed this." He was surprised by his own honesty. "It was good running into you again."

"So have I," Samantha replied, a soft smile playing at her lips. "It seems we keep crossing paths."

"Maybe it's not just a coincidence," he suggested before he could stop himself.

A hopeful light flickered in Samantha's eyes. "Maybe not." She hesitated, then seemed to make a decision. "I don't usually do this, but... would you like my number? Just in case you need help finding any other elusive grocery items?"

The teasing note in her voice made Daniel smile. "I'd like that." He took out his phone. "You never know when another salmon salad emergency might arise."

As she dictated her number, Daniel felt a strange mixture of excitement and trepidation. This step was as small as it was significant. It was the first time since Teresa's death that he had willingly opened the door to a possible new connection.

"I should warn you," Samantha said as he saved her contact information. "I work odd hours at the hospital, so I might not always be able to answer right away."

"No worries. I always have at least one or two stacks of essays to grade that reach the ceiling. So, believe me when I say that I understand completely."

The diner's door jingled again as a petite woman with light-brown hair hurried in. She scanned the room until she spotted Samantha.

"That's Olivia," Samantha said, gathering her purse. "She's my Bible study partner and official best friend."

Daniel nodded, standing as well. "I should get going. I have lots of papers to grade and some football plays to review."

"It was really nice seeing you again, Daniel."

"Likewise," he replied, meaning it deeply.

Samantha had already turned toward Olivia, caught in an animated conversation, but Daniel lingered a second longer, watching her.

He stepped outside and took a deep breath. The weight would return soon enough with the grief, anger, and doubts that had become his constant companions. But for now, with the taste of cinnamon still on his tongue and Samantha's smile fresh in his mind, he allowed himself to feel lighter.

The rain clouds gathering overhead promised an afternoon shower, but for the first time in two years, Daniel didn't mind the thought of getting a little wet.

Chapter 10

THE CRISP SCENT OF antiseptic filled the ER as Samantha checked Mrs. Abernathy's vitals. The elderly woman's frail fingers curled around Samantha's hand, her anxiety lingering even though the numbers were stabilizing on the monitor.

"Now, Mrs. Abernathy," Samantha said gently. "Your blood pressure is looking much better than when you came in. Dr. Lawson wants to run just one more test before we send you home."

"Are you sure I'll be okay, dear?" The woman's voice trembled. "My Harold's been gone three years now. If something happens, there's no one waiting for me at home."

Samantha gave her hand a reassuring squeeze. "You're not alone, Mrs. Abernathy. In Deuteronomy, God promises never to leave or forsake us. I'll make sure you're well before you go home."

Relief softened Mrs. Abernathy's features. "You remind me of my granddaughter. She has the same gentle spirit as you. Thank you for the scripture, child. It does help to an old woman's heart."

As Samantha adjusted the IV line, Hanna Vaughn's familiar voice cut through the ER's hum. "You're still the patients' favorite, I see."

Samantha turned to find Hanna, the mentor who had guided her through her first months in the ER. At fifty-two, she carried the seasoned confidence of a nurse who had seen it all.

"When you're done here, do you mind handling the laceration in bed three?" Hanna's eyes twinkled. "You still have the steadiest hands in the ER."

"You flatter me," Samantha teased. She patted Mrs. Abernathy's arm. "I'll be back to check on you soon."

As they stepped into the corridor, Hanna nudged her. "You seem a bit distracted today. Is something on your mind? Or... maybe, someone?" She smirked. "Could it be that handsome man I saw you with at the counter in Heavenly Delights last week?"

Samantha laughed, shaking her head. "You're impossible."

"I like to think of myself as observant," Hanna corrected, winking. "And if that man's the reason you're distracted, then I approve."

Samantha rolled her eyes but couldn't stop the warmth from spreading through her chest. Maybe, just maybe, she was finally ready to admit that Daniel had been on her mind more than she wanted to acknowledge.

"We're still getting to know each other." Samantha checked a patient's chart to hide her flustered reaction. "But there's something special there. I just... " She hesitated, the words caught in her throat.

"Just what?"

Samantha sighed. "I don't know. But sometimes, he gets this look when I mention anything about church or faith. It's like he's hiding something. But then he'll just smile at me and say all the right things."

Hanna's experienced eyes studied her. "You need to trust your instincts, Sam. And remember what you always tell our patients who are afraid... take it to the Lord in prayer."

"I will," Samantha promised, grateful for the reminder.

Jessica Whitaker appeared around the corner, her auburn hair escaping from her ponytail after hours of rushed care. "We have a trauma coming in... a car accident with multiple victims. ETA five minutes."

The next hour blurred into organized chaos as the ER team worked in seamless coordination. Samantha moved between patients with focused efficiency, her earlier concerns temporarily set aside. This was where her calling felt clearest. Her hands were steady despite the urgency, her voice calm amid the storm, and her faith was an anchor when unexpected outcomes hung in the balance.

As she helped stabilize a teenage girl with a fractured femur, Samantha whispered reassurances, noting how the girl's panicked breathing slowed in response. Sometimes, ministry happened without a single scripture being quoted. It was simply presence and compassion flowing from the wellspring of faith within her.

By six o'clock, she was finalizing her notes when her phone vibrated against the desk. Daniel's name appeared on the screen, sending a flutter through her chest.

Are you free this evening? I was thinking of stopping by Hearthside Reads around 7:45. Would love to see you there if you're not too tired after your shift.

Samantha's fingers hovered over the keyboard. There was a shift between them since their chance meeting at Heavenly Delights. The connection she felt was undeniable, but so was the uneasiness whenever their conversations approached matters of faith.

I'd love that. I actually need to pick up a new devotional. My old one is almost filled with notes. See you around 7:45ish!

Tucking her phone away, Samantha closed her eyes briefly. "Lord," she whispered, "Please guide my heart. Help me see clearly where this relationship is heading. Is Daniel the man You've chosen for me?"

No thunderous response came. Just the quiet certainty that God heard her concerns, and the peace that settled over her was enough for now.

Daniel tapped his red pen against the stack of essays, his gaze unfocused on the words sprawling across the page. A tenth grader's analysis of *The Great Gatsby* lay in front of him, but the inked paragraphs blurred together. His thoughts kept pulling him elsewhere. Samantha.

Three hours. That's how long until he would see her.

The classroom stood empty, afternoon sunlight streaming through the windows. He had been distracted all day, replaying their conversation at the diner, remembering how her eyes lit up when she spoke about her patients.

But beneath the warmth of those memories lay a cold knot of dread. Every time she spoke of faith, it pressed against him like a weight he couldn't shake. She assumed they shared the same beliefs and that their foundation was built on something solid.

And he had let her believe it.

"Still burning the midnight oil?"

Daniel looked up as Stanley filled the doorway, his usually easy stance edged with curiosity. The head football coach's sharp gaze never missed much.

"I'm just trying to get through these essays." Daniel gestured to the stack. "I want these kids to have their grades before the weekend."

Stanley shook his head, as if unconvinced. "You've got that same look you had Saturday after practice." He stepped into the classroom, pulling up a chair across from Daniel's desk.

"You're thinking about the woman you met at the grocery store... Sam, right? How are things going?"

Daniel set down his pen, knowing Stanley wouldn't let this go. "Fine, I guess. We ran into each other at Heavenly Delights last week. And we've talked a few times on the phone."

"And?" Stanley prompted, leaning forward.

Daniel sighed heavily. "She's even more incredible than I first thought. The way she cares for people, her intelligence, her compassion... " He trailed off.

"But something's bothering you."

The observation hung. Stanley was among the select few privy to the devastating effect Teresa's death had on Daniel's beliefs. He also knew how Daniel had walked away from the church and the God he once trusted.

"Her faith is everything to her. Scripture, prayer, God's plan. It's in every conversation." He exhaled sharply. "And I just... go along with it."

"You haven't told her," Stanley stated rather than asked.

"How can I?" Daniel ran a hand over his face. "When I'm with her or talk with her on the phone, I feel alive again. For the first time in two years, I look forward to the next day, and the day after that." He leaned back in his chair, staring at the ceiling. "If I tell her the truth, I might lose the chance to get to know her better."

"And if you don't tell her?" Stanley's voice was steady, not accusing. "How long before pretending turns into lying?"

Stanley's question pressed against the silence as Daniel shuffled his papers.

He still didn't have an answer.

"Look," Stanley said, his voice gentler now. "I've known you since you started teaching here. You're a man of integrity. That's why this is eating at you." He leaned forward, elbows on his knees. "Teresa's death... it broke something in you. I get that. But building something new on a foundation of half-truths?" He shook his head. "That's not the Daniel Forrester I know."

Daniel's jaw tightened. The truth in Stanley's words stung because they echoed his own internal conflict. "I just need more time. I need time to figure out how to tell her without losing her completely."

Stanley stood, clapping a hand on Daniel's shoulder. "Just don't wait too long, brother. The longer this goes on, the harder that conversation becomes."

As Stanley left, Daniel stared at the essays before him. The students' interpretations of Gatsby's illusion-filled life suddenly struck him as being too close to home.

Hearthside Reads Bookstore welcomed Daniel with the comforting scent of paper and coffee. The independent bookstore had been a fixture in Brookside for decades, its wooden shelves lined with everything from bestsellers to rare first editions. A café nestled in the corner offered readers a place to linger over their discoveries.

He arrived early, nervous energy propelling him through the door at 7:30. He wandered to the classics section, his fingers tracing leather-bound spines as he waited. The familiar titles grounded him—Dickens, Austen, Hemingway—their worlds unchanged by grief or doubt.

The bookstore was quiet, the kind of hush that invited lingering. A couple stood close in the travel section, fingers tracing maps as they whispered about their next adventure. In a reading nook, a college student sat cross-legged, lost in a world of equations and ink-stained margins.

At exactly 7:45, the bell over the door chimed. Samantha stepped inside, her post-shift exhaustion evident in the way she rolled her shoulders. But when she spotted him, her face lit up, seeming to push away the weariness.

She had changed out of her work clothes and into a flowing burgundy top and dark jeans, and a colorful scarf was looped artfully around her neck. Gold hoops glinted at her ears, catching the warm bookstore lighting.

Their eyes met, and her smile illuminated her entire face. He watched as she spoke briefly with Mr. Finch before making her way toward him.

"Hi," she said softly, as if they were sharing a secret.

"Hi." Daniel resisted the urge to pull her into an embrace, settling instead for a gentle touch to her arm. "Long shift?"

"The longest," she confirmed with a small laugh. "But it was worth it to end the day here." She glanced at the books behind him. "Hmm... the classics section? I should have guessed an English teacher would be here."

He grinned. "Busted. However, I'm actually looking for something new. What about you? You mentioned needing a devotional?"

A shadow of uncertainty flickered in her eyes, quickly replaced by warmth. "Yes, I try to start each morning with scripture and prayer. My current journal is almost full." She tilted her head. "Do you have a particular devotional that you use?"

The innocent question landed like a blow. This was his opportunity and chance to be honest about his estrangement from God. Instead, Daniel heard himself say, "Not currently. Maybe you could recommend one?"

Her face brightened. "I'd love to! The Christian section is this way."

As he followed her through the store, shame burned in his chest. Each step deeper into deception made his eventual confession more difficult. Yet the alternative, watching her expression change from affection to disappointment, was unthinkable.

They spent the next hour browsing shelves together, sharing discoveries and recommendations. Samantha's excitement was infectious when she discovered a meaningful devotional. They cozied up in the café with their chosen selections—a devotional for her, a novel for him—and steaming mugs of coffee.

"I've been thinking," Samantha said after a companionable silence. "It's really something how we keep running into each other. First at the grocery store, then at the diner... it almost feels like it's more than a coincidence."

Daniel nodded, captivated by the hope in her eyes. "I've thought the same thing."

Samantha's searching gaze held his. "My mother used to say there's no such thing as coincidence, only God-incidences. Do you think He brought us together for a reason?"

The moment stretched, heavy with possibility. Her question invited him into her world of faith and providence. A world he had abandoned when Teresa died.

"I... " Daniel started, his throat constricting.

Just as he gathered the courage to speak the truth, a loud crash from the front of the store startled them both. A display had toppled, sending books cascading to the floor. The moment shattered, leaving Daniel both relieved and disappointed.

The opportunity for honesty slipped away as they helped Mr. Finch clean up. By the time they said goodbye in the parking lot, Daniel had retreated behind the safety of small talk and shared interests. The weight of his unspoken truth grew heavier with each passing moment.

Walking back to his car, Daniel paused, looking at the star-scattered sky. Two years ago, he might have seen divine order in those constellations, evidence of a Creator's hand. Now, he saw only the cold distance, beautiful but indifferent to human suffering. Yet Samantha could still look at those same stars, see God's fingerprints, and feel His presence even in the silence.

The gap between them felt wider than ever.

"I don't know, Olivia," Samantha murmured into her phone, curling deeper into the couch. "Sometimes, it feels like we're perfectly in sync. And then, just like that, he's a million miles away."

"All right. You need to tell me what happened at the bookstore?" Olivia's voice was steady, but Samantha could hear the concern beneath it.

Samantha tucked her feet beneath her, tracing the worn edges of her mother's Bible. "We were having a great time. Laughing, sharing books. But then I mentioned how I felt like God brought us together, and... he just froze."

"Did he say anything?"

"He was about to, but then we were interrupted." Samantha traced the worn cover of the Bible, finding comfort in its familiar texture. "That's what worries me. Every time our conversation turns to spiritual matters, he finds a way to change the subject, or something interrupts us. It's like he's hiding a part of himself."

Olivia was silent for a beat. "Sam, you know I love you. But... do you think that maybe your feelings for Daniel might be running ahead of your spiritual discernment, and you having to make a tough decision about continuing this relationship?"

The question stung, but Samantha knew it came from a place of love. For the past five years, Olivia had been her spiritual anchor, the friend who spoke the truth, even when it was difficult to hear.

"Maybe, but there's something special about him. When I'm with him, I feel... I feel like I'm seen. It's like he understands parts of me that most people don't even bother to notice."

"That's beautiful, Sam. But a relationship needs more than just a connection. Especially for you. You've always said that your faith is nonnegotiable in a partner."

"Believe me, I remember how things went with Paul," Samantha admitted, her fingers tightening around the Bible. The pain of his betrayal wasn't as sharp anymore, but the lesson still burned. "I hate that I compromised so much, thinking I could change him. But with Daniel... it just feels different with him."

"Different how?" Olivia asked, her tone thoughtful.

Samantha hesitated. "When I was with Paul, I always felt like I was chasing something that never existed between the two of us. But, when I'm with Daniel... I don't know. It's like his faith isn't completely gone, just buried somewhere deep inside of him."

Samantha opened her Bible to where she had left off that morning in Proverbs 4:23, which was highlighted in yellow: *Above all else, guard your heart, for everything you do flows from it.*

"I know," she whispered. "I just... I think God is working something out in his life. I can just sense it."

"Then you need to pray for him and be patient. If Daniel is the man God has for you, God will make that clear in His own time."

After they had hung up, Samantha knelt beside her bed as she had since childhood. The wooden floor was hard against her knees, a physical reminder of her submission to the One greater than herself. Tears welled in her eyes as she prayed:

Father, I believe You're moving in Daniel's heart, even if he isn't aware of it yet. Lord, I ask that my will not be led astray by my desires. Let him know You've always been by his side through everything he's faced. Show me how to love him as You would... patiently, unafraid, trusting in Your perfect plan.

Rising, Samantha felt peace settle over her. Whatever uncertainty lay between her and Daniel, she wasn't facing it alone. God would guide her steps. She just needed to be still enough to follow.

Outside her window, the first stars of the evening appeared, bright against the deepening blue. Perhaps these were the same stars Daniel was looking at right now. She wondered if he ever looked up at them and remembered what it felt like to believe they were hung there with a purpose. A guarded truth hid behind those warm brown eyes of his. A wound, a secret, a loss of faith, perhaps. But Samantha felt certain that with time and prayer, all would be revealed.

Whatever it was, she would confront it with the same compassion she offered her patients, not with judgment, but with healing hands and an open heart.

Chapter 11

THE HUM OF THE fluorescent lights barely registered as Daniel stepped into the teachers' lounge, drawn by the rich aroma of slow-cooked chili. His shoulders ached from grading essays all morning, but his mind wasn't on work. It was on Samantha and the question she had asked at the bookstore three nights ago.

"Perfect timing, Daniel!" Meghan Townsend called, waving a wooden spoon like a scepter. "I was about to launch a full-scale search operation to look for you."

The history teacher stirred a large crockpot, steam rising in fragrant tendrils. Her dark curls were pulled back with a headband, and her colorful shirt declared, *Teach, Feed, Inspire,* across the front. Meghan, a thirty five year-old history teacher at Greater Pines, was known among the faculty for her legendary cooking.

"Is that your famous chili?" Daniel asked, his stomach responding with an eager rumble. He had barely touched breakfast, his appetite lost in the echo of Samantha's words: *Do you think He brought us together for a reason?*

"It certainly is." Meghan's shrewd eyes assessed him. "You look like you could use some comfort food."

The teachers' lounge was surprisingly empty for the lunch hour. Audrey Sinclair, an art teacher, and Coach Michaels sat in the corner, deep in discussion about the upcoming spirit week. And Mr. Simmons, the calculus teacher, was hunched over a stack of tests in the far corner, his red pen flying across the papers.

Daniel accepted the bowl Meghan handed him, the steam warming his face. "Thanks, Meghan. Your cooking can make any day better."

He settled at an empty table, taking his first bite. The chili was perfect, with just the right balance of spices, beans, and meat. But even as he ate, his mind drifted back to Samantha.

"Earth to Daniel." Meghan slid into the seat across from him with her own bowl. "I just asked you three times if you wanted any cornbread."

Daniel blinked. "I'm sorry. I just have a lot on my mind today."

"Hmm." Meghan's eyes narrowed, the same way they did when catching students bluffing their way through an assignment. "Do you want my unsolicited opinion?"

Daniel sighed. "Do I have a choice?"

"Not really." Meghan leaned in. "Stanley says you met someone recently. Are you still seeing her?"

A slow burn spread up Daniel's neck. "It's... complicated."

"Complicated how?" Meghan's teasing tone softened. "Daniel, it's been two years. Teresa would want—"

"Please." His voice came out sharper than he intended. Spoon forgotten, Daniel exhaled, rubbing his temple. "I know what everyone *thinks* Teresa would want. But that doesn't mean they're right."

Meghan reached across the table, patting his hand. "You're right, and I'm sorry I overstepped." She hesitated. "It's just that it's good to see some life coming back into your eyes. We've all been worried about you."

Daniel exhaled slowly, his irritation fading. "I know. And I appreciate it. It's just... "

"Just what?"

He considered how much to share. Meghan was one of the few colleagues who had kept her distance after Teresa's death, respecting his need for space without disappearing completely. Her kindness now deserved some honesty.

"Her name is Sam," he admitted. "She's a nurse at Lakeside Hospital. We've run into each other a few times now, and talked some over the phone."

A warm smile played on Meghan's lips. "That's wonderful, Daniel."

"She's... " He searched for words. "She's not what I expected. There's this light about her. But she's very spiritual, and I'm... " He trailed off, stirring his chili absently.

Understanding dawned in Meghan's eyes. Few people, Stanley among them, knew the depth of Daniel's despair after Teresa died.

"I see," she said quietly. "She doesn't know about your... current relationship with the Almighty?"

Daniel shook his head. "I haven't exactly lied about it. But I haven't been entirely truthful either."

"That's a thin line to try and walk on, Daniel," Meghan observed without judgment.

"I know." Daniel took another bite of chili, needing a moment to gather his thoughts. "Every time I think about telling her, I imagine that look. You know the one. The disappointment and the pity." He set his spoon down again. "Or worse, she might try to *fix* me."

"And I take it that you don't want to be fixed," Meghan stated.

"I don't know what I want. Except maybe I want more time with her before everything gets complicated."

"Speaking of time," Meghan said, deliberately changing the subject. "Do you have any plans for Thanksgiving? It's coming up fast."

Daniel was grateful for the shift. "Just the usual. I'll be driving to Bristol Heights to be with my parents and siblings." He pictured the familiar scene—his mother's kitchen filled with delicious aromas, his father watching football in the living room, and his brothers arguing good-naturedly about politics. "My sister, Mandy, and her husband, Noah, will be there too."

"That sounds nice," Meghan said. "Family traditions are important."

Daniel nodded, but the word *"traditions"* sparked another pang of guilt. Thanksgiving had been one of Teresa's favorite holidays. She had loved the gathering of family, the expressions of gratitude, and the focus on blessings. In the years since her death, he had gone through the motions, showing up for his family's sake while feeling nothing but emptiness where gratitude should be.

"What about your new friend, Sam? Does she have family nearby?"

"I doubt it," Daniel responded, aware of his limited knowledge of Samantha's holiday plans. "She mentioned losing her parents some years back."

"You should ask her," Meghan suggested. "People like to know someone's thinking about them during the holidays, especially if they don't have any family to spend that time with."

The idea settled in Daniel's mind. It would be a natural question, wouldn't it? Friends asked each other about holiday plans all the time.

As the lunch period ended, Daniel found himself genuinely smiling as he thanked Meghan for the chili. For the first time in weeks, he had a clear next step with Samantha. He would initiate a simple, nonthreatening conversation about Thanksgiving and ask if she had any plans.

It wasn't a solution to his larger dilemma, but it was something.

The hospital cafeteria hummed with conversation, and the clatter of trays and silverware filled the air. Samantha sank into the seat across from Jessica, balancing a tray of wilted salad and a lasagna that looked more suspicious than satisfying. After six straight hours of emergencies, even a questionable meal felt like a luxury.

Jessica arched a brow at Samantha's tray. "Please tell me that's not your entire lunch. That's not food, it's a cry for help." The red-headed nurse had been at Lakeside longer than Samantha, and her caregiving instincts extended to all her colleagues.

Samantha shrugged. "It was either this or the mystery meat sandwich."

"You should have texted me. Don't worry, I brought extra." Jessica pushed half her turkey sandwich across the table. "Dr. Lawson said you handled three cardiac arrests before I even clocked in. How are you still vertical?"

Samantha took a grateful bite of the sandwich. "God gives us strength when we need it most." Simple truth. Steady truth. The kind that kept her going when exhaustion clawed at her.

Jessica nodded, her expression softening. "That family in room four couldn't stop praising you. The grandfather said you were an angel."

Heat rose to Samantha's cheeks. "I was just doing my job."

"You're so modest," Jessica smiled. Then her voice lowered. "Speaking of miracles," Jessica teased, her eyes glinting. "Hanna says she spotted you with an extremely handsome man the other day. Spill it. I want to hear all the juicy details."

Samantha laughed despite herself. The hospital grapevine was more efficient than any communication system they used for patient care.

"His name is Daniel. We met at the grocery store a few weeks ago."

"And?" Jessica prompted, leaning forward eagerly.

"And... we're still figuring things out." Samantha took a slow bite, buying time. "He teaches English at Greater Pines and helps to coach football after school. He's kind. Thoughtful. He's the kind of man who listens more than he speaks."

"Sounds promising. But I hear some hesitation in your voice."

Samantha sighed wearily. Jessica was familiar enough with her to pick up on any subtle changes in her behavior. "There's something between us that I just can't place my finger on. I don't know how to put it into words. Whenever I bring up church or spiritual matters, it's like a door closes behind his eyes." She struggled to articulate her concerns. "He says all the right things, but it sometimes feels as if he's holding something back."

"Have you asked him directly about his faith or what he thinks about God?"

"No, not explicitly," Samantha admitted. "It hasn't seemed like there's been a right time to bring it up."

"But it's important to you," Jessica stated rather than asked.

"You know it is." Samantha absently touched the cross pendant at her throat. "After what happened between me and Paul... I promised myself I wouldn't compromise on this again. Being equally yoked isn't just a nice-to-have for me."

"Then you need to ask him, Sam." Jessica's voice was firm but gentle. "And you need to do it before your heart writes a future for the two of you that your faith can't follow."

The wisdom in Jessica's advice was undeniable, but the thought of potentially ending what had barely begun with Daniel made Samantha's chest ache. There was a connection between them that felt like it had been divinely orchestrated.

"You're right. I just need to find the right moment."

"Speaking of moments," Jessica said, glancing at the clock. "Our break is almost over. Do you have any exciting plans for Thanksgiving? It's coming up quickly next week."

"I'll be with Olivia and her family. Olivia and the Stewarts have practically adopted me into their family since my parents passed."

"That's nice," Jessica smiled. "Family doesn't always have to be blood related."

"What about you? Are you still hosting your entire extended family at your house?"

Jessica groaned dramatically. "Please don't remind me. There will be seventeen people in my little home. My mother-in-law will be critiquing my cooking. And my brother-in-law's wild children will use my living room as their personal jungle gym." Despite her complaints, affection shone in her eyes. "And I will love every minute of it. I wouldn't have it any other way."

As they gathered their trays to return to the ER, Samantha's phone vibrated with a text message. She glanced down to see Daniel's name on the screen.

Any chance you're free for coffee at Heavenly Delights around 6? No pressure if you're too tired after your shift.

Warmth spread through her chest. Even after a grueling day, the prospect of seeing Daniel lifted her spirits.

Just finishing lunch. My shift ends at 5:30 today. Would love to meet you there around 6:15.

She tucked her phone away, aware of Jessica's knowing smile.

"Daniel?" Jessica asked.

Samantha nodded, unable to suppress her own smile.

"Just remember," Jessica said gently as they headed back to the ER. "A relationship built on anything less than complete honesty won't last, no matter how good the man looks in his jeans."

Samantha laughed, but Jessica's words settled deep. Honesty. Clarity. Trust.

Tonight, she would find the right moment, because some conversations couldn't wait forever.

A rush of warmth greeted Daniel as he stepped into Heavenly Delights, the bell above the door chiming softly. This place had quickly become one of his favorites in Brookside. Though if he was honest, it had little to do with the food.

"Well, well, look who's practically family now," Willow teased from behind the counter, hands on her hips. "Would you like your usual black coffee?"

"Yes, please." Daniel settled into a booth near the window where he could watch for Samantha's arrival. "And could you also make one of those caramel-vanilla lattes for Sam when she gets here?"

Willow paused, then smiled. "Well, that's something. Sam's got you remembering people's favorite drinks now?"

Caught off guard, Daniel blinked. Before Samantha, he never noticed things like that. Teresa was the one who always remembered birthdays, preferences, and the little things that made people feel special. The thought sat with him longer than he expected.

"I suppose she is," he acknowledged. Willow brought his coffee, the ceramic mug warming his hands.

The bell jingled again, and Daniel looked up just in time to see Samantha step inside. Despite the tired slope of her shoulders, her face lit up the moment their eyes met. She wore her royal blue scrubs, and her hair was pulled back in a practical ponytail, yet there was a grace about her that made his heart skip.

"I'm sorry I'm late," she said, sinking into the booth with a tired sigh. "We had a last-minute emergency with a five-year-old who had an allergic reaction to a spider bite."

"Is the child okay?" Daniel asked, concerned.

"She will be," Samantha confirmed. "But her poor parents were terrified."

Willow appeared with the latte, setting it down without a word. "On the house. You look like you need it."

Samantha gratefully accepted the warm mug. "You're a life-saver!"

Willow walked away, leaving a silence in her wake. The situation wasn't awkward, exactly, but a definite tension was present.

Daniel ought not to have been staring. Nevertheless, he was. The graceful curve of her cheek and the delicate curl of her fingers around the mug held him spellbound. Even her quiet existence in the room held his attention completely.

"You're staring," Samantha teased, raising an eyebrow over her mug.

Daniel didn't flinch. "I know." He leaned back, a slow smile tugging at his lips. "It's just good to see you."

"It's good to see you, too." She took a sip of her latte, leaving a smudge of foam on her upper lip. Before she could reach for a napkin, Daniel had the absurd urge to wipe it away himself. But he clenched his fingers into a fist instead.

They reached for a sugar packet at the same time.

Her fingers grazed his. They were warm and soft against his calloused skin. The touch was brief, but it sent a sharp current through him that was unexpected and unsettling. He should have pulled away immediately, but for a fraction of a second, neither of them moved.

He noticed Samantha's breath catch, her eyes flitting to their hands and then back to his. Heat licked at the edges of his composure.

She pulled back, tucking a loose curl behind her ear. "I'm sorry." Her voice was quieter than before.

Daniel exhaled, forcing a chuckle. "No problem," he said, though the sudden tightness in his chest told him otherwise.

Samantha cleared her throat and took another sip of her latte. "So... how was your day? Better than mine, I hope."

"It was certainly less dramatic," Daniel replied. "Though I did have to confiscate three cell phones during my third-period class. Apparently, I'm *literally the strictest teacher ever.*" He mimicked his student's exaggerated tone.

Samantha laughed, the sound warming him more than the coffee. "Oh, my goodness! I remember the trauma of adolescence. I'm sure they'll recover."

"Eventually," Daniel agreed. "Though probably not before they've told everyone on social media how I've ruined their lives."

Their conversation flowed easily, moving from work anecdotes to a discussion of the book Samantha had purchased during their bookstore visit. Daniel found himself relaxing, the guilt that had plagued him earlier receding in the simple pleasure of her company.

When Willow brought them each a slice of apple pie *"for sustenance,"* as she put it, Daniel remembered Meghan's suggestion.

"I just realized," he said, "Thanksgiving is next week already. Do you have any special plans for the holiday?"

A flicker of pleasure, perhaps at his interest, quickened Samantha's gaze. "I do. I'll be spending it with my friend Olivia and her family. The Stewarts have included me in their holidays since my parents passed away."

"That sounds really nice," Daniel said sincerely.

Samantha's expression softened with affection. "It is. Mrs. Stewart makes the most amazing sweet potato casserole you've ever tasted, and Mr. Stewart insists on watching every football game possible." She tilted her head. "What about you? What are your Thanksgiving plans?"

"I'm driving to Bristol Heights to be with my family. It's about a two-hour drive from here. It will be my parents, siblings, their spouses, and a few nieces and nephews running around the house, causing havoc."

"That sounds wonderful," Samantha said. "Big family gatherings can be chaotic, but there's something beautiful about them too."

"There is," Daniel admitted. "Though I usually end up in my old bedroom, grading papers for at least part of the day."

Samantha laughed. "The dedicated teacher, even on holidays."

"Speaking of which," Daniel ventured, "I was wondering if you might be free the weekend after Thanksgiving? There's a classic film festival at the old theater downtown. They're showing *To Kill a Mockingbird* Saturday afternoon."

Samantha's face lit up. "I'd love that. It's one of my favorites."

"Mine too," Daniel said, unreasonably pleased at this shared preference. "Gregory Peck as Atticus Finch... no one will ever do it better."

"Absolutely," Samantha agreed enthusiastically. "The way he embodies moral courage without seeming self-righteous. It's a powerful performance." She took another bite of pie, considering. "You know, that's a deeply spiritual film in many ways."

Daniel's fork paused halfway to his mouth. "How so?"

"Well, Atticus's sense of justice comes from a moral framework bigger than himself. He stands against an entire town because he believes in a truth that transcends social opinion." Her expression grew contemplative. "I've always thought it illustrates what Paul writes about in Romans. You know, about not conforming to the pattern of this world."

The biblical reference hung between them, and Daniel scrambled for an appropriate response.

"I've never thought about it that way," he said carefully. "But now that you mention it, I can see the connection."

Samantha studied him for a moment, and Daniel had the uncomfortable feeling she was seeing past his careful deflection.

"Daniel," she began, her voice gentle. "I was wondering... can I ask you something?"

His throat tightened. "Of course. You can ask me anything."

"When was the last time you went to church?"

He was taken aback by the directness of the question, despite its unbiased tone. He put down his fork, stalling for time.

"To be honest, it's been a while," he admitted finally. The truth, but not the whole truth.

"Has it been since your wife, Teresa, passed?" Samantha's intuition was unsettling.

Daniel found kindness rather than condemnation in her gaze. Her openness encouraged him to be more truthful than planned.

"Yes, it has," he said quietly. "Honestly, my church attendance has been limited to funerals."

Samantha nodded. "I know that faith can be complicated when we're grieving. After my mother died, I questioned my faith a lot, too."

It wasn't the same, Daniel thought. Questioning wasn't the same as turning your back completely. But he couldn't bring himself to correct her assumption. Not yet, and not here in the warm diner with apple pie between them and plans for next weekend taking shape.

"Please know that I'm not trying to pry." Samantha reached across the table to touch his hand. "And I'm definitely not judging. I just... I just believe that faith is meant to be lived in a community. And I wonder if maybe that's something you've been missing."

Her touch was warm and her intentions pure. It was clear to Daniel that he needed to tell her everything. He should tell her about the graveside rage, the prayers that had gone unanswered, and the God that he no longer believed watched over them. But the words stuck in his throat.

"Maybe," he said instead, turning his hand to hold hers properly. "But right now, I'm focused on other things." He held her gaze meaningfully. "Like getting to know you better."

Samantha smiled, but a shadow of uncertainty lingered in her eyes. "I'd like that too," she said softly. "Very much."

A shift to more casual conversation made Daniel regret not being entirely truthful earlier. But the fear of losing what was beginning between them outweighed the guilt of his continued evasion. There would be time for the whole truth later, he told himself. He would confide in her after their relationship matured and she had come to understand his history of broken trust.

The little voice inside called this rationalization what it was—cowardice. But the voice grew quieter beneath the warmth of Samantha's smile and the gentle pressure of her hand in his.

That night, Daniel stood at his living room window, bathed in the pale glow of the crescent moon. The house behind him felt cavernous, the warmth of the diner and Samantha's laughter already fading into memory.

The church flyer sat untouched on the coffee table, the edges curling as if time itself were trying to erase them. He had kept it. And he still didn't know why. Maybe he kept it as a reminder of the man he used to be.

The man Samantha believed he still was.

Samantha's voice whispered through his thoughts: *When was the last time you went to church?*

Such a simple query had opened a door he wasn't ready to walk through. She had offered understanding, not judgment. But would that understanding extend when she learned the full truth about his estrangement from God?

Daniel picked up the flyer, studying the smiling faces of the congregation. He had once been part of something larger. Something that made suffering bearable. Now, unfulfilled promises left the world feeling hollow.

He set the flyer down and turned away from the window. Tomorrow, he would focus on his students, lesson plans, and the tangible responsibilities that structured his days. And he would look forward to seeing Samantha again and exploring whatever was growing between them.

But tonight, in the quiet of his home, Daniel faced the truth he hadn't been able to speak aloud. This was the truth he couldn't escape. He and Samantha were building something, but on what?

The foundation was sand, and sooner or later, the tide would rise, and possibly take it all out to the vastness of the sea.

Samantha knelt by her bed, the pages of her mother's Bible bearing witness to her quiet contemplations. She was overwhelmed with fatigue, yet sleep remained elusive. The evening's events replayed in her mind. She couldn't help but think about Daniel's guarded responses.

Her hands rested on the open Bible, finding strength in its familiar texture, and she prayed:

Father, I need Your wisdom. Please, help me be patient and a light, not a burden. If this isn't Your will, show me before my heart is too far gone. Not my will, but Yours.

The night stretched quiet and still, yet Samantha felt the presence she had known since childhood. She felt a peace not born of answers but of knowing she was heard. Her prayers were not lost. They had found their way to the heart of a loving Father.

Rising from her knees, she closed the Bible and placed it on her nightstand. As she prepared for bed, her thoughts drifted to Thanksgiving, to the Stewarts' warm home, and to the traditions they had welcomed her into after her parents' deaths.

She was truly grateful for so many blessings. She was thankful for her work at the hospital, her friendship with Olivia, and the church community that had supported her through loss and heartbreak. And now, perhaps, there was Daniel.

But as sleep claimed her, Samantha couldn't shake the feeling that a crucial truth remained unsaid between them. Daniel's hesitation when she mentioned church and the way his expression had closed off briefly before he redirected the conversation bothered that small voice inside of her.

"Trust your instincts," Hanna, her colleague, had advised.

Her instincts told her there was more to Daniel's relationship with God than he was revealing. Maybe there was a deeper wound than a grief-induced absence that prevented him from attending church. The question was whether that wound could heal and whether she was prepared for what might emerge in the process.

Only time would tell. And until then, she would continue to pray. She would pray for Daniel, for wisdom, and for the courage to face whatever truth eventually came to light.

Chapter 12

As the credits rolled, Daniel fished for the last kernels of popcorn in his empty container. Beside him, Samantha dabbed at her eyes with a napkin, still caught in the film's emotional weight.

"I've seen this movie a dozen times," Samantha murmured, blotting her eyes. "But at the point when the gallery stands for Atticus? It gets me. Every time."

Daniel nodded. "Gregory Peck was perfect. That quiet dignity—" He paused, searching for the right words. "There's something about standing firm on what you believe, even when the whole world pushes you back."

Their shoulders brushed as they gathered their belongings. The simple contact sent a current of warmth through him, a feeling that had grown familiar yet still thrilled him each time.

"I'm glad you suggested this," Samantha said as they made their way up the carpeted aisle. "It was the perfect post-Thanksgiving activity."

"It sure was better than fighting for sales with the Black Friday crowds," Daniel replied with a smile that didn't quite reach his eyes.

Since returning from Bristol Heights, something had felt... off. His mother's cooking, his father's constant presence, and the familiar laughter of his siblings and friends all brought him comfort. And surprisingly, he had managed to have a real conversation with his high school buddy, Colton Knight. Yet, at its core, a void remained, a quiet sense of isolation that wouldn't leave him.

"You seem distracted, little brother," Joshua had said, his eyes sharp with knowing. "Is it the woman you mentioned? Sam?"

Daniel tried to avoid the issue, but Joshua saw right through him. "You're keeping something from her, aren't you? Something important."

The memory of that talk lingered as they stepped out into the crisp late November evening. Samantha's breath formed delicate clouds as she tightened her scarf against the chill.

"I don't know about you, but that soda and popcorn didn't quite do the job. I'm still a little hungry."

Daniel checked his watch. "It's still early. The Village Eatery's open. I may have called ahead, just in case." He gave her a small smile. "What do you say?"

Her smile lit up her face. "That's perfect. I've been craving their fabulous chicken marsala for ages."

They walked in step, the sidewalk echoing their rhythm. As Daniel opened her door, a soft trace of jasmine and vanilla wrapped around him. It calmed him just as much as it unsettled him. How much longer could he pretend when every moment with her made the truth harder to ignore?

The drive to the restaurant was short, filled with their impressions of the film. Samantha animated the conversation with her insights into Scout's character development, her hands gesturing enthusiastically as she spoke. Commenting on Atticus's unwavering ethics, Daniel was internally focused on a pressing secret he needed to reveal.

The Village Eatery welcomed them with its warm lighting and rustic charm. Wooden beams crossed the ceiling, and the walls were adorned with local artwork. A hostess greeted them with a smile and led them to a corner booth that was slightly removed from the busier sections of the dining room.

"This is perfect," Samantha said as they settled in. "I love this little nook."

Daniel unbuttoned his coat, draping it on the hook beside their booth. "I thought you might appreciate a quieter spot."

The truth was, he had specifically requested this table when making a reservation earlier. He needed privacy for what he planned to share tonight. His brother Joshua's parting words had haunted him throughout his drive back from Bristol Heights: *If you care about her, Daniel, then you need to be honest. You need to be honest about everything.*

A server approached with menus and took their drink orders—water for both of them. As the server walked away, Samantha reached across the table and squeezed Daniel's hand.

"Thank you for suggesting the movie. It was the perfect way to ease back after the holiday."

"How was your Thanksgiving with the Stewarts?" Daniel was grateful for the momentary reprieve from his thoughts.

Samantha's face brightened. "It was wonderful. Mrs. Stewart outdid herself with the food. There was turkey with all the fixings, and three different kinds of pie... " She laughed. "I think I'm still full, despite claiming to be hungry now."

"It's the company of the people you love and who love you that matters most," Daniel said, thinking of his own family gathering.

"Exactly. Olivia and I stayed up half the night talking after everyone else went to bed." She paused, studying his face. "How was your family gathering?"

Daniel traced the rim of his water glass. "It was good. My mom's cooking hasn't changed. She still makes the best mashed potatoes you'll ever taste. And my dad insisted on watching every minute of the football games."

"That sounds nice. Family traditions are special."

"They are." He cleared his throat. "My brother Joshua and my friend Colton cornered me, though. They wanted to know all about you."

A flush colored Samantha's cheeks. "Oh wow! What did you tell them?"

"The truth. That I've met someone extraordinary." The sincerity in his voice surprised even him. Despite his internal struggle, this much was entirely true.

Their server returned with drinks and took their food orders—chicken marsala for Samantha and porterhouse steak for Daniel. As she walked away, silence stretched between them. The air was thick with expectancy, though not uncomfortable.

Daniel took a deep breath. The moment he had been dreading and postponing had arrived. "Sam, there's something I need to tell you. There's something I should have told you from the very beginning."

She set down her glass, eyes soft with concern.

He stared down at the table, gathering his courage. "It's about my wife, Teresa. I want to tell you how she died." His voice caught on the last word, but he forced himself to continue. "And I need to tell you about what happened to my faith afterward."

Samantha reached across the table, her fingers grazing his. "I'm listening."

The gentle touch nearly undid him. How long had it been since he had spoken openly about that day? His bottled grief and anger threatened to spill over, but he steadied himself.

"It was an ordinary day," he began, his voice low. "Teresa had woken up that morning complaining of a headache. She mentioned she was feeling nauseated, but we thought it might have been something she ate at the church potluck the night before." He swallowed hard. "She always had a sensitive stomach."

Samantha nodded, her eyes never leaving his face.

"I kissed her goodbye before leaving for school. I told her I'd text and check on her during my lunch break." A bitter laugh escaped him. "When she didn't respond, I just assumed she was taking a nap."

Their server approached with a basket of fresh bread, but sensing the gravity of their conversation, she set it down quietly and retreated without a word.

"The house was so silent when I got home, and for a moment, I thought Teresa was probably still napping. But when I entered the bedroom, I knew. She lay curled on her side, peaceful, but... I knew she was gone."

Samantha's grip on his hand tightened. Her eyes shimmered with the tears she was fighting to contain.

"The doctors said it was an aneurysm," Daniel continued, the clinical term feeling foreign on his tongue. "It had most likely been there all along, undetected. They said the headache was the first sign, that there was nothing anyone could have done. But knowing that didn't make it any easier."

He couldn't meet Samantha's eyes, focusing instead on their joined hands. "The night before, we'd been at church. Praising God, and sharing a meal with our congregation." His voice hardened. "Everything was so perfect! How could God let this happen? How could He take her without any warning? Without even giving me a chance to say goodbye?"

The grief he thought he had contained rose like a wave, threatening to drown him again. "We had our whole life planned out. Children, growing old together... " He trailed off, unable to continue.

When Daniel finally looked up, he saw tears streaming down Samantha's face. She made no move to wipe them away, allowing herself to share in his pain.

"I haven't spoken about this to anyone in so long," he admitted, his voice raw. "Honestly, I haven't wanted to let myself think about that day. But you deserve to know... to understand why this is so hard for me."

He turned his hand beneath hers, allowing their fingers to intertwine. "After Teresa died, I just couldn't pray anymore. Each time I tried, all I felt was anger. How could a loving God let this happen? Why didn't He protect her? Why didn't He protect *us*?" The words scraped his throat like broken glass. "I walked away from church, from prayer, from everything I once believed in. And I hate Him for it! To tell you the truth, I haven't spoken to God since the day of her burial."

The admission was heavy and irrevocable. Daniel watched Samantha's face, searching for rejection or disappointment, but found only compassion mingled with her tears.

"I understand now why you're angry and why you've seemed so distant when I talk about church and faith," she said softly.

"I know I should have told you sooner." Guilt washed over him. "Every time you mentioned your faith, I let you believe I shared it. I didn't correct you when you assumed I still went to church or when you talked about God's plan for us." Shame colored his words. "I was afraid that if you knew the truth, that I've turned my back on God, you wouldn't want anything to do with me."

Their food arrived, steam rising from the perfectly prepared dishes, but neither made a move to eat. The server quietly set down their plates and withdrew without interruption.

Samantha studied him for a long moment, her expression unreadable. "Thank you for trusting me with this," she finally said, her voice gentle. "I can't imagine how difficult and awful it must have been to lose your wife so suddenly."

Daniel waited, steeling himself for what would come next—her inevitable disappointment, perhaps even her decision to end things between them. How could she, with her unwavering faith, possibly want to continue a relationship with someone who had rejected everything she held dear?

"I need to ask you something, Daniel, and I need you to be completely honest with me."

He nodded, unable to speak.

"Are you *angry* at God, or do you no longer believe He exists?"

The question took him by surprise. He expected judgment or a gentle dismissal, not this probing inquiry that cut to the heart of his struggle.

"I—" he faltered, searching for words. "Yes, I'm angry. I'm so angry I can barely breathe sometimes. But I guess... I guess I still believe that He's there. I just don't believe He cares about what happens to me."

Samantha's expression was thoughtful. "That makes a difference, you know."

"Does it?"

"Yes. Having faith isn't about never doubting or questioning what happens to us," she said. "It's about finding your way back to God after you do."

Daniel shook his head. "I don't know if I can find my way back, Sam. Or if I even want to."

The admission hung between them, its weight almost tangible. Samantha looked down at their still-joined hands, then back up to meet his eyes.

"My faith is the center of everything I am, Daniel," she said quietly. "It guides every decision I make, how I treat others, how I see the world." Her voice wavered slightly. "I don't know if I can build a life with someone who doesn't share that foundation."

Even though he was expecting it, the words really knocked him for a loop. He started to pull his hand back, but she kept a firm grip.

"But I also care deeply for you," she continued. "What we have... it feels special. It feels rare." She took a deep breath. "I think I just need some time to think about what this means for us. And what this means for me."

"I understand." The weight in his chest both lighter for having shared his truth and heavier for the uncertainty it created. "Please, take all the time you need."

They sat in silence for a moment, their untouched food cooling between them. Finally, Samantha picked up her fork.

"We should eat. And maybe... can we just talk about normal things for now?"

Daniel nodded in relief. As they ate, their conversation became easier. They talked about the week ahead at work, Samantha's latest book, and Daniel's upcoming football practices. The tension lessened but did not completely go away. Things were changing between them.

As they finished their meal, avoiding dessert by mutual unspoken agreement, Daniel paid the bill despite Samantha's protest. They walked to his car in silence, the night air sharp and clear. Stars speckled the sky above them, distant and cold.

The drive to Samantha's apartment was quiet, punctuated only by the soft music from the radio. When they arrived, Daniel walked her to her door, uncertainty hanging between them like a veil.

"Thank you for tonight," Samantha said as they reached her apartment. "For the movie, dinner, and... " she paused. "Especially for trusting me with the truth."

"I should have told you sooner, but I was afraid of losing you."

Samantha looked up at him, her expression earnest. "Whatever happens, I want you to know that I admire your honesty. It took courage for you to share something so painful."

They stood facing each other, the hall light casting soft shadows across their faces. Daniel wanted to pull her close and feel the reassurance of her in his arms. But he held back, uncertain if the gesture would be welcome.

"Goodnight, Daniel," she said softly, reaching up to brush her fingers against his cheek. The touch was feather light, yet it anchored him.

"Goodnight, Sam."

She unlocked her door and slipped inside, casting one last glance at him before closing it gently. Daniel stood there for a moment, the ghost of her touch lingering on his skin, before turning to leave.

As he walked back to his car, he felt oddly unburdened despite the uncertainty ahead. The truth about Teresa and his fractured faith no longer lay hidden between them. Whatever came next, whether Samantha chose to continue their relationship or not, at least it would be based on honesty.

The night sky spread vast and infinite above him as he drove home, stars scattered like distant promises. After two years, Daniel wondered if somewhere in that vastness, God was still listening, still waiting for him to find his way back—not for Samantha's sake, but for his own.

Chapter 13

RAIN DRUMMED SOFTLY AGAINST the window, matching the storm churning inside her. Droplets streaked down the glass, distorting the streetlights into golden smudges. Samantha curled on her sofa, fingers wrapped around a mug of chamomile tea that had long since grown cold, like the certainty she once held.

Daniel's words echoed in her mind, a haunting refrain that refused to be silenced.

I hate Him for it! To tell you the truth, I haven't spoken to God since the day of her burial.

The words had shattered something in her. How had she missed it? She had assumed their faith was shared. She prayed with him before meals, and they frequently spoke about church. But now she saw it had all been an illusion, built on sand instead of stone.

Samantha set the mug on her coffee table and reached for her mother's Bible. The leather cover was worn soft from years of handling, its pages holding not just scripture, but her mother's handwritten notes in the margins. It was a legacy of faith passed down. Her fingers traced the words her mother had underlined in 2 Corinthians 6:14: *Do not be yoked together with unbelievers.*

The verse stared back at her, uncompromising in its clarity.

Samantha's grip tightened around the edges of the Bible. The room was quiet, too quiet, except for the steady tick of the clock on the wall, each second amplifying the war inside her heart.

"Lord, what do I do?" Samantha whispered, her voice raw. "I think I'm falling in love with him. But is that enough?"

The question hung in the quiet, unanswered.

She sank onto the couch, pressing the heels of her hands against her eyes. Loving Daniel felt as natural as breathing, but so did her faith. And she couldn't ignore the warning signs flashing in her mind. Her mother's voice drifted through memory, gentle but firm:

Baby girl, love is beautiful, but it's not enough if you're walking two different roads.

She opened her eyes, the familiar weight of loneliness settling in her chest. Her glance rested on the framed photograph near her. The memory was perfectly preserved. Her mother hugged her tightly, beaming with pride as she graduated from high school. Samantha could almost hear her mother's whispered prayers from that morning, filled with the steadfast faith that had sustained their family through every storm.

Would her parents understand her dilemma now?

The thought sent a fresh wave of sorrow through her. Raised in a devout home, where her parents' faith formed the bedrock of their marriage, she believed that God should be central to all relationships. She had vowed to do likewise. But what would she do now?

Now, she was falling for a man who had turned his back on God. She was left breathless by the sudden, overwhelming realization. She wrapped her arms around herself, rocking slightly, seeking comfort in the only place she knew.

"Lord, please guide me," she whispered, her voice shaking. "Help me to choose wisely. Because right now, I don't know if my heart is leading me toward love... or toward heartbreak."

Samantha rose and paced to her kitchen, her slippered feet making no sound on the floor. The mundane act of filling her kettle to prepare another cup of tea and setting it to boil gave her restless hands something to do while her mind continued to race.

She sensed a specialness about him from that first encounter in the grocery store. Not just his good looks or the charming way he fumbled for words, but a deeper kindness and integrity that drew her in. Even with her current knowledge, she couldn't deny their bond.

The kettle's whistle jolted her from her thoughts. As she prepared a fresh cup of tea, Samantha faced the truth she had been avoiding. She might be falling in love with a man who had turned his back on God. The realization both frightened and saddened her.

But hadn't she once been distant from God, too? Finding out about her ex-boyfriend's infidelity caused her to reassess her beliefs about love and faith. It had taken time, support, and grace to find her way back. Was Daniel so different? His anger stemmed from grief and loss, not a willful rejection of the truth.

Still, she couldn't ignore the voice of caution. Relationships were challenging enough when couples shared the same values. How could she build a future with someone who resented the very foundation of her life?

Samantha returned to the sofa and picked up her phone. She needed wisdom beyond her own limited perspective. Her finger hovered over Olivia's number before she tapped the call button.

"Hey, Sam," Olivia answered warmly after two rings. "Is everything okay? It's getting kind of late."

Samantha was unable to mask the tremor in her voice. "I need to talk. Are you free for breakfast tomorrow? Can we meet at Heavenly Delights?"

"Of course. Are you okay? Is this about Daniel?"

Samantha sighed. "How did you know?"

"Because I know you," Olivia replied. "What happened?"

"It's complicated and too much to go over on the phone. But... " Samantha paused, gathering her thoughts. "He's been hiding something important, and I don't know if we'll be able to move forward from here."

"Oh, Sam. How about meeting at eight o'clock tomorrow? I'll be there," Olivia promised. "You just try to get some sleep, okay? Whatever it is, we'll figure it out together."

After they had hung up, Samantha felt marginally better. Olivia had been her rock through so many storms. Her friend's unwavering faith and sound advice helped her overcome the difficult time following her ex-boyfriend's betrayal.

Samantha set her Bible down and closed her eyes, pressing her palms together, and silently prayed. And though her prayer didn't instantly resolve her uncertainties or offer miraculous solutions, it eased her anxiety. No matter what tomorrow brought, she wouldn't face it alone.

Heavenly Delights was unusually quiet for a Monday morning. The breakfast rush had yet to begin, leaving the diner peacefully subdued. Willow moved unhurriedly behind the counter, preparing for the day ahead while the rich aroma of brewing coffee filled the air.

Samantha sank into a booth by the window. Sleep had eluded her, and her night had been spent wrestling between prayer and restless thoughts. The dark circles beneath her eyes felt like shadows of uncertainty, poorly concealed beneath a thin layer of makeup she had eventually abandoned.

The bell jingled, breaking the quiet. Olivia breezed in, shaking the cold from her coat as she unwound a colorful scarf. Her gaze instantly landed on Samantha, and concern flickered across her face.

She slid into the booth, eyes scanning Samantha's face. "Sam, you look like you pulled an all-nighter and lost the battle. Please, tell me what happened?"

Before Samantha could speak, Willow arrived, coffee pot in hand.

"My favorite early birds," she said, pouring steaming coffee into both mugs before either of them asked. "The usual?"

Samantha nodded gratefully. "Thanks, Willow. And could you maybe throw in an extra cinnamon roll? It's been that kind of morning."

"You got it, honey." Willow's gaze lingered on Samantha for a moment, her intuition clearly picking up that there was an underlying distress, but she didn't pry. Instead, she gave Samantha's shoulder a gentle squeeze before heading back to the kitchen.

"Okay, spill it," Olivia said, stirring cream into her coffee once they were alone. "Tell me what's going on with you and Daniel."

Samantha wrapped her hands around her mug, drawing comfort from its warmth. "Yesterday, we went to dinner after we watched a movie. It was a perfect evening. Until it wasn't." Samantha swallowed. "He told me he hasn't prayed or gone to church since his wife died. Then he told me that he... that he hates God for taking her away from him."

Olivia's eyes widened. "Oh, Sam."

"All this time, I thought we were on the same page spiritually. He held my hand during prayers and talked about growing up in a faith-filled family. But it was all—" Samantha's voice caught. "I don't even know what it was. A lie? A mask? I just don't know. But what I do know is that he let me believe we shared the most important part of my life."

Olivia exhaled, setting her coffee down. "Sam, that's... heavy. It's no wonder that you're shaken."

"And do you want to know what the worst part of this is?" Samantha's voice dropped. "I care about him even more. I don't know why. Maybe it's because of what he's been through." Samantha looked down at her coffee. "Is that crazy? Is it crazy for me to love someone who rejects everything I believe in?"

"It's not crazy at all," Olivia replied. "Love isn't a light switch that we can just turn off when things get complicated."

They fell silent as Willow returned with plates of steaming pancakes, crispy bacon, and an extra cinnamon roll glistening with icing, as promised. Samantha managed a smile of thanks, though her appetite had vanished.

"Hey," Samantha said once they were alone again, making an effort to shift the focus. "I just realized I've been so wrapped up in my own drama that I never asked how things are going with you and Dr. Lewis. How is it? Are you two still seeing each other?"

Olivia laughed, the sound brightening the somber mood. "Oh, that fizzled out pretty fast. We went for coffee a few times, and he's a nice guy, but... " She shrugged. "We realized we're better as friends. Besides, his true love is that veterinary clinic. I'm not sure there's room for anything or anyone else in his life right now."

"I'm sorry," Samantha said. "I know you were excited about getting to know him."

"Don't be. Some things aren't meant to be, and that's okay." Olivia cut into her pancakes. "Which brings us back to your situation. What exactly did Daniel say last night? Walk me through everything."

Samantha recounted their conversation, the pain in Daniel's eyes as he spoke about his late wife, and the crushing realization that they viewed faith so differently.

"I just don't know what to do," she finished. "The Bible's pretty clear about being unequally yoked. And faith is everything to me. It's shaped who I am and what I value. I can't compromise on that, not even for him."

Olivia took a thoughtful sip of her coffee. "Can I offer you a different perspective?"

"Please do. That's why I'm here."

"Sometimes, God brings people into our lives not because they're perfect, but because they need healing," Olivia said carefully. "Just think about it. What if you're *exactly* what Daniel needs right now? Not to *'fix'* him or change him, but to show him what living a life of faith looks like."

Samantha frowned. "But that's not a good foundation for a relationship. I can't be his spiritual savior."

"No, you can't," Olivia agreed. "That's God's job. But you might be part of how God works in his life." She reached across the table to grasp Samantha's hand. "Listen, I've seen how you light up when you talk about him. There's something real there."

"But what if it's not enough?" Samantha pushed her untouched food around her plate. "What if I invest my heart now, only to find out later that we can never truly connect on the deepest level?"

"But that's the risk we take in any relationship," Olivia pointed out. "There are no guarantees. Even if you were dating the most devout Christian on the planet, there would still be a risk of getting your heart broken."

Samantha sighed. "It's just... I keep hearing my mother's voice in my head. She always warned me about giving my heart to someone who doesn't share my faith."

"And that's wise advice." Olivia nodded. "But consider this... Daniel had faith once. He grew up going to church with his family. His grief and anger have created a wall between him and God, but that doesn't mean the foundation isn't still there, buried underneath."

"Maybe," Samantha conceded. "But I can't base a relationship with him on what might happen someday."

"Tell me, what does your heart tell you to do?" Olivia asked.

Samantha was quiet for a long moment. "My heart wants to be with him. But my mind keeps flashing warning signs to me."

"Then maybe there's a middle ground," Olivia suggested. "Set some boundaries. Be honest with him about what you need. But don't close the door completely, not when you clearly care about him so much."

A memory surfaced. She recalled Daniel's face when they prayed together before their meal at The Village Eatery, and the way his expression had softened when she reached for his hand. A flicker of vulnerability had been there beneath his composed exterior that suggested his heart wasn't as closed as he claimed.

"Do you remember what our pastor said last month?" Olivia continued. "He said that faith isn't about never doubting or never struggling. It's about continuing to seek God in the midst of those doubts and struggles."

"But Daniel's not seeking," Samantha pointed out. "He's deliberately turned himself away."

"You're right. For now, he has turned away. But people change, Sam. God works in ways we can't imagine." She paused, her expression growing serious. "But that doesn't mean you should ignore your own needs and convictions. If being with Daniel means compromising your relationship with God, that's a different story."

Samantha pushed her plate away, untouched. "I don't know what to do," she repeated, frustration edging into her tone.

"You should continue to pray about it. And maybe talk to Daniel again. Really listen to where he is, but be honest about your concerns."

Willow approached with a coffee refill, her instincts clearly sensing Samantha's distress. "Is everything okay with you two?" she asked, focusing primarily on Samantha.

"We're just trying to sort through some life stuff," Samantha offered with a weak smile.

"Well, whatever it is, you've got this," Willow said, giving Samantha's shoulder a reassuring squeeze. "And that cinnamon roll isn't going to eat itself. Sugar makes everything a little clearer, I always say."

Despite everything, Samantha laughed. "I'll keep that in mind."

Olivia gave Samantha a searching look once Willow was gone. "What are you going to do?"

Samantha took a deep breath. "Right now, I'm going to finish breakfast with my best friend. Then I'm going to take a walk and think more about what we've talked about. And I'm going to pray. A lot."

"And what about Daniel?"

"I don't know yet," Samantha admitted. "But I need to talk to him, and we need to talk soon."

Olivia nodded, understanding in her eyes. "Whatever you decide, I'm here for you. You know that, right?"

Samantha was incredibly thankful for her friend's constant support. "I do, and that means everything to me."

As promised, Samantha picked up her fork and took a bite of the cinnamon roll. The sweet, spicy warmth spread through her, a small comfort amid the confusion.

The lakefront path at Providence Park wound along the water's edge, its beauty shifting with the seasons. Today, a crisp wind stung Samantha's cheeks as she buried her hands deep in her coat pockets.

After leaving Olivia, she had driven here, craving solitude and clarity. The park was quiet, save for the distant rhythm of joggers' footsteps and an elderly man strolling with his dog.

Samantha found a bench overlooking the water and sat, watching a pair of ducks glide across the lake's surface. Their peaceful movements contrasted with the storm in her heart.

She pictured Daniel. His warm laugh, the quiet strength in the way he held her hand, and the way his eyes came alive when talking about his students. And then the shadows crept in. She also pictured his grief and the way that losing his late wife had shattered the foundation of his faith.

Above all else, guard your heart, for everything you do flows from it. The verse surfaced unbidden, a quiet whisper in her spirit. But hadn't she already given Daniel a piece of her heart? Hadn't she, deep down, imagined a life with him?

Samantha closed her eyes, letting the sounds of nature wash over her. She thought about what Olivia said about Daniel having faith once and about grief creating a wall between him and God. She remembered her own journey and how her faith had been tested by loss and betrayal, yet it was ultimately strengthened.

Perhaps that was it. It wasn't that she should walk away, but that she should walk forward with caution and clarity. Not compromising her own faith, but not condemning Daniel for his struggle either.

Samantha exhaled, her breath misting in the cold air. Her thoughts weren't suddenly clear. There was just the steady lap of water and the whisper of wind through the trees.

But deep in her spirit, she knew. She understood that walking away wouldn't solve the problem. She would continue seeing

Daniel. She would continue with honesty, with caution, and with unwavering faith in God's plan.

Samantha pulled out her phone, hesitating only a moment before typing:

I've been thinking about what you shared. It took courage to be honest, and I respect that more than you know. I care about you, Daniel. That hasn't changed. When you're ready, let's talk.

She hesitated a moment before pressing send, then tucked the phone back into her pocket. Whatever came next, she had taken the first step toward an authentic relationship that was based on truth rather than assumptions.

As Samantha rose from the bench to continue her walk, she felt a fragile peace settle over her. She didn't have all the answers, and the path ahead wasn't clear, but she had faith that God was guiding each step. And for now, that was enough.

Chapter 14

DANIEL GRIPPED THE STEERING wheel, his pulse thrumming in his ears. The glow of The Sweet Tea Tavern spilled into the evening darkness, inviting yet intimidating. Seven days. That's how long it had been since he had seen Samantha and told her his painful revelation. It had been seven days of wondering if he had lost her.

He spotted Samantha's silver sedan, parked neatly near the entrance. His chest tightened. Did she regret asking to meet? Had she spent the last week reconsidering everything?

He had told her the truth, the hardest truth. He had told her that his faith had fractured, and that his anger at God was still raw. He had given her space, just like she asked, but the distance had been unbearable.

Each day without her voice or presence had been a struggle, but he respected her need to process everything. When she finally texted him and suggested they meet, relief had washed over him so strongly that he had to sit down.

Daniel checked his reflection in the rearview mirror, running a hand over his locs. The shadows under his eyes betrayed his restless nights of wondering if he had lost her for good. He straightened his collar and sent up a thought that felt dangerously close to a prayer:

Please let this go well.

Inside the restaurant, the savory aroma of burgers and fries mingled with the hum of conversation and soft country music. Vintage signs advertising sweet tea and homemade pie adorned the rustic wood-paneled walls. A waitress balanced a tray of milkshakes with glasses frosted and topped with whipped cream.

Daniel scanned the room, his heart doing a familiar flip when he spotted her in a corner booth. She wore a deep blue sweater that complemented her skin perfectly, and her hair was pulled back in a simple ponytail. Even from a distance, he could see the slight tension in her shoulders.

Samantha looked up, and their eyes met. Following a pause, a small, genuine smile graced her face. The tension in Daniel's chest loosened just enough for him to take the first step toward her.

"Hey." He slipped into the booth. The vinyl seat squeaked, a small, awkward detail in a moment that felt impossibly big.

Samantha studied him, head tilting slightly. "Hey, yourself." A pause. "You look tired."

"You do too." His lips twitched. "I guess we've both been thinking too much."

Daniel reached for a paper napkin, folding the corner absently between his thumb and forefinger. "Honestly? I've been missing you. Worrying about you. And wondering if... " He trailed off, unable to finish the thought.

"You've been wondering if I'd decided you weren't worth the trouble?" Samantha finished for him, her directness surprising them both.

He nodded, his throat suddenly tight. He wasn't used to this vulnerability or feeling completely exposed.

"I won't try to pretend the past week has been easy," she admitted, twisting her mother's silver ring around her finger. "I've been doing a lot of praying and soul searching. And I wanted to see you."

The overhead light caught the subtle highlights in her hair, creating a soft halo effect that seemed almost symbolic. Daniel realized how much he missed just looking at her and taking in the small details that made her uniquely Samantha. He missed seeing the slight arch of her eyebrows when she was deep in thought, and the way her hands were always in motion when she spoke.

Before he could respond, their server arrived—a cheerful college-aged girl with a bright smile and a name tag that read *"Jessie."*

"Welcome to Sweet Tea! Can I start you off with something to drink?" Her ponytail bobbed as she pulled out her notepad.

"Sweet tea for me, please," Samantha said.

"I'll have the same."

As Jessie bounced away, a moment of awkward silence fell between them. The jukebox in the corner switched to an old Johnny Cash song, filling the void with tales of love and redemption that hit a little too close to home. They both reached for the laminated menus, grateful for the temporary distraction.

"The bacon cheeseburger here is amazing," Samantha offered, an olive branch of normalcy. "They use this special maple-pepper bacon that'll change your life."

Daniel managed a smile, feeling a little better as the knot in his stomach loosened. "That sounds good. I'm really hungry right now... I haven't had much of an appetite this week."

Samantha's expression softened, the nurse in her momentarily assessing him. "It's been the same way with me, too."

Their drinks arrived, ice clinking softly against the glass. Daniel sipped his tea slowly, but the cool sweetness did little to calm his nerves.

Across the table, Samantha added a lemon wedge, squeezing it before stirring with her straw, a simple gesture, yet something about it felt strangely intimate.

They ordered matching bacon cheeseburgers and a shared basket of fries, but Daniel barely registered the exchange. He tried to focus on the easy rhythm of conversation, but the question that had haunted him all week refused to be ignored.

"Sam." Daniel set his glass down carefully, as if bracing himself. His voice was low, nearly swallowed by the hum of the restaurant. "I know you've needed time to think and process everything that I've told you. I just want to know where we stand. I get it if my... if my struggle with faith is a deal-breaker for you. If I were in your shoes, maybe I'd feel the same way."

Samantha placed her hands flat on the table as if gathering her thoughts before responding. A burst of laughter from a nearby family sharply contrasted with the serious nature of their conversation.

"It's not a deal-breaker," she said at last, her fingers tracing the rim of her glass. "But I won't pretend it doesn't matter. My faith isn't just a part of my life. It shapes everything for me. It shapes how I see the world, how I make decisions. And how I love."

Relief flickered through Daniel, brief and fragile, before giving way to the weight of what followed. The bright fluorescent lights seemed to intensify his unspoken fears and doubts.

His voice was quieter now. "I get that, and I'd never ask you to compromise your faith or your beliefs for me." His fingers brushed over the condensation ring left by his glass. "That wouldn't be fair to you, or to us."

"I know that you wouldn't." Samantha's warm hand reached across the table. "And I'd never try to impose my faith on you. That's not how it works. But I do need to know that you respect it, even if you don't share it right now."

"I do respect it," Daniel insisted. "And I respect you. How could I not? Your faith is part of what makes you... you. The kindness you show, the way you care for people... I see the connection."

Their food arrived, momentarily pausing their conversation. The burgers were piled high with toppings, the aroma of seasoned meat and maple bacon making Daniel's mouth water despite the seriousness of their discussion. He was grateful for the interruption, needing a moment to collect his thoughts.

Daniel watched as Samantha bowed her head, her lips moving in a silent prayer. It was a simple gesture, yet it felt like a canyon between them. Once, he wouldn't have thought twice about bowing his head in gratitude. Now, watching her, it felt like he was witnessing something distant—something lost, or worse, something he had willingly walked away from.

As they ate, their conversation drifted to safer waters—hospital stories, an amusing essay from one of Daniel's students, and movies they both wanted to see. It felt easy and comfortable. But beneath it, tension hummed like an unresolved chord.

"So, how's the coaching going?" Samantha asked, stealing one of his fries despite the full basket between them. "The football season must be wrapping up soon, right?"

Daniel nodded, grateful for the familiar territory. "Yes, and state championships are next weekend. The guys are working hard, but we're up against Jefferson High, and their running game is incredible."

"I'm sure you'll come up with some brilliant strategy," she said with such genuine confidence that it warmed him. "You're an amazing coach."

"But you've never even seen me coach," he pointed out, unable to suppress a smile.

"I don't need to. I see how those boys look up to you when we run into them around town." She popped another fry into her mouth. "That doesn't happen by accident."

Daniel was halfway through his burger when Samantha laughed, her eyes lighting up in a way that made his heart ache with tenderness. Ketchup smeared the corner of her mouth, and without thinking, he reached across with his napkin to dab it away.

Her laughter stopped, but her smile remained, a sense of quiet connection replacing the momentary mirth.

Right then, he realized he had made his decision days ago. He wanted to be with her and try to make this work, even with the complications. The world made more sense with Samantha in it, even if his faith no longer did.

"What are you thinking?"

"I was thinking that I've missed your laugh," he admitted, folding his napkin and setting it aside. "And that I want to keep hearing it, if you'll let me."

Her smile was warm but cautious, like someone approaching a treasure they feared might disappear. "I've missed you, too. But Daniel, we need to be honest about what we're walking into here. It won't always be easy."

"When has anything worth having ever been easy?" he countered, surprised by his own conviction.

They finished their meal, talking about boundaries and expectations. Daniel committed to expressing his thoughts on faith openly and honestly, without hiding his uncertainties or questions. While assuring him she wouldn't push, Samantha also made it clear she wouldn't conceal her beliefs. It was a precarious balancing act, yet Daniel felt a surge of hope for the first time in days.

After paying the bill, they stepped into the crisp evening air. The stars were beginning to wake, scattered across a sky deepening to indigo. The restaurant's sign bathed the parking lot in a golden glow, flickering slightly in the breeze. A dog barked in the distance, but otherwise, the night was still and waiting.

Neither moved toward their cars. Neither seemed ready to say goodbye.

"Will you walk with me?" Daniel asked, nodding toward the small park beside the restaurant. A cobblestone path curved through lamplit gardens, the lights casting gentle shadows over the leaves.

Samantha hesitated only a second before pulling her cardigan tighter and falling into step beside him.

They walked in a quiet rhythm, shoulders brushing just enough to spark an awareness that neither chose to address. Their hands drifted close, fingertips almost touching before retreating again, like a silent question neither dared answer. The night was quiet with just the distant sound of traffic and the crunch of gravel beneath their feet.

Samantha broke the comfortable silence. "There's this elderly woman who comes into the ER often. She has congestive heart failure. Every time she's admitted, she brings crocheted crosses for the staff."

Daniel glanced at her, intrigued. Ahead, the path curved around a still, small, man-made pond, and the moon rippled over its surface like a whispered promise.

"Last week, she was worse than I'd ever seen her. She was so pale and struggled to breathe. But before we could get her into a room, she asked if any new nurses had started since her last visit. She wanted to make sure that they got one of her crosses."

Samantha halted and turned to face him beneath the soft glow of a lamppost. Golden light illuminated one side of her face, while the other was shrouded in shadow. It echoed the doubt and uncertainty in their relationship.

"I asked her once why she does it. Why, when she's gasping for breath and when the pain is unbearable, why does she still think of others?"

Samantha's voice softened. "*'Honey,'* she told me. *'Faith isn't what you do when life is easy. It's what you hold on to when nothing makes sense.'* I've never forgotten that she said that."

Daniel swallowed hard. "She sounds... remarkable."

Her gaze searched his. "She is. It made me think of you. I thought about how you lost your wife, and how you've been carrying that pain all alone."

Daniel stiffened. He wanted to brush past it and change the subject. But Samantha's eyes held him in place.

"It's hard," he said finally. "It's hard to hold on to something that you wanted so bad when it's been ripped away from you."

"I know. And I want you to know that I hear you. And I'm not dismissing what you've been through."

They resumed walking, the path leading them beneath a row of old oak trees. Their branches formed a canopy overhead, dappling the moonlight like a living cathedral. The comparison wasn't lost on Daniel, and he wondered if Samantha had chosen this spot intentionally.

She paused for a moment, then inhaled. "Daniel, there's going to be a Christmas Cantata at my church to celebrate the holidays." She spoke carefully and deliberately. "The choir will perform the

Christmas story through song, music, and poetry. It's going to be really beautiful."

Daniel felt a tightening in his chest, a premonition of things to come. He fel his pulse accelerate.

"I'd love for you to come with me. Not as a test and not to fix you or push you. But just... just because it matters to me. And I'd like to share it with you."

The invitation hung heavy in the cool night air. This wasn't just about a church service. If he went, he would be stepping toward her, toward faith, and toward questions he wasn't ready to answer.

But what if he refused? He feared the gap between them might become irreparable.

"When is it?" he asked, buying himself time to think. A fallen leaf crunched beneath his shoe, the sound unnaturally loud in the quiet night.

"It's scheduled for the Sunday evening right before Christmas." She tugged at the sleeve of her cardigan. "The music is wonderful. Even if you still don't believe in Jesus anymore, I think you might still appreciate it."

They had reached the end of the pathway, and a small gazebo lit by strings of lights marked the park's boundary. An empty bench inside offered a place to sit, but they remained standing at the entrance, the moment too pivotal to be seated.

"Look, you don't have to give me an answer now," she said gently, finally meeting his eyes. "Just think about it and pray about it, if you're willing. But I want you to know that whatever you decide, it won't change how I feel about you."

The sincerity in her eyes undid him. Without thinking, Daniel stepped forward and pulled her into his arms. It wasn't romantic or passionate. It was a deeper recognition of the delicate, precious connection growing between them despite the obstacles.

Samantha's arms wrapped around his waist, and her head rested against his chest. He could feel her warmth through his jacket, and the steady rhythm of her breathing aligned with his own. He inhaled the fresh, floral scent of her shampoo. In the silent moment, the unspoken emotions flowed between them, communicated not through words, but through touch.

Daniel closed his eyes, feeling a sense of peace he hadn't experienced in years. Whatever happened next, whatever decision he made about the Cantata and all it represented, this moment was real. The connection between them was real.

When they finally pulled apart, Samantha's eyes were bright with unshed tears, but she was smiling. A strand of hair had escaped her ponytail, and Daniel gently tucked it behind her ear.

"I should get going," she said softly, checking her watch. "I have an early shift at the hospital tomorrow."

"I'll walk you to your car."

Returning to the restaurant parking lot, they walked in silence, their shoulders occasionally brushing. The night had grown colder, and their breaths were visible in small clouds. At her car, Samantha looked at him, her expression serious again.

"Thanks for meeting me tonight. And thanks for being honest and listening."

He spoke from the heart. "And thank you for giving me a chance." His words came from deep within his soul.

He watched her drive away, her taillights disappearing around the corner, before moving toward his vehicle. Inside, with the engine running but the car still in park, Daniel sat with his thoughts.

A Christmas Cantata. He could already picture it. Her church would be filled with families, carols he had grown up singing, and the nativity story he once believed with his whole heart. Could he sit there without feeling like a fraud? Could he go for Samantha's sake without reopening the wound of his anger at God?

As he finally put the car in drive and pulled onto the road toward home, Daniel realized the decision before him was about far more than a single Christmas service. It was about whether he was willing to take the first tentative step back toward the faith he had once cherished and whether he was brave enough to let Samantha walk beside him on that journey, however uncertain the path might be.

In the darkness of his car, surrounded by the familiar sounds of the engine and the heater, Daniel found himself whispering words he hadn't uttered in two years.

"God, if You're still listening... please help me figure this out."

The prayer, small and uncertain as it was, felt like the first crack in a wall he had built brick by agonizing brick around his heart. Whether anyone was listening on the other side remained to be seen, but somehow, the act of reaching out eased him. And that, perhaps, was the first miracle of his Christmas season.

Chapter 15

Darkness blurred the ceiling above Daniel as he lay awake, the red glow of his alarm clock highlighting another sleepless night. It was seventeen minutes past two in the morning. The weight of Samantha's invitation felt heavy and stifling on his chest.

Two days had passed since she had asked him to attend the Christmas Cantata. Her eyes had been bright with hope, her voice warm with quiet expectation.

He had smiled and nodded, words failing him. Now, in the silence of his bedroom, that simple request exposed a fault line between them. Despite finally telling Samantha about his anger toward God, the thought of sitting in those pews, surrounded by worshippers whose faith still burned bright, sent a wave of dread through him.

She had been more understanding than he deserved, but under-standing wasn't the same as acceptance. How long would it take for her to see their differences as insurmountable?

With a frustrated groan, Daniel threw back the covers and sat on the edge of the bed. The hardwood floor was cold beneath his feet, grounding him in the weight of his own thoughts. The confession he had made to Samantha had been raw, cutting through the fragile peace they had been building.

He had watched her face fall at his words: *I hate Him for it! I haven't spoken to God since the day of her burial.*

And yet, she hadn't walked away. Her grace both humbled and terrified him. It was one thing for her to know about his struggles in theory. It was another to witness them firsthand. How would it be for her to see him in a place of worship with his heart walled off against the very God she loved? Would she still believe in them as a couple once she saw how far he had fallen?

Each moment with Samantha felt like both a gift and a test. She breathed warmth into the hollow spaces of his life, but every mention of God reminded him of the chasm between them. A chasm she sensed but perhaps didn't fully comprehend.

Morning arrived with no answers, only a restless urgency. After a shower and a hastily swallowed cup of coffee, Daniel got into his car with no clear destination in mind. As if guided by instinct, he soon found himself pulling into a place he had avoided for months.

Silent as sentinels, the wrought-iron gates guarded the Whispering Pines Burial Grounds. A heavy December sky, thick with the promise of snow, hung above him as he walked the familiar path to the gravesite.

Teresa Lynn Forrester. Beloved Wife, Daughter, Sister, Friend. Forever in our hearts.

Daniel knelt, his fingers tracing the engraved letters, the polished granite cold beneath his touch. The chill seeped through his skin, settling deep into his bones as if the grief that had never fully left him was rising to meet him again.

"I met someone, Teresa," he said at last, his voice breaking the hush of the cemetery. "Her name is Samantha. Sam." A dry, humorless chuckle escaped him. "You'd probably like her. She's kind, smart, and beautiful. She's a nurse. She helps people, just like you did."

The wind whispered through the trees, offering no reply.

He rubbed a hand over his face. "She invited me to go with her to her church. And honestly, I don't know what to do."

Silence stretched around him, vast and unyielding.

"But there's a problem." His voice dropped, though no one was close enough to hear. "She believes in God... I mean, she really believes. Just like you did, and like I used to."

He exhaled sharply, his breath misting in the cold air. "It took a while, but I finally told her how I feel about Him." His shoulders slumped, the weight of that truth pressing down on him. "And you know what? She didn't walk away. Not yet, anyway. But I keep wondering... when she truly sees how lost I am, will she walk away from me then?"

Daniel sat back on his heels, staring at the headstone as if it might offer guidance. "She invited me to church for a Christmas service." He let out a bitter chuckle, shaking his head. "But I don't belong there, Teresa. Not anymore." His fingers curled into fists, nails digging into his palms. "How can I stand in a place that preaches about God's love when He stole you from me? How can I sing to a God who let you die all alone?"

The familiar anger surged through him, hot and consuming despite the chill. His jaw clenched so tightly that pain radiated up through his temples. The taste of metal filled his mouth. Had he bitten his cheek, or was it the bitterness rising from somewhere deep inside?

"After all this time, I'm still so angry." His voice cracked. "I'm angry at God, I'm angry at the doctors who couldn't save you, and sometimes—" He stopped, the truth too painful to voice.

Sometimes I'm angry at you for leaving me.

The unspoken thought hung between them, sacrilegious in its honesty. Guilt followed immediately, a familiar companion that had walked with him since the day he found her lifeless body in their bed.

A drop of moisture hit the back of his hand, then another. Daniel glanced up, expecting rain, but the sky remained a solid sheet of gray. With surprise, he realized the wetness came from his own eyes. He hadn't cried in months, had thought himself emptied of tears, yet here they were. Tracking silently down his cheeks as a physical manifestation of the grief he had tried so hard to contain.

"I don't know how to do this without you," he whispered, no longer certain if he meant navigating his dwindling faith or building a new relationship. Perhaps both. "How do I sit in that church with Sam, knowing she loves a God I can barely stand to think about? How do I bridge that gap without hurting her?"

The distant sound of a car door slamming pulled him back to the present. He had lost track of time, and his legs had gone numb from kneeling on the frozen ground. With effort, Daniel pushed himself upright, his bones protesting the movement. His knee had fallen asleep, and pins and needles shot through his calf as circulation returned.

"Somehow, I'll figure this out," he murmured, even though he wasn't sure if he believed it.

As he turned to leave, a flicker of red caught his eye. It was a cardinal perching lightly on the next row of headstones. Its feathers stood out, vivid against the bleak winter sky. Teresa had loved cardinals, calling them messengers from heaven. He had always dismissed it as sentimentality, but now... now, he wasn't quite so sure.

The bird tilted its head, regarding him as if waiting.

Daniel exhaled, shaking his head. "If this is a sign, you're going to have to be clearer than that," he muttered. But his voice lacked the sharp edge of before. Just for a moment, the weight on his chest didn't feel quite as heavy.

Miranda opened the door, eyes widening as she took in Daniel's rumpled clothes and hollow expression.

"Daniel? Oh, my goodness!" She didn't wait for an answer. She just grabbed his wrist and pulled him inside.

He barely remembered the drive. One moment, he was at Teresa's grave, and the next, he was standing in Miranda's kitchen, surrounded by the scent of cinnamon and fresh coffee. The warmth of the house pressed in on him, a stark contrast to the icy numbness that was seizing within his chest.

"Hey, Mandy. I hope it's okay that I dropped in. I need to talk and get some things off my mind," he rasped.

Miranda didn't hesitate. She poured a mug of coffee and pressed it into his hands. "Noah's at work right now, so it's just us. Sit and have a drink first. You look like you're halfway frozen. We'll talk after."

The ceramic was hot against his palms, and the heat slowly seeped into his stiff fingers. He wrapped both hands around the mug, letting the warmth anchor him. Miranda sat across from him, silent, waiting. She didn't push. Didn't pry. She just waited patiently, which made it easier to speak. The first sip scalded his tongue, but he welcomed the pain. He craved a way to shatter the numbness that had taken hold.

"I wanted to talk about Sam," he said at last, staring into the coffee's dark swirl.

"I figured as much. You've been different ever since you met her. Happier even. But, you also seem more... more conflicted in some ways."

Daniel's grip tightened around the mug. "She invited me to go with her to her church."

Miranda raised an eyebrow. "Her church is having a Christmas Cantata, right?"

He blinked. "How did you—"

"It's December, Daniel. Churches do this kind of thing," she teased, offering a small smile.

Daniel set the mug down with a dull thud. "I don't think I can do it, Mandy."

"You mean go to church?"

He exhaled sharply. "I don't think I can sit there and hear them sing about God's love and mercy when I don't believe in either." He swallowed, his throat tight. "I don't think I can do it. Not after everything that's happened."

Miranda studied him, her silence heavy with thought. The kitchen clock ticked, steady and unbothered, as sparrows bickered over seeds in the backyard feeder. Life moved forward, whether he was ready or not.

"You've told Sam how you feel about God, didn't you? How did she take it?"

Daniel exhaled, the weight of the moment pressing against his ribs. "She took it better than I expected. She was hurt, but... she didn't walk away." He ran a hand across his jawline. "She said she needs time to think things through. But she still wants to try to continue working on building a relationship between the two of us."

"Well, that sounds good, doesn't it?" Miranda asked, though her brow furrowed. "So, there has to be something more on your mind. What's really bothering you?"

Daniel hesitated. "My going to church with her feels... wrong. It feels like I'm pretending." He traced the rim of his coffee mug. "She's so full of faith, Mandy. It's who she is. And I'll be sitting there, next to her, feeling nothing but anger at the God she worships."

"Are you afraid of losing her?"

His fingers tightened around his mug. "Every day. What if she sees the truth and realizes that the gap between us is just too wide to overcome? What if she realizes that she deserves someone better in her life than me?"

He dragged a hand down his face. "You haven't seen her talk about God, Mandy. It's like she's speaking to someone she personally knows. And me?" He let out a bitter laugh. "Just saying his name fills me with resentment."

"Daniel, let me ask you something. Do you love her?"

The question knocked the air from his lungs. Did he? He thought of Samantha's laughter, the way she listened without judgment, and how just being near her made the world feel less heavy.

"Yeah," he murmured, voice rough. "I think I do."

Miranda smiled. "Then stop trying to protect her from your truth. If she loves you, she won't run from it."

Daniel's gaze dropped to his hands, where the coffee had gone cold. "But what if it's too much for her?" Daniel whispered. "What if she realizes I'll never be the man she needs me to be?"

"But what if you're exactly the man that she needs?" Miranda countered. "What if your honesty isn't a deal-breaker for her, but the foundation of something real for the two of you to build on?" She held his gaze. "And what if, through all of this, God is reaching out to you?"

Daniel scoffed, the old bitterness rising. "God didn't bring her into my life, Mandy. That was a chance. Coincidence. Nothing more."

Miranda arched an eyebrow, unfazed. "Do you really believe it was just chance? That of all the grocery stores, in all the towns, in all the world, she just happened to walk into yours?"

The unexpected *Casablanca* reference nearly made Daniel smile. Nearly. "It's not my grocery store."

Miranda sighed. "You know what I mean. You've spent two years being angry at God for taking Teresa. But what if—" She held his gaze steady. "What if He sent Sam into your life in order to bring you back to Him?"

Daniel wanted to brush off her words, to reject the idea outright. But they stuck and settled into that empty, aching space inside him. What if there was a reason Samantha had entered his life now?

He clenched his jaw, and his fingers tightened around his coffee mug. He didn't want to believe it. But he also didn't know what to believe anymore.

"I just don't know," he admitted, voice barely above a whisper.

Miranda reached across the table, covering his hand with hers. Her warmth steadied him, the way it always had. Like when they were kids, facing thunderstorms together.

"Look, you don't have to figure it all out tonight. But you do have to be willing to try. Try for her, and try for yourself."

Daniel swallowed, staring into his coffee. Could he really do this?

Slowly, deliberately, he nodded. "I'll go with her."

"Are you going because you want to, or because you think it's what she wants?"

Daniel paused before admitting, "I want to understand both. And I want to see what she sees." He exhaled. "And yeah... I want to make her happy." His voice dipped lower. "Is that so wrong?"

Miranda squeezed his hand. "No. But don't lie to her, Daniel, even if it's a lie by omission. If you're struggling, you need to let her know. Keep that door open, because once it closes, it's hard to pry back open."

"I will," he vowed, the responsibility heavy upon him. "Telling her the truth was the first step. Now, I need to show her that I'm willing to try."

Miranda's smile softened. "I'm proud of you, you know. You're facing this head-on, and that takes courage."

Daniel swallowed hard. Courage? That wasn't what he felt. He felt terror, doubt, and the fear of stepping into a church and feeling nothing.

But Miranda's faith in him sparked something small, but real. Maybe, just maybe, there was a way forward through the maze of grief, love, and doubt.

Rising from the table, he pulled her into a tight hug. "Thank you, little sister."

"For what?"

He exhaled, his voice quieter. "For not giving up on me. Even when I gave up on everything else, you've always been there for me."

She hugged him back fiercely. "Never, big brother. Not ever in a million years."

That evening, Daniel sat on the edge of his bed, thumb hovering over the call button. Samantha's name glowed on the screen.

He exhaled, his chest tight with uncertainty. The conversation with Miranda still echoed in his mind, tangling with the unexpected peace he had felt at Teresa's grave. Could he really do this?

Taking a steadying breath, he pressed the button. She answered on the second ring.

"Daniel... hi!" Her voice was inviting and familiar. It was a restraining tether preventing him from venturing into the vast unknown.

"Hey, Sam. I was calling to talk to you about the Christmas Cantata... "

"Oh." A beat of silence. "Daniel, if it's too much, I understand. I don't want you to feel pressured—"

"I want to go."

The words left his mouth before he fully understood them, and for a moment, he sat with the shock of it. But it was true. He wanted to go. Not just for her, but because somewhere deep inside, something in him was reaching for more.

"I want to experience this celebration with you," he said, softer this time.

The silence that followed was brief but weighted with emotion. When she spoke again, her voice was hushed, as if sharing a precious secret.

"Really? You'll come with me, even though... ?"

"Yes," he said, hesitant but sure. A smile tugged at the corner of his mouth. "I can't promise how I'll feel, but I want to try. For us."

He heard the breath she let out, as if she had been holding it. When she spoke again, her voice was softer, reverent, as if she recognized this moment for what it was. "Daniel... thank you."

They talked through the details, but Daniel barely registered the logistics. There was a shift inside him—not a dramatic revelation, not faith returning all at once, but a crack—a willingness.

He wouldn't pretend to others that he believed. But he would show up. And maybe, for now, that would be enough.

It was a start. A small step back toward the light, even if he couldn't yet see where the path led.

The night stretched quiet as Daniel set his phone down. Outside, stars burned against the black sky, distant but steady.

He recalled what Teresa had once said while looking up at the stars as her fingers gently traced the constellations: *The stars remind us that we're not alone. They remind us that there's something greater out there.*

He had stopped believing in something greater the day he lost her. But now, staring at those same stars, he wondered. Not faith.

Not yet. But maybe, just maybe, the silence wasn't as empty as he once thought.

Chapter 16

THE WARM GLOW OF her bedside lamp softened the edges of Samantha's small apartment. On the bed, she had laid out a deep burgundy dress, black heels, and the pearl earrings her mother had given her at her high school graduation. Her fingers traced the cool pearls, grounding herself in their quiet significance.

She perched on the edge of the bed, hands twisting together. "Lord, I don't know if he's ready. Maybe I shouldn't have pushed." Her voice wavered. "But I believe You placed him in my life for a reason. Please... open his heart. Even a little."

The memory of Daniel's hesitation when she invited him to the Christmas Cantata still unsettled her. She had heard his apprehension and felt his tension before he agreed. Yet beneath his reluctance, she heard a longing, perhaps, or at least a willingness to step outside his comfort zone for her sake.

Her phone chimed with a text notification, jolting her from her thoughts. Olivia's name appeared on the screen:

Praying for you and Daniel tonight. Call me after! Love you!

Samantha smiled, typing back a quick thank you. Olivia had been her sounding board these past weeks, offering wisdom when Samantha questioned whether she should continue seeing a man whose faith lay dormant. She read Olivia's next message of advice: *Be patient. God's timing isn't always our timing.*

As Samantha slipped into her dress, she fought against the nervous flutter in her stomach. This evening wasn't just about a Christmas service. It was about inviting Daniel into the most essential part of her life, about sharing her faith in a way that words alone couldn't express.

She paused before her mirror, smoothing the fabric over her hips. "Help me be a light, Lord," she prayed. "And not a spotlight."

The church parking lot was alive with the movement of families making their way inside, and their laughter was carried by the crisp December air. Samantha stood near the entrance, coat pulled tight against the cold, her breath curling in the night.

She scanned the passing cars, her fingers tightening around the strap of her purse.

What if he changed his mind?

She checked her phone again—no messages. Daniel promised to meet her fifteen minutes before the service, but that time had come and gone. Each passing minute stretched her nerves tighter, until she found herself bargaining with God in silent desperation.

Just let him come, Lord. Even if nothing changes, and even if he's just here to be polite. Please, just let him come.

Headlights flashed as a familiar car pulled into the lot. Samantha's breath hitched. Relief crashed over her, but she forced herself to stay still, watching as Daniel stepped out.

"You came."

"Yeah," he said, voice low. Uncertain. But here.

Up close, Samantha could see the effort he had made. His charcoal dress pants and navy button-down were crisp, and his locs were neatly groomed. But it was his posture that caught her attention. His shoulders were squared yet stiff, and his gaze flickered to the church doors like an outsider looking in.

"By the way, you look beautiful," Daniel said, his voice quieter than before.

Warmth spread through her. "Thank you. You clean up pretty well yourself." She resisted the urge to adjust her earrings. "Are you ready?"

His hesitation was brief, but she caught it. Then, with a slight smile, he extended his arm. "Lead the way."

As they reached the top step, the church doors swung open, revealing Sister Madeline, a silver-haired fixture of the congregation. Her warm smile deepened with curiosity as her gaze landed on Daniel.

"Sam, what a joy to see you!" Then, with a knowing tilt of her head, "And who is this fine young man?"

"This is Daniel Forrester," Samantha said, feeling a peculiar mix of pride and nerves. "Daniel, this is Sister Madeline Jackson."

Daniel extended his hand, his voice effortlessly smooth. "It's a pleasure to meet you, ma'am."

Sister Madeline beamed. "Well, aren't you just a blessing! We're so glad you could join us tonight."

They wove through the foyer, occasionally stopping for the introductions that came in waves. There were smiling faces, firm handshakes, and warm greetings wrapped in phrases like "*God bless you*" and "*Praise the Lord.*"

Daniel handled it with ease, his responses polite, and his smile intact. But Samantha noticed how his fingers curled at his sides, how his nods became sharper, and how he glanced toward the sanctuary as if needing an escape route.

When they finally entered the sanctuary, Samantha guided them to a pew about halfway down. It was close enough to feel engaged, but not so close as to make Daniel feel exposed. The space breathed with anticipation, decorated in deep greens and rich reds, with poinsettias lining the altar and white candles glowing in tiered stands.

"Is this okay?" she whispered, gesturing to their seats.

Daniel nodded, his expression softening as he took in the transformed sanctuary. "This reminds me of the Christmas Eve services from when I was younger," he admitted quietly.

The wistfulness in his tone gave Samantha hope. She squeezed his hand lightly as they settled into their seats. Her heart lifted a silent prayer of thanks that they had made it this far.

The first notes of *O Come, O Come Emmanuel* drifted through the sanctuary, the choir's rich and reverent voices layered like a prayer woven in harmony. Candlelight flickered against the stained-glass windows, casting soft halos along the pews.

Samantha stole a glance at Daniel. His expression was unreadable, but his grip on the program had tightened. He wasn't just sitting in a pew. He was standing in a place that once held meaning, and maybe, somewhere deep inside, it still did.

As the choir's voices swelled in *O Holy Night,* Samantha noticed the shift. Daniel's posture softened, and his shoulders were no longer stiff with hesitation. His breathing slowed and deepened. Then, as the soloist's voice soared on, *Fall on your knees,* his fingers clenched around the program. It was barely noticeable, but enough.

Was he remembering? Was he thinking of other Christmases, and other nights filled with worship, before grief had rewritten everything he once believed?

When the congregation rose for *Joy to the World,* Daniel stood, too, without any hesitation. He didn't sing, but he didn't withdraw either.

Samantha glanced at him, her chest tightening. This man, who had once turned his back on faith, stood in a house of worship, surrounded by voices lifted in praise. He didn't do it because he believed, but he did it because she had asked him to come.

Pastor Wilson's voice carried through the sanctuary, steady and sure. "The Christmas story reminds us that God works in ways we don't expect. A king was born in a stable. A savior arrived as a helpless infant. And divine light broke through even the darkest nights of our lives."

Samantha felt the words settle deep. Hadn't she prayed for Daniel's heart to open? Hadn't she asked God for hope in the places she couldn't reach?

Maybe it was happening. Maybe, even now, Daniel was stepping toward something neither of them fully understood.

The sanctuary glowed with candlelight as voices hushed for *Silent Night*. Samantha accepted the flame, then turned to Daniel, tilting her candle toward his.

Their eyes met above the flickering light. The world fell silent for a brief moment, revealing the sight to her. A tiny fissure appeared in his guarded composure, disclosing a fleeting glimpse of his unspoken yearning. Maybe, there was even the faintest whisper of surrender.

With the lights dimmed, only candlelight remained, and as their hands holding the candles trembled, Daniel's fingers brushed hers. Slowly, he then intertwined their fingers. The simple act created a bridge of genuine human connection, its tenderness and truth spanning the distance between their contrasting spiritualities.

"There's nothing quite like eating breakfast food at night," Samantha said, smiling across the laminated menu at Daniel. The twenty-four-hour diner was unusually busy, a hive of activity at close to eleven o'clock on a Sunday night. The restaurant was a blend of churchgoers finishing their evening service and regulars looking for a comforting meal before beginning the work week.

"I couldn't agree more," Daniel replied, the awkwardness from earlier in the evening fading into something more comfortable. "There's something almost rebellious about ordering pancakes after dark."

A waitress brought a pot of coffee. "Good evening. My name is Denise, and I'll be your server. Do you know what you'd like to eat?"

"I'll have the blueberry waffle special with a side of bacon, please," Samantha ordered. "And a glass of orange juice."

"Make that two," Daniel added. "But I'll have mine with sausage links instead of bacon."

Denise nodded approvingly. "Good choices. I'll be right back with those drinks."

The fluorescent lights buzzed softly, contrasting with the candlelit sanctuary they had left behind. Yet, somehow, the hush between them still felt sacred.

Samantha traced the rim of her glass, gathering her thoughts. "Thank you for coming tonight," she said at last. "I know it wasn't easy for you, and I appreciate that you made the effort."

"It was..." He hesitated, rubbing a hand over the back of his neck. "It was different from what I expected."

Samantha studied him. "Different good or different bad?"

He exhaled. "I don't know. I guess I thought I'd feel nothing when I walked into the sanctuary. I thought that it would be just another church service. I thought it would be just more songs about a God that I had stopped believing in."

She remained silent, letting him work through the words.

"But then..." He swallowed. "Then they started singing, and for a second, I—" His voice caught, and he shook his head. "I don't know, Sam. It was like something stirred inside of me. Something that I thought was dead. And I hated it."

Samantha's brow furrowed. "Why?"

His voice was barely above a whisper. "Because it made me wonder if all this time... if all this time I've been wrong. And I don't know if I'm ready to face that."

Samantha's heart quickened at this small revelation. "But, that's how faith can be sometimes. Even when we think we've left it behind, it still has a claim on us."

His response was gentle. "Well, I don't know about that. But I do know that watching you tonight, seeing how deeply you believe, and how naturally you worship... it made me wonder. I started thinking about how it would feel to embrace that certainty for myself once again."

The waitress returned with their orange juice, momentarily interrupting their conversation. When she left, Samantha sipped the tart sweetness before responding.

"I'm not always certain, Daniel," she admitted. "Some days, my faith feels like I'm hanging on to a rope in the dark, and I'm not always sure if it's even tied to anything."

She traced a drop of condensation down the side of her glass. "After I lost both of my parents, there were moments when I questioned everything. But I kept holding on because letting go of my faith seemed worse than the struggle itself."

Daniel's expression softened. "How did you find your way back to... to that peace I saw in you tonight?"

"I did it one day at a time and one prayer at a time." She met his gaze directly. "And I had lots of help. I had my friend Olivia, her parents, and my church family. They carried me during the times when I couldn't walk on my own."

Their food arrived, steam rising from the golden waffles piled with fresh blueberries and crowned with dollops of whipped cream. The conversation paused as they each took their first bites, savoring the sweet-tart combination.

"This is amazing," Daniel declared, gesturing with his fork. "Breakfast at night was definitely the right call."

Samantha laughed, grateful for the lighter moment. "My dad used to say breakfast food works for any meal because it's just that good."

"Your dad sounds like he was a wise man."

She smiled at the memory. "He was. He had this saying... *Life's too short for soggy cereal.*' It was his way of telling me not to settle for less than I deserved."

Daniel's smile faded. He glanced down, fingers tapping against his glass. "Is that what I am to you, Sam?" His voice was quieter now, more raw. "Am I your consolation prize of soggy cereal?"

The question caught her off guard. "What? No, of course not."

Daniel's grip tightened around his fork. "But you deserve better, Sam. You deserve someone who shares your faith completely. You deserve someone who doesn't hesitate when you ask them to pray. Someone without all this... baggage."

Samantha set her fork down, searching for the right words. "Daniel, faith isn't a checkbox on some relationship qualification list. It's a journey."

Reaching across the table, she covered his hand with hers. "And to tell you the truth, I'd rather be with someone who's honestly wrestling with their faith than with someone just going through the motions to impress me."

Uncertainty shone in his eyes as they locked with hers. "What if I never make it back to where I was? What if... this is as far as I can go?"

The question hung between them, weighted with implications for their future. Samantha felt the familiar tug-of-war in her heart—her deep desire for a partner who shared her faith versus her growing feelings for this man whose spiritual path remained uncertain.

She exhaled slowly. "I don't have all the answers, Daniel. I wish I did. But I know what we have. This connection matters. You showed up tonight, even when it wasn't easy. That means something."

She squeezed his hand. "And I know that I'm not ready to walk away from this or from us, just because the road might be complicated."

Their fingers laced as he gently turned his hand under hers.

"I don't know where this journey will take me. But I promise you, Sam... I won't hide anything from you. I'll be honest every step of the way."

Her heart swelled. "That's all I'm asking for."

They finished their meal in comfortable conversation, sharing stories from their childhoods and discovering new common interests beyond their initial connection.

After paying their bill, they found the diner deserted. The murmur of conversation died away, leaving them in a rare, profound silence that amplified the moment's importance beyond what either dared to confess.

Outside, the night air nipped at their skin, each breath curling in the cold. Daniel fell into step beside Samantha, their shoulders brushing, not by accident, but as if neither of them quite wanted to pull away.

The warmth between them lingered, defying the winter chill.

"I had a good time with you tonight," Daniel said as they reached her car, his voice lower, more certain than she expected. "Not just at the diner, but at the service too. Thank you for inviting me."

Samantha turned, her pulse stuttering at his nearness. "I appreciate that you were willing to come."

The parking lot lights bathed him in a soft glow, casting shifting shadows across his face. She was transfixed, though, by the warmth and focus in his eyes. A silent current hummed between them, unspoken but undeniable.

His hand lifted to her face, and his thumb grazed her cheekbone with exquisite tenderness. It was a single touch, yet it sent a shiver coursing through her. "Sam," he whispered, her name a question, a promise, a prayer.

Her heart pounded so loudly, she swore he could hear it. The rational part of her whispered that she should slow down and keep her guard up. But the moment stretched, charged with something she couldn't fight. She tilted her face upward, drawn to him by a force she didn't fully understand but had no desire to resist.

The scent of his cologne, the subtle notes of sandalwood, and a hint of warm spice enveloped her, heightening her awareness of how close they stood. And then, finally, he closed the distance.

When his lips met hers, it was soft at first. Tentative, as if he were waiting for her to pull away. But she didn't. She dissolved into him, her hands instinctively rising to caress his neck, her fingers playing with his short locs. His heartbeat thundered beneath her touch, matching her own.

The kiss deepened, a slow unraveling of restraint. Heat bloomed low in her belly, spreading outward until her skin tingled in the cold evening air. Daniel's arm encircled her waist, drawing her closer, and she let him. She let herself fall just a little deeper into something she had tried so hard to guard against.

The world faded. The cars. The distant murmur of voices. The chilly breeze against her skin. None of it existed. Only this. The warmth of his body, the unspoken longing in the way he held her, and the dizzying realization that she was falling. Hard.

When they finally parted, their breaths mingled in the cold air, their foreheads resting against each other's. Daniel's eyes were still closed as if he were gathering himself, and the barely restrained longing in his expression sent another shiver through her.

"I should go," he murmured, though his arm remained around her waist, contradicting his words.

Samantha nodded, not trusting herself to speak as she struggled to slow her racing heart. She recognized the dangerous territory they approached and how easily physical attraction could cloud judgment and blur carefully drawn boundaries. Yet she couldn't deny the powerful chemistry between them, a force as real and undeniable as gravity.

But all she could manage was, "Goodnight, Daniel."

His thumb brushed against her lower lip in a gesture so intimate it stole her breath. And then, with visible reluctance, he pulled away, as if staying another moment would make leaving impossible.

She climbed into her car and exhaled shakily, gripping the steering wheel. She had spent so long guarding her heart, building walls of faith and caution. But tonight, Daniel Forrester had slipped past every single one.

As she drove home, the memory of the kiss lingered like a prayer on her lips. For all their differences, for all the uncertainty of the path ahead, something true had awakened between them tonight—something worth nurturing, worth fighting for, worth believing in.

Samantha's apartment welcomed her with familiar shadows and silence. As she readied for bed, her evening routine culminated as it always did. She kneeled beside her bed, her mother's Bible open before her.

"Lord, thank You for tonight." She touched her lips lightly, still feeling the imprint of his kiss. "I don't know where this journey leads, but I trust You're with us both, every step of the way."

As she climbed into bed, Samantha felt a peace that transcended understanding. Daniel might not share her faith completely. Not yet, and perhaps, not ever. But tonight had shown her glimpses of the man he had been and could be again. Their paths had converged from different directions, and whether they would continue together remained in God's hands.

But for now, for tonight, that was enough.

Chapter 17

THE CRISP JANUARY AIR nipped at Daniel's skin as he stood beside Samantha on the steps of Cottonwood Faith Community Center. Around them, voices blended in a hum of warm greetings, laughter punctuating the morning chill.

Samantha's hand curled around his arm, her warmth bleeding through his wool coat. He exhaled, watching his breath dissipate in the cold.

"Thank you so much for coming," she whispered, squeezing his arm lightly. Her eyes shone with something close to joy.

Daniel forced a smile, but it felt strained. These past few weeks had been a delicate balancing act. Samantha was trying her best to give him space. Yet, Daniel felt lost, stumbling amidst the ruins of his shattered trust. He had agreed to this service as a peace offering.

But now, standing at the threshold, it felt like he was stepping into a house that no longer felt like a home. The walls were too tight. And the air was too thick.

"It meant a lot to me to be here with you," he said, and that much was true. The joy on Samantha's face when he met her outside the church had been worth the discomfort of the hour that followed.

Pastor Scott Wilson approached, his silver-rimmed glasses catching the pale winter light. His handshake was firm, his eyes carrying the steady warmth of a man well-acquainted with life's storms.

"Good afternoon, Sam," he greeted warmly before turning to Daniel. "And you must be Daniel. Sam's told me so much about you."

Daniel nodded, feeling an odd prick of unease.

"I couldn't help but think of your namesake during the service today," Pastor Wilson added.

"My namesake?" Daniel echoed.

"Yes." The pastor smiled. "The prophet Daniel from the Bible. Daniel was a man who stood firm in faith, even while he was in the lion's den. You have a name that carries great strength and power."

The words sat heavy in Daniel's chest. He didn't feel strong. He felt lost. And if standing firm meant trusting a God who had let him down, then maybe the name didn't fit him at all.

A poignant recollection stirred in Daniel's memory. He recalled his mother's soft and reverent voice as she told him bedtime stories from her well-worn Bible.

"It was nice to meet you, sir," Daniel managed, discomfort tightening his chest.

The pastor nodded, sensing his unease. "I hope to see you again soon." With a gentle pat on Samantha's shoulder, he moved on to greet other members.

As they walked toward Daniel's car, Samantha glanced at him. "What did Pastor Wilson mean about your name?"

He opened her door before circling to the driver's side, grateful for the momentary reprieve from her question. The dashboard clock read 12:17 p.m. as he settled behind the wheel.

"My mother named me after Daniel in the Bible," he finally said, turning the key in the ignition. The car rumbled to life, and the heat slowly dispelled the chill. "The story of Daniel was one of her favorite stories."

"Would you mind telling me about it?" There was a gentle curiosity in her voice.

Daniel pulled onto the road, his eyes fixed ahead. "She used to read it to me at bedtime. Daniel was taken captive in Babylon, but he never abandoned his faith... not even when it meant certain death. They threw him into a den of lions for praying to God instead of the king." His grip tightened on the wheel. "But God sent angels to shut the lions' mouths, and Daniel came out unharmed."

Samantha sighed. "It's a beautiful story of faithfulness. Your mother chose well."

Daniel exhaled sharply, fingers flexing against the wheel. "She always wanted me to have that kind of faith. But look at me now." He let out a humorless chuckle. "I guess I've fallen pretty far from living up to my namesake's example, huh?"

Lightly, she touched his arm. "The path of faith isn't always straightforward, Daniel. Sometimes, it's full of detours and dead ends."

His retort, laced with bitterness, took them both aback. "But not everyone stops talking to God altogether."

A heavy silence settled between them as Daniel drove. Samantha gazed out the window, her reflection thoughtful in the glass.

"My church has a couples' Bible study that's starting next week," she finally said. "It meets on Tuesday evenings. I thought... I thought maybe we could go together?"

Daniel felt a knot form in his stomach. Attending a church service was one thing, but a weekly commitment to discuss his faith with strangers was entirely different.

"I'm not sure that's a good idea. My schedule's pretty packed with semester planning, and the basketball team needs extra help with coaching."

He sensed her disappointment, even though she attempted to sound upbeat. "Oh. Sure. I understand. Maybe another time."

But did she really? Daniel wondered as he drove toward her apartment. How could she understand when he himself couldn't explain the contradictions that were tearing him apart? He cared for Samantha. He might even be falling in love with her, but the spiritual gap between them seemed to widen with each passing day.

"Yes, maybe another time," he offered lamely, knowing the words rang hollow.

Samantha nodded, but the light had dimmed in her eyes.

A faint hum from the heater was the only sound as Daniel sat alone in his classroom. The January sun shone brightly across the deserted desks, highlighting the same turkey sandwich he had eaten nearly every day since Teresa's passing.

His phone vibrated with a text from Samantha: *Hope your day is going well. Praying your meeting with the principal goes smoothly.*

Daniel stared at the message, particularly the word *"praying."* It was such a simple word, yet it stirred an uncomfortable mixture of warmth and resistance within him. Unlike him, Samantha mentioned praying so naturally.

He typed back: *Thanks. I'll let you know how it goes.*

Setting his phone aside, Daniel took a bite of his sandwich, the flavors bland and uninspiring. His gaze landed on the Bible verse calendar a student had given him for Christmas. January's verse was Jeremiah 29:11: *For I know the plans I have for you, declares the LORD, plans to prosper you and not to harm you, plans to give you hope and a future.*

Plans to prosper, not to harm. Daniel's mind drifted to Teresa and to the aneurysm that took her without warning. Where was the prosperity in that? Where was the hope?

Yet, Samantha had lost both her parents and somehow maintained her faith. She didn't just go through the motions. Her belief was absolute and heartfelt.

Daniel brushed crumbs from his desk, a question forming that he had been avoiding for months. Had his anger at God become a habit rather than a genuine feeling? Was he holding on to it because letting go felt like he was betraying Teresa's memory?

The biblical Daniel refused to abandon his faith, even when faced with imminent death. He stood firm in his beliefs despite overwhelming pressure. Why couldn't he, Daniel Forrester, find the same courage? Why couldn't he find the courage to either fully reject his faith, or fully embrace it?

He was caught in the middle, neither believing nor disbelieving, and the tension was starting to wear on him.

"So then Mrs. Young says, *'Noah, I don't care if you've been selling houses for ten years! My granddaughter's dollhouse is not for sale!'*" Noah Bolton laughed, covering his wife's hand with his.

Miranda chuckled and leaned into her husband's shoulder. "You should've seen his face when he figured out she was just kidding."

Daniel smiled, grateful for the lighthearted moment. The Italian restaurant Miranda had suggested for dinner was warm and inviting. Red-checkered tablecloths and soft lighting created an intimate atmosphere despite the Friday night crowd.

"It sounds like your real estate business is doing well," Samantha observed, reaching for her water glass.

"It's actually doing better than expected for January," Noah confirmed. "People seem eager for fresh starts in the new year."

"Speaking of fresh starts," Miranda said, turning to Samantha. "Our church book club is starting a new book next month. We're reading *Redeeming Love* by Francine Rivers. You should join us. And don't worry. You don't have to be a member to be a part of it. And I'd love for you to be my guest."

Daniel tensed, his fork pausing midway to his mouth. New Hope Baptist was his former church, the place where he and Teresa had worshipped and where they had built a community. The thought of Samantha there without him created a strange dissonance.

"Thank you for the invitation. That sounds lovely. When does it meet?"

As Miranda explained the details, Daniel's attention drifted to the careful way his sister avoided mentioning his absence from church. Since Teresa's death, Miranda and Noah had invited him countless times, but each gentle suggestion was met with increasing resistance until they finally stopped asking.

"Daniel, you remember Francine Rivers, right?" Miranda nudged. "We read her books in that couple's Bible study. You and Teresa loved them."

"Vaguely," Daniel replied, though the memory was crystal clear—the Bible study had been three months before Teresa died, a time of fellowship that now seemed to belong to someone else's life.

"Her books are amazing," Noah commented. "They really offer comfort and guidance in trusting God through difficult periods."

An uncomfortable silence fell, and everyone at the table was acutely aware of the elephant in the room. Daniel reached for his wine, taking a long sip to avoid meeting anyone's eyes.

"How's the emergency department these days, Sam?" Miranda asked, skillfully changing the subject.

As Samantha described a challenging case from earlier that week, Daniel studied her animated expressions and the way her hands moved expressively as she spoke. She radiated such genuine compassion, which she gave to her patients and everyone she encountered.

"... so I told Dr. Lawson I'd been praying about the treatment plan, and he agreed we should try the alternative approach," Samantha was saying. "Thankfully, the little boy's fever broke the next morning."

"That's wonderful," Miranda exclaimed. "God works in such amazing ways."

Noah nodded in agreement. "The Lord always comes through, doesn't He?"

Daniel felt a familiar discomfort creep up his spine. They spoke with such unwavering conviction. He had once shared that certainty. Now, he felt like an impostor, pretending to be someone he wasn't, someone who still believed in divine intervention and answered prayers.

Miranda spoke with excitement. "Oh! Before I forget. Pastor Morrison asked about you last Sunday, Daniel. He said to tell you the basketball team could use an assistant coach if you're interested."

"I'm pretty busy with the school's basketball team," Daniel replied, the excuse sounding hollow even to his own ears.

Miranda's smile dimmed slightly. "Of course. I just thought I'd pass along the message."

The rest of dinner passed pleasantly enough, but Daniel couldn't shake the feeling of disconnection. His sister, his brother-in-law, and the woman he was falling for were all people he cherished. But an invisible barrier separated him from them. Their shared faith was one he had abandoned, and their language, one he had unlearned.

By the time they stepped out into the chilly night air, the strain of maintaining appearances had left Daniel exhausted.

"Your sister and brother-in-law are wonderful," Samantha said as they drove away from the restaurant. "I can see why you're so close to them."

Daniel nodded, keeping his eyes on the road. "Noah and Mandy have always had a gift for seeing the good in people."

"I'm really looking forward to the book club. It'll be nice to connect with some of the women at your church."

"It's not my church anymore." His words were more cutting than he meant them to be.

Samantha turned to look at him. Her expression was a mixture of surprise and hurt. "I know you haven't been attending, but I thought... I thought you'd been going there for some years with Noah and Mandy, right?"

His grip tightened on the steering wheel. "Just because I'd been going there for a long time doesn't make it my home forever."

A tense silence fell between them. Daniel could feel Samantha's questioning gaze on him, but he kept his eyes fixed ahead.

Finally, she spoke. "It's almost February, and Valentine's Day is coming up in a few weeks."

The unexpected change of topic threw him. "Yes, I suppose it is."

"My church is hosting a couples' retreat at Lake Windemere Resort that weekend," Samantha said hesitantly. "I've heard it's beautiful. They have hiking, candlelight dinners, and couples' devotionals planned as part of the itinerary."

The word *"devotionals"* tightened something in Daniel's chest. He couldn't believe she wanted him to share his broken faith, or rather, his lack of faith, in front of strangers. That was just too much.

"Sam... " He exhaled, hearing the tension in his own voice. "I really don't think I can do that."

"We don't have to participate in everything," she offered quickly. "We could skip some of the devotional sessions if you're not comfortable."

A sigh escaped Daniel's lips as his frustration grew. "That's not the point. The retreat is centered around faith... a faith I'm still trying to figure out. I would feel like I would have to pretend the whole time I was there."

"You wouldn't have to pretend. Everyone would be on their own journey, just like you and me."

Daniel shook his head. "You don't get it. These people... they're like you. Faith isn't a battle for them. They haven't had it torn away like I have."

Samantha spoke softly. "Daniel, believe me, faith isn't always easy for me either. I lost my parents. I had my heart broken. And I have struggled, more than you know. But I make a choice to choose to trust God anyway."

Daniel remembered their conversation weeks ago, when Samantha had opened up about finding her ex-boyfriend Paul with another woman. He remembered how devastated she had been, not just by the betrayal, but also by how far she had strayed from her faith during that relationship. He had been moved by her vulnerability and touched by her willingness to share that painful chapter of her life.

"So, what are you saying?" Daniel's defenses shot up, despite that memory. "That I'm weak because I lost my faith when Teresa died?"

"That's not what I meant at all. I'm just saying that faith is a choice that we have to make, not a feeling."

Daniel pulled the car to the side of the road, putting it in park before turning to face her. "Do you think I *wanted* to lose my faith?" Daniel's voice cracked despite his effort to stay in control. "*I prayed for Teresa every day!* I thanked God for her every morning. And then, just like that, she was gone! No warning, no goodbye. Just... gone."

Samantha's eyes filled with tears. "Daniel... I can't pretend to know exactly how that feels—"

"No, you don't," Daniel said sharply, interrupting. "You can't know what it's like to have everything... your whole life ripped away in an instant. To walk through the door and find your wife... " His voice broke, and he had to look away.

The silence stretched, thick with unspoken grief. Outside, a streetlight flickered, slicing shadows across the dashboard like cracks in fragile glass.

"I'm sorry. And you're right," Samantha said softly. "I can't fully understand what you experienced. But I do know what it's like to lose people you love. And I know that shutting people out won't bring them back."

Daniel closed his eyes, steeling himself against the impact of her words. However, they went down, resting in spots he wasn't prepared to confront. He glanced back at Samantha, her expression inscrutable, a delicate blend of pain and empathy.

"I care about you, Daniel, more than I can even explain. But I can't pretend that your non-relationship with God doesn't matter to me. That's just part of who I am."

Daniel's response was immediate. "And my struggle with faith is part of who I am right now. I can't just flip a switch and become the man of faith you want me to be."

"I'm not asking you to flip a switch," Samantha said. "I'm asking you to be open to the journey. I just want you to consider that maybe, just maybe, God is still there, waiting for you to turn back to Him."

Daniel stared out the windshield, the night stretching dark and vast beyond. "And what if I can't? What if I'm never able to find my way back? What then, Sam?"

The question remained unanswered. The silence from Samantha resonated deeply, causing a painful fracture in Daniel's composure.

"I think I should go ahead and take you home." He shifted the car into drive.

The remainder of the journey passed in silence, each lost in their own thoughts. When they reached Samantha's apartment building, Daniel walked her to the door, the distance between them feeling greater than the physical space.

"Good night, Samantha," he said formally, unable to meet her eyes.

"Daniel." Her voice stopped him as he turned to leave. "I'm not giving up on you. Or us. I just need you to know that."

He nodded once, not trusting himself to speak, and walked back to his car.

Later that night, Daniel sat alone in his living room, his untouched glass of water reflecting the dim light. The house was still, save for the occasional creak of settling wood and the distant hum of the refrigerator. This was all a reminder that life, however unchanged, continued moving forward.

His argument with Samantha looped through his mind, each word cutting deeper. She wasn't wrong. Her faith shaped and defined her. How could he ask her to compromise that?

Yet how could he pretend to be someone he wasn't? The biblical Daniel had refused to bow to false gods and had maintained his integrity even when it would have been easier to conform. There was courage in that stance, a courage Daniel wasn't sure he possessed.

He couldn't let go of faith entirely, and he couldn't bring himself to declare that God had abandoned him. But neither could he reach for it again, knowing the sting of silence, the ache of unanswered prayers.

Daniel picked up his phone, his thumb hovering over Samantha's name. He wanted to call and apologize for his sharp words. But then what? The distance between them wasn't just hurt feelings. It was faith and the absence of it, and that fundamental challenge remained unresolved.

With a heavy sigh, he set the phone down. The image of the biblical Daniel standing firm amid the lions haunted him. His namesake possessed an unwavering certainty and a foundation that couldn't be shaken.

Daniel wondered if he would ever find that kind of certainty again. Or, what if he was destined to remain caught in this limbo, neither believing nor disbelieving, while the woman he was growing to love slipped further from his grasp?

Chapter 18

Samantha's apartment felt unnaturally quiet. She had spent the past hour trying to focus on a medical journal article about new trauma protocols, but the words kept blurring before her eyes as her mind replayed their argument from earlier.

Setting the journal aside, she reached for her mother's Bible. As she opened it, a pressed flower, a memento from her mother's garden, fluttered to her lap. Samantha picked it up gently, its dried petals fragile against her fingertips, a reminder of how carefully one must handle precious things. She whispered to the empty room:

I handled this all wrong, didn't I?

Their argument about the couple's Valentine's Day getaway had escalated, revealing a deep rift in their relationship. The look of pure agony in Daniel's eyes when he stopped the car stayed with her. He was clearly frustrated, accusing her of not understanding his grief. She understood his words weren't malicious, yet they still deeply wounded her.

But what troubled her most wasn't his anger. It was the realization that despite their growing closeness, she couldn't bridge the gap between his spiritual estrangement and her own deeply rooted faith. How could they build a future together when they viewed the most important aspects of life through such different lenses?

Samantha closed her eyes, letting the gravity of the situation sink in. After her experience with betrayal, she promised herself she wouldn't compromise on her spiritual journey. But Daniel wasn't Paul. His struggle with faith stemmed from a place of profound loss, not a selfish disregard.

Opening her eyes, Samantha reached for her phone. Her screen showed a photo of them at Heavenly Delights, both laughing over something Willow had said. The memory lodged in her throat. Would they ever share such easy joy again?

Taking a fortifying breath, she started typing a message to Daniel:

I've been thinking about our conversation. I care about you deeply, but I need time and space to reflect on what this means. I hope you can understand.

Her finger loomed over the send button before she finally pressed it, releasing a breath she hadn't realized she was holding. Whatever came next, she needed this clarity, not just for him, but for herself.

Setting her phone aside, Samantha knelt beside her bed and prayed:

Father, I don't know what to do. I care for Daniel, but I'm afraid I'm not strong enough to help him find his way back to You without losing my own path. Please show me how to love while staying true to the beliefs I cherish in my heart.

As she rose, a peculiar peace settled over her. She didn't have all the answers, but she had taken the first step toward finding them. For now, that would have to be enough.

The buzzing of her phone woke Samantha from a fitful sleep. Reaching for it in the darkness, she saw Daniel's response to her message:

I understand. Take all the time you need. I'll be here when you're ready.

His words were simple, but she could feel the restrained emotion behind them. A lump formed in her throat as she set the phone back on her nightstand.

She awoke earlier than she wanted to, the gray morning light barely penetrating her curtains as she started getting ready for work. The hospital would be a welcome distraction. Caring for others always helped her to put her own troubles in perspective.

When she arrived, the emergency room was unusually quiet, a rare lull that the staff knew better than to comment on for fear of tempting fate. Hanna greeted her with a concerned look that told Samantha that her internal turmoil was more visible than she had hoped.

"Rough night?" Hanna asked, handing her a patient chart.

Samantha managed a weak smile. "I didn't sleep very well."

Hanna studied Samantha for a moment, her experienced eyes seeing more than she wanted to reveal. "Sometimes, the hardest part of loving someone is knowing when to hold on to them, and when to let them find their own way."

The insight caught Samantha off guard. "How did you—"

"I've had thirty years of marriage and fifty-two years of life to look back on," Hanna replied with a gentle smile. "After a while, you learn to recognize the look."

The emergency doors slid open before Samantha could respond, and the tranquil morning was shattered by the controlled chaos of paramedics bringing in a man clutching his chest. The conversation was forgotten, and both nurses sprang into action, their personal concerns set aside for the service of someone whose need was more immediate.

Hours later, as Samantha documented the successful resuscitation, she thought about Hanna's words. Perhaps that was the heart of her dilemma. Should she hold on to Daniel while he struggled spiritually? Or, should she let him find his way back to his faith on his own?

She felt her phone vibrate in her pocket. Looking at the screen, she saw it was a text from Olivia. After their conversations, her friend had been a constant source of support without judgment. Samantha quickly typed a reply:

Just taking it one day at a time. Still need space to think.

As she slipped her phone away, Dr. Lawson approached, his expression serious. "Samantha, we have a situation in Room 8 that could use your specific skills."

She followed him to find a young mother clutching a rosary, her face streaked with tears as her child underwent treatment for a severe asthma attack. The woman's panic was obvious. Her prayers were interspersed with frightened questions about her son's condition.

"Mrs. Rolston," Samantha said gently, moving to the woman's side. "My name is Samantha. I'm one of the nurses who'll be helping Dr. Lawson care for Jonathan."

The woman looked up, desperation in her eyes. "Will he be okay? Please, help him! I can't lose him!"

"We're doing everything we can," Samantha assured her, carefully avoiding false promises. She noticed the rosary beads twisted around the woman's fingers. "Would you like to pray together while the doctor works?"

Relief flooded Mrs. Rolston's face. "Yes, please. I would like that."

As they bowed their heads, Samantha's doubts receded. This was what faith looked like in action. It wasn't about perfection. Instead, it was about reaching out to God in moments of fear and finding the strength to face whatever may come.

She supported the young mother by taking her trembling hand. "We pray for your healing hand upon Jonathan, Lord. Please, give the doctors wisdom, give his body strength, and give his mother peace in knowing You are here with us. We trust in Your goodness, even when we're afraid."

Mrs. Rolston squeezed Samantha's hand tightly. Her whispered *"Amen"* carried her gratitude.

Together, they watched Dr. Lawson and the respiratory thera-pist work to stabilize Jonathan. As the boy began to breathe easier and his complexion improved, a sense of relief washed over the room.

"He's responding well to the treatment," Dr. Lawson explained, his calm voice reassuring as he updated Mrs. Rolston. "We'll need to admit him overnight for observation, but I'm very optimistic that he'll make a full recovery."

"Praise the Lord." Mrs. Rolston wept openly. She turned to Samantha. "And thank you for praying with me. Most nurses don't... they don't understand how much it helps."

Samantha assisted the woman in collecting her things for the transfer to the pediatric floor. "It was my pleasure. Faith is a part of healing. It reminds us that we're never alone in our struggles."

The words left her mouth before she realized their significance for her own situation. All day, she had been wrestling with how to reconcile her faith with her feelings for Daniel. But perhaps the answer wasn't in choosing between them, but in understanding that faith itself was designed to help navigate life's most difficult passages, including loving someone who was lost.

Samantha changed out of her scrubs at the end of her shift, feeling more clearheaded than she had in days. She hadn't resolved everything, but watching Mrs. Rolston cling to faith reminded Samantha of what truly mattered.

Driving home under a sky painted with sunset colors, she found herself praying not just for guidance about Daniel, but also for Daniel himself. She prayed not that he would change to fit her expectations but that he might find peace with God on his own terms and in his own time. And that, whatever happened between them, they would both emerge stronger in their faith.

Daniel stood in his kitchen, staring at the untouched coffee growing cold in his mug. Four days had passed since Samantha asked for space. It was four days of silence that seemed to stretch into an eternity. He respected her request, limiting himself to a single text to let her know he understood and would wait. But the waiting was proving harder than he imagined.

He took his coffee into the living room, setting it beside a stack of ungraded essays. Normally, immersing himself in his students' work provided a welcome distraction, but today, even that couldn't hold his interest.

Instead, he thought about the argument that had driven them apart. He had lashed out, defending his anger toward God as if it were a precious thing to be protected. But now, with distance, he could see it differently. His anger wasn't a shield. It was a prison. And it was costing him a chance at happiness with Samantha.

It dawned on him. He had spent two years in this vacuum of spiritual desolation, telling himself it was God's fault for taking his wife away from him. But what if, as Samantha suggested, having faith wasn't about him never doubting or never struggling? What if the emphasis were on his perseverance in seeking God, in spite of his questioning and difficulties?

Restless energy propelled Daniel as he paced the room. He needed some space to think. On autopilot, he reached for his jacket and car keys.

Muscle memory guided him as he drove to Providence Park, his mind preoccupied with other thoughts. He and Teresa used to stroll there during brisk autumn afternoons. After her death, he had stayed away. The memories were simply too painful to confront. But today, he felt compelled to face what he had been avoiding.

When he arrived, the park was quiet because most visitors were deterred by the overcast sky that threatened rain. Gravel crunched beneath his shoes as he followed the path around the lake, his hands buried deep in his pockets.

He reached a clearing with benches overlooking the water. On impulse, he sat on the one Teresa had always preferred, its weathered wood familiar beneath him. In the past, sitting here had been an exercise in torture, each memory a fresh wound. Today, though painful, it felt different. It was like visiting an old friend rather than confronting a longtime enemy.

"I've made a mess of things," he said aloud, as if Teresa might hear him. "I found someone who makes me want to live again, and I'm pushing her away because I'm still angry at God for taking you."

A pair of ducks glided across the water, their movements serene against the rippling surface. Daniel watched them, envying their simple existence.

"The thing is," he continued, the words coming easier now. "I think Sam might be right. Maybe God hasn't been the one keeping His distance all this time. Maybe it's been me."

"It usually is," a voice said from behind him.

Daniel turned, startled to find a man standing nearby. The stranger's weathered face was etched with deep lines that spoke of wisdom gained through experience. His silver hair caught what little sunlight broke through the clouds. And his hands, gnarled but strong, rested on top of a polished wooden cane. A small silver cross hung from a chain around his neck, glinting as he moved.

The man's voice was gentle. "I didn't mean to intrude, but sometimes a stranger's ear is exactly what we need. Do you mind if I join you?"

Daniel hesitated, then nodded, shifting to make room on the bench.

"My name's Liam." He lowered himself with a slight groan of effort.

"Daniel," he replied, oddly comfortable with this unexpected company.

"It sure is peaceful here." Liam gazed at the lake. "It's a good place to sort through troubled thoughts."

Daniel studied him, curious about this strange intrusion into his solitude. There was a captivating duality to Liam. He evoked both familiarity and wonder. It was reminiscent of a grandfather who dispensed candy and profound insights in equal measure.

"You said *it usually is*' when you walked up," Daniel recalled. "What did you mean by that?"

Liam's eyes crinkled at the corners. "It's just that when we feel a distance between ourselves and God, it's rarely Him who's moved away." He adjusted his grip on the cane, the wood smooth from years of use. "Were you talking to someone special? Someone you've lost?"

Daniel was taken aback by how perceptive the question was. "Yes. Sometimes I still talk to my late wife. She died a little over two years ago from a ruptured brain aneurysm."

Liam nodded, compassion in his gaze. "I'm so sorry to hear that, and I'm sorry for your loss. That kind of grief can really change a person."

Daniel's nod indicated his agreement. "You're right, it did change me. But I think I've let my grief change me in all the wrong ways."

"How so?"

Daniel found himself telling this stranger what he had only recently admitted to Samantha. He shared how Teresa's death had shattered not just his heart but his faith. And he told Liam how anger had become his constant companion, blinding him to the possibility of finding joy again.

"And now, there's someone new in my life," he concluded. "She sees the world through the lens of faith, and she believes that God has a purpose for us all, even during the times of our suffering. But I don't share that same perspective as she does. And because I don't, it's created this gulf between us."

Liam listened without interruption, his expression thoughtful. When Daniel finished, he was quiet for a moment, as if weighing his response.

"You know," he finally said. "There's a difference between being abandoned by someone and choosing to walk away from them. Which one do you think happened between you and God?"

Daniel was profoundly troubled by the question. He opened his mouth to argue, then closed it again, finding no adequate response.

"I was so angry." He clenched his hands in his lap. "My wife meant the world to me. We had plans and dreams. And then she was just... gone. It felt like God had ripped it all away from me. I felt as if He didn't care about my pain at all."

"Sometimes, grief can blind us to our blessings." Liam's observation was gentle despite the challenge in his words. He fingered the silver cross around his neck, a gesture that seemed habitual. "It can cause us to become so focused on what we've lost, that we fail to see what still remains."

Daniel considered this. The truth of Liam's statements was uncomfortable, but it was also undeniable. "Sam says something similar," he admitted. "She lost both her parents, but she somehow kept her faith through it all. She sees God's hand everywhere... in her patient's recovery, in a beautiful sunset, even in our meeting at the grocery store."

Liam asked a question. "Tell me, what do you see when you look at your life now? Where do you find light and joy while you're in the darkness of your grief?"

The question prompted Daniel to reflect. Despite his grief and anger, there *had* been bright spots in his life. He enjoyed his students' enthusiasm when they connected with literature, the camaraderie of coaching football with Stanley, and the unwavering support of his sister Miranda and her husband, Noah.

And then there was Samantha. Her smile lit up the darkest corners of his heart. Her compassion extended to everyone she met. And her faith shone brightly, even in his presence, despite his skepticism.

"I see... I see the blessings," he drawled, the realization dawning. "Even during my pain, there have been many gifts I didn't deserve to receive."

"Well, if you ask me, that doesn't sound like the life of a man whom God has forgotten," Liam remarked, his insight striking at the core of Daniel's assumptions.

"But Teresa—" Daniel's voice cracked, years of grief pressing in.

Liam nodded, his gaze steady. "Her loss was heart-wrenching, Daniel. No one should diminish that. But let me ask you this. If God didn't love you, would He have given you all those years that you had with her? And then, would God have brought this amazing woman, Samantha, into your life if He had truly abandoned you?"

The question lingered between them, and struck something deep inside Daniel, shaking the foundation of his pain.

Liam continued speaking. "You've spent so long looking at what was taken *away* from you, that you haven't stopped to see what was given *back* to you."

Daniel's fingers curled into fists. Could it be true? Had God been present all along, even in his darkest moments?

"Honestly, I've never thought of it that way," he admitted. "I've been so focused on what I've lost that I couldn't see what was being offered to me."

"Don't worry, we all do it at one time or another. It's a common human failing," Liam said with a smile. "But it's never too late to open our eyes to see the gifts that we really have in our lives."

A raindrop splashed against Daniel's hand, then another. Clouds had gathered overhead, darkening the sky during their conversation.

"I should get going before this weather gets worse." Liam rose with a slight grimace. "My old bones don't care too much for the damp weather anymore."

Daniel stood as well, suddenly reluctant to end this unexpected conversation. "Thank you," he said sincerely. "Thank you for listening. And thank you for helping me to see some of the things that I couldn't see before."

Liam smiled gently in reply. "That's the beauty of talking to a stranger. Sometimes, they have the clearest view of being able to see a situation without all the other stuff that can muddle the mind." He extended his hand, and Daniel shook it, struck by the strength in those gnarled fingers.

"Remember, never let the past blind you to the present," Liam advised as he turned to leave. "You've been given some precious gifts. Don't let anger obscure the beauty and love that's surrounding you."

With that, he walked away, his cane making soft impressions in the damp earth. Daniel watched him for a moment, then turned back to the lake, needing to process this unexpected encounter.

The rain began to fall more steadily, but Daniel hardly noticed. Liam's words struck a chord deep within him, challenging his entire narrative of abandonment. What if God hadn't left him? What if, all this time, divine love had continued to work in his life, even as he denied its existence?

When he finally turned to leave, Daniel noticed an item on the bench where Liam had sat. It was a single silver feather, gleaming with an impossible luminescence despite the gray day. He picked it up, surprised by its warmth against his skin.

A memory surfaced. His mother was reading bedtime stories of angels appearing as ordinary people, bringing messages of hope and guidance. As a child, he had accepted these tales without question. But as an adult, he had dismissed them as myths.

Now, holding this inexplicable feather, he wasn't so sure.

Drawn by an impulse he couldn't explain, Daniel sank to his knees on the damp earth. For the first time since Teresa's death, he allowed himself to truly pray.

Emotion choked his voice. "God, I don't know if You're listening. I've been angry for so long, blaming You for taking Teresa away from me just when I needed her most." Rain mingled with tears on his face. "I walked away from You, convinced You had abandoned me first. But I was wrong."

The admission shattered a long-held barrier within him, like ice cracking after a long winter. "I see now that You've been with me all along, sending people to comfort me even when I pushed them away. And then You sent Sam... " His voice cracked. "She reflects Your love in everything she does."

Daniel took a shaky breath, the silver feather warm in his palm. "I don't know if I can find my way back to You completely. I still have questions and doubts. But I'm willing to try. Please help me become the man Sam deserves... and help me become the man You created me to be."

As he finished his awkward prayer, Daniel felt a shift inside him. It wasn't a dramatic revelation or a sudden return to unwavering faith, but a quiet sense of peace, as if a burden he had carried too long had finally begun to lift.

Rising from his knees, he brushed the damp earth from his pants and glanced around, half-expecting to see Liam watching from a distance. But the park was empty, with no sign of the silver-haired stranger who had changed everything with a few simple questions.

The rain continued to fall, but Daniel barely felt it. For the first time in two years, he felt hope. Hope for reconciliation with God, for healing from his grief, and maybe, if he wasn't too late, hope for a future with Samantha.

He carefully slipped the feather into his pocket, a tangible reminder of this moment, and walked back toward his car. The path ahead wouldn't be easy. He had much to learn, much to repair, and much to prove. But Daniel no longer felt lost in the darkness. A light had been kindled, small but persistent, guiding him back toward faith, and back toward the woman who had helped him see it.

Chapter 19

THE DRIVE HOME FROM Providence Park blurred past Daniel in a haze of streetlights and shadows. His hands trembled slightly on the steering wheel, and his mind replayed the encounter with Liam in an endless loop. He pondered the enigmatic man's disappearance, the words that pierced through two years of anger and grief, and the inexplicable silver feather left behind. It all seemed impossibly surreal and more authentic than anything he had experienced in years.

There's a difference between being abandoned by someone and choosing to walk away from them.

The gentle challenge in Liam's voice echoed in Daniel's thoughts, and it was impossible to dismiss.

By the time he pulled into his driveway, the night had settled firmly over the town. His house stood dark and quiet, reflecting how he had lived these past two years. He had been existing without truly living, nursing his anger and pain like precious possessions he couldn't bear to surrender.

Daniel sat motionless in his car, the engine ticking as it cooled. The silver feather lay on the passenger seat, its surface catching the dim glow of the dashboard lights. He picked it up, marveling at its unnatural warmth and the way it seemed to pulse with an inner light.

"Just who *was* Liam?" Daniel whispered to the empty car. "And what in the world just happened?"

He entered his house, shutting the door behind him. Everything was the same, yet somehow different. His anger had cast a gray film over his perception of the world, like a darkened lens that filtered all experience through the prism of loss and abandonment. But now, that filter had cracked.

In the living room, Daniel stood before his small bookshelf, his eyes landing on a leather-bound volume pushed to the back, half-hidden behind stacks of teaching materials and literary criticism. With tentative fingers, he pulled out his Bible, a layer of dust marking how long it had sat untouched. The cover was smooth beneath his fingertips, worn in places from years of handling before grief had rendered it untouchable.

Daniel carried the Bible to his kitchen table and set it down gently, as if it might vanish if handled too roughly. He stared at it as memories flooded back. He remembered his mother's voice reading him stories of faith and courage, youth group meetings that stretched into the night with friends who felt like family, and sitting beside Teresa in church, their hands linked as they sang hymns that felt like personal conversations with God.

He swallowed hard. Teresa. Her name brought the familiar pang of loss, but for the first time, it wasn't immediately followed by the surge of rage that had become his reflexive reaction. Instead, he felt a quiet sadness mingled with something he hadn't allowed himself to acknowledge before. He felt an immense gratitude for all the years they had shared together.

"I've been so busy being angry at God for taking her away from me," he said into the silence of his kitchen. "And I forgot to be thankful for the time I had with her."

The realization was painful and freeing. He thought of the blessings still present in his life—his students whose minds opened like flowers to literature, the thrill of coaching alongside Stanley, Miranda's unwavering support, and Samantha's gentle presence that had somehow breached the walls around his heart.

Samantha. The thought of her sent a different ache through him, and he realized that his anger might have cost him yet another chance at happiness.

Daniel's hand trembled as he opened the Bible, the pages falling to the book of Psalms, as if the volume remembered where he had once sought comfort. His eyes caught on Psalm 34:18: *The Lord is close to the brokenhearted and saves those who are crushed in spirit.*

The words blurred as unexpected tears filled his eyes. For two years, he believed himself abandoned, forsaken by the God he once trusted. But what if, as Liam suggested, he had been the one to walk away? What if God had remained close all along, waiting for him to turn back to his faith and belief?

His throat tight with emotion, Daniel bowed his head, clasping his hands awkwardly in a gesture that had once been so natural.

His voice was raspy and hesitant. "God, I don't know if You're listening. I wouldn't blame You if You weren't. I've been... " He swallowed hard, searching for words. "I've been so angry. At You. At the world. At myself for not being able to save her."

Tears slipped down his cheeks, but he continued, the words coming easier now that he had begun. "I blamed You for taking her and leaving me alone. But I think... I think maybe I was the one who left. I walked away because it was easier to be angry than to face the pain."

Daniel took a ragged breath, the weight of two years of silent fury beginning to lift from his shoulders. "I'm so sorry. For the anger. For turning my back on You. And for closing my heart to everything good You were still trying to give me."

The silver feather lay on the table beside his open Bible, its impossible glow casting soft light on the pages. "And thank You for not giving up on me, and for sending people into my life who kept showing me Your love, even when I couldn't see it." His thoughts turned to Stanley's patient friendship, Miranda's quiet faith, his students' innocent enthusiasm, and Samantha's generous heart.

"Especially Sam. She reflects Your light in everything she does. Please don't let my stubbornness cost me the chance to... " He paused, a sudden clarity revealing his true desire. "Please don't let my stubbornness cost me the chance to love again and share a life with someone who sees the world through Your eyes."

When he finished speaking, Daniel remained still, half-expecting some dramatic sign or sensation. But there was only the quiet of his kitchen, the soft ticking of the wall clock, and the distant hum of the refrigerator. Yet a door that had been locked tight now stood ajar, letting in the first tentative rays of hope.

With gentle reverence, he closed the Bible and carried it to his bedroom. He placed it on his nightstand where it had once resided alongside his alarm clock and reading glasses. He set the silver feather atop it as a reminder that divine encounters could happen on ordinary park benches and that mysteries existed in a world he had come to view as coldly rational.

As he readied for bed, Daniel felt a lightness he hadn't experienced in years. He wasn't naive enough to believe that one conversation and prayer had erased all his doubts or healed all his wounds. But it was a beginning, and an acknowledgment that there might be more to his story than the chapter of grief that had consumed him for so long.

His phone sat on the dresser, Samantha's contact information a tantalizing temptation. Daniel wanted to call her and share this new spiritual awakening, and he wanted to ask her forgiveness for the harshness of his earlier words. But respect for the space she had requested held him back. And, perhaps, it was the humility to know that his journey back to faith had only just begun.

Instead, he composed a message that he saved to drafts, promising himself he would send it in the morning when his thoughts were clearer:

Sam, I had the strangest experience today, one I can't explain, but it's changed something in me. I'm ready to talk when you are. I miss you, and I'm trying to find my way back—to faith, and I hope, to you.

Sleep came easier than it had in months, deep and dreamless at first. But then, in the darkest hours before dawn, Daniel jerked awake, his heart pounding with inexplicable dread. Samantha's face filled his mind, her expression fearful, reaching out to him from some unknown danger.

"Sam," he gasped into the darkness, instinctively reaching for his phone before remembering the late hour and their agreement for space.

However, the sense of urgency didn't fade. The weight of it pressed against his chest, an almost tangible force, until he found himself doing the unthinkable. He was praying again, fervently and without self-consciousness.

"Lord, please watch over her," he whispered, the words coming naturally now. "Protect her from whatever danger I can feel but can't see. Keep her safe until I can... until I can tell her what I should have said weeks ago."

The premonition was so strong that Daniel nearly dressed and drove to her apartment, consequences be damned. But respect for her boundaries won out. Instead, he lay awake, the silver feather catching moonlight from his window, his whispered prayers continuing until exhaustion finally claimed him once more.

The soft murmur of the television filled Samantha's apartment as she curled on her couch with a fleece blanket wrapped around her shoulders. On the screen, a weathered cowboy rode across the endless plains, his face stoic beneath a wide-brimmed hat. She had turned to her collection of classic Westerns, seeking the simple comfort of stories where good and evil were clearly defined, justice prevailed, and faith was an uncomplicated certainty.

It wasn't working.

Despite her favorite film's familiar dialogue and sweeping landscapes, Samantha's thoughts continually circled back to Daniel. Asking for space had seemed necessary after their argument, but the days of silence weighed heavily. She missed his quiet laughter, the warmth in his eyes when he looked at her, and even their challenging conversations about faith and doubt.

"This isn't helping," she muttered, reaching for the remote to adjust the volume. She had hoped the movie would provide a welcoming distraction, but even John Wayne couldn't compete with the questions that plagued her. Had she made a mistake in stepping back? Was she asking too much, expecting Daniel to embrace the faith he had abandoned while he was in so much turmoil? And was she being fair to either of them?

Her phone vibrated with an incoming text. Samantha's heart jumped, but it was Olivia's name on the screen, not Daniel's.

Just checking in. How are you holding up with the Daniel situation?

Samantha appreciated her friend's concern, but she wasn't in the mood for another deep analysis of her relationship. She typed back quickly:

Hanging in there. Watching "The Searchers" and eating too much popcorn. Rain check on the heart-to-heart? Breakfast on Thursday?

Olivia's response came swiftly:

Deal. But call if you need me, day or night. Love you.

Samantha replied: *Love you too.*

She set her phone aside with a sigh. On screen, the cowboy protagonist stared across the valley at his long-lost niece, his face a study in restrained emotion. Samantha had always been moved by this scene. It was the part when there was the moment of recognition and a connection that was restored after years of searching. Now it struck her differently, resonating with her own situation.

She realized that Daniel was also searching. He may not have been searching for faith itself, perhaps. But he was searching for a way to reconcile his loss with the possibility of receiving divine love from the One who had allowed that loss to happen. So really, who was she to demand that he find the answers to all his doubts and concerns on her spiritual timetable?

The credits began to roll, and the sweeping orchestral score filled her living room. Samantha muted the television and closed her eyes, feeling the familiar tug in her spirit that always preceded prayer.

"Lord, I don't know if I'm being patient or foolish. If I'm holding too tightly to what I want Daniel to be, or if I'm right to stand firm in my faith." She took a deep breath, trying to quiet her racing thoughts. "I miss him so much. And I believe you brought him into my life for a reason. If that reason is only for me to show him what unconditional love looks like, then please give me the strength to do that well. And if it's something more..."

She exhaled, her voice trailing off with emotions too complex to articulate.

"Then please show me the next steps that we can take for the both of us to become even closer to You," she finally concluded.

As she finished her prayer, a curious peace settled over her. She didn't have all the answers, but she did have the assurance that whatever happened, she wasn't walking this path alone. Whether her future included Daniel or not, God's presence would remain her constant.

Samantha switched off the TV and moved through her evening routine. She locked the door, adjusted the heat, and changed into comfortable pajamas.

As exhaustion pulled her under, her gaze landed on her mother's Bible. It had carried her family through storms far greater than this, and it would also carry her through this uncharted situation.

"Tomorrow," she murmured, her eyes already closing. "I'll figure it all out tomorrow."

Outside her window, the winter wind whispered against the glass, promising more cold days ahead. The old apartment building creaked and settled around her, its familiar sounds a lullaby that had accompanied her sleep for years.

But beneath the peaceful quiet of her home, danger lurked in the forgotten basement of the aging complex. The building's outdated electrical panel, neglected by cost-cutting management, contained wires frayed by time and strained by the increased energy demands of winter heating. A loose connection sparked briefly before fading away, serving as a warning that went unnoticed and unheeded.

The small anomaly would have been easily addressed if seen by knowledgeable eyes. Instead, the compromised wiring heated further, melting ancient insulation bit by imperceptible bit, creating the perfect conditions for a cataclysmic catastrophe.

Above this brewing danger, Samantha slept deeply, her breathing even and peaceful. Her dreams were gentle landscapes populated by those she loved. She dreamed of her parents walking by a sunlit lake, Olivia laughing over breakfast, and Daniel, his face no longer shadowed by grief but illuminated with a joy she had rarely glimpsed.

The night deepened with stars hidden behind the thickening clouds. In the silence interrupted only by distant traffic and the hum of electronics, the small spark in the basement panel flared again, brighter this time, a harbinger of the devastating crisis to come.

Chapter 20

Daniel jerked awake, his heart hammering against his ribs. The bedroom was still shrouded in darkness, but the sense of dread that jolted him from sleep clung to him like a physical presence. Sweat dampened his t-shirt, and his pulse raced with an urgency he couldn't explain.

He couldn't get Samantha's face out of his head. Fear widened her eyes as she reached for him through the smoke and shadows. The vision was too incredibly realistic to write off as a typical nightmare.

"Sam," he whispered into the darkness as he fumbled for his phone on the nightstand. The screen illuminated, showing that it was 2:36 a.m. There were no messages and no missed calls.

Daniel lingered, his thumb poised above her number. They had agreed to allow each other some breathing room. Would calling her in the middle of the night over a bad dream seem obsessive or irrational? He dropped the phone, and with the heels of his hands, rubbed his eyes.

"You need to get it together," he muttered, but the knot of anxiety in his chest only tightened.

Rising from his bed, Daniel moved to his window, drawing back the curtain. The street below was quiet, and the houses dark except for the occasional porch light. Nothing seemed amiss in this pre-dawn world, yet the feeling of impending danger refused to subside.

He paced his bedroom, trying to rationalize the sensation away. Just yesterday, his encounter with Liam in the park had opened a crack in the wall he had built against having faith. Perhaps this strange premonition was part of that awakening, and his mind was processing the change.

The silver feather gleamed on his nightstand, catching the moonlight in ways that defied explanation. Daniel picked it up, its warmth surprising against his palm.

"Lord," he prayed, the word still foreign on his tongue after two years of silence. "I don't know if this feeling means anything, but please... please watch over Sam and keep her safe."

The simple prayer brought no immediate relief, but it felt right and necessary. Saying the words aloud seemed to make them more powerful. Daniel returned to bed, but sleep eluded him. Dawn's pale gold light filled his room, but he remained awake, haunted by an unshakeable feeling of foreboding.

Morning brought no respite. Daniel followed his routine precisely, like a machine. He showered, had coffee, and ate breakfast, though he couldn't taste it. The news played in the background as he gathered papers for school, but even the weather forecast couldn't penetrate his distraction.

His phone buzzed on the counter. It was Samantha's friend, Olivia. Her name flashed on the screen, and Daniel's blood ran cold before he even answered.

"Olivia? What's wrong?" He answered without preamble, the words tumbling out, sharp with fear.

"Daniel!" Her voice was taut with worry. "I'm so glad I was able to reach you! There's been a fire at Sam's apartment complex! It was awful! The ambulance took her to Lakeside Community Hospital!"

The world tilted beneath his feet, the kitchen spinning in nauseating circles. "Is she—" The question lodged in his throat, impossible to complete.

"She's alive," Olivia said quickly. "But she's inhaled a lot of smoke. They're treating her in the emergency department."

"I'm on my way." Daniel was already moving, grabbing keys and wallet, the phone pressed against his ear.

"Daniel." Olivia's voice softened slightly. "She was asking for you before they took her to the back. Even after everything... she was calling out your name."

A dam of restraint broke within Daniel at those words. "Tell her I'm coming. Tell her to hold on."

The drive to the hospital passed in a blur of traffic lights and honking horns. Daniel barely registered cutting off a delivery truck or running a yellow light that was more red than amber. His mind was filled with one thought: *Please, God, not her, too. Not when I've just started finding my way back to You... and to her.*

The prayer formed without conscious thought, rising from a place he thought had withered and died when Teresa passed away. But now, faced with potentially losing Samantha, his instinct wasn't rage or bargaining. It was prayer. Simple, desperate, and more sincere than anything he felt in years.

Lakeside Community Hospital loomed ahead, its red-brick facade reassuring and terrifying in its familiarity. Two years ago, he had raced to these same emergency doors only to have his world shattered. The parallel wasn't lost on him as he parked haphazardly and sprinted toward the entrance.

The antiseptic smell hit him first, and the distinct hospital aroma of disinfectant and illness triggered an avalanche of memories. The emergency waiting room was crowded with anxious faces. Many of them showed signs of the fire. You could see it in their soot-stained clothes, their shell-shocked expressions, and their bandaged hands.

"I'm looking for Samantha Kelly." Daniel approached the reception desk, his panic barely contained. "She was brought in from the apartment fire on Westmoreland Avenue."

The clerk tapped at her computer. "Are you family?"

"I'm—" Daniel faltered. What was he to Samantha? After their argument and days of silence, he couldn't claim to be her boyfriend, and saying he was her friend seemed woefully inadequate. "She's my... "

"Daniel!" Olivia appeared beside him, her face drawn with fatigue and worry. She turned to the clerk. "He's with me. I'm listed as Samantha's emergency contact."

Relief flooded through him as Olivia led him away from the desk. "How is she? Can I see her?"

"Dr. Lawson is with her now." Olivia led him to a quieter corner of the waiting area. "She was conscious when they brought her in, but she was having some trouble breathing. They've admitted her for further treatment."

"What on earth happened?" His voice, roughened by feeling, was strained.

"According to the firefighters, the fire started in the electrical panel in the basement of her building. It was the middle of the night, and almost everyone was asleep." Olivia's composure cracked. "Sam woke up to the sound of the alarms. Instead of just getting herself out, she went door to door, making sure her neighbors were awake. By the time she got to the stairs, the smoke was really thick."

Daniel pictured Samantha bravely navigating the smoky hallways, prioritizing others' safety over her own. That was so characteristic of her. She was selfless to a fault.

"Daniel?"

Daniel turned to find Samantha's attending ER physician and colleague, Brandon Lawson, approaching. He was still dressed in scrubs and had a stethoscope hanging around his neck. They had met briefly at a community fundraiser, where Samantha had previously introduced them.

"Dr. Lawson," Daniel searched the physician's face for clues about Samantha's condition. "Tell me... how is she?"

"She's stable right now." Dr. Lawson's voice was calm but firm. "But smoke inhalation is serious. Her oxygen levels are lower than we'd like them to be, and she has some inflammation in her lungs."

"What does that mean?" Fear constricted Daniel's throat.

Dr. Lawson's expression was professional but compassionate. "We've admitted her for continued oxygen therapy and monitoring. Sometimes, smoke inhalation can cause delayed effects. There's a risk of pulmonary edema and chemical pneumonitis from the toxic compounds that are found in the smoke. There's also a risk of secondary bacterial infections as the damaged tissues start to heal."

Daniel felt a lump in his throat. "She'll be okay, won't she?"

"Her age and overall excellent health work in her favor," Dr. Lawson confirmed. "But we'll need to keep her for at least a couple of days. She'll be on supplemental oxygen until her levels stabilize. And we've started her on a regimen of corticosteroids to help reduce the inflammation."

"When will I be able to see her?" Daniel's question came out more desperate than he meant.

Dr. Lawson checked his watch. "Right now, she's in the process of being moved to a room. Give the nurses about twenty minutes to get her settled in, then you can go up. She'll be in room 412."

"Thank you," Daniel said, meaning it more deeply than the doctor could possibly understand.

As Dr. Lawson walked away, Olivia touched Daniel's arm. "I need to make some calls. I need to contact my parents and let them know what's happened to Sam."

Daniel nodded, remembering how Samantha spoke of the Stewarts as being her surrogate family after her own parents passed away.

"Will you be alright staying with her?" Olivia looked intently into his eyes. "I know things between you two have been a bit... complicated."

Daniel met her gaze. "This is where I need to be."

His tone must have convinced her because Olivia squeezed his arm before heading toward the exit. "Okay. When she wakes up, tell her that I'll be back soon."

Left alone, Daniel sank into an uncomfortable waiting room chair, the events of the past twenty-four hours crashing over him. First, he had the unexplainable encounter with the mysterious Liam, which led to his halting return to faith and prayer. Then, there was the disturbing premonition that kept him awake through the night. And now this—Samantha had truly been in danger, just as he had feared.

It couldn't be a coincidence. The timing was too precise, and the parallels too exact. For the first time in years, Daniel faced a thought he had long buried: *What if God had never stopped speaking to him? What if it was he who had stopped listening to the Lord's voice?*

The thought should have frightened him, yet it brought an unexpected calm. If God had warned him about Samantha, then perhaps God was also protecting her. The realization settled over him like a mantle, stilling his panic and clearing his mind.

When the nurse arrived to escort him to Samantha's room, Daniel rose with purpose. His fingers brushed against the silver feather tucked safely in his pocket. It was a quiet reminder that no matter what happened, he wasn't alone.

Samantha drifted through layers of consciousness, more aware of sensations than any coherent thoughts. There was an oxygen mask against her face, a steady beep of monitors, and an ache in her chest with each breath. Voices swirled around her—medical terms she recognized from her nursing experience as she floated in and out of focus.

Behind her closed eyelids, images flashed in a disjointed sequence. She remembered flames licking up walls, Mrs. Coleman from apartment 3B clutching her cat to her chest, and the terrifying moment when the hallway filled with black smoke so thick she couldn't see her hand before her face.

Through it all, she had prayed. Not flowery, formal prayers, but desperate pleas for protection. Protection for herself and her neighbors. And somewhere in those smoke-filled corridors, as panic threatened to overwhelm her, Samantha had felt an inexplicable peace. A certainty that, regardless of the outcome, she wasn't facing the danger alone.

Now, in the fuzzy space between waking and dreaming, she sensed a familiar presence beside her bed. Familiar somehow, though her mind couldn't quite grasp why. The weight of someone's hand covered hers, warm and steady. The scent of sandalwood and coffee tickled her nose beneath the oxygen mask.

With monumental effort, Samantha forced her heavy eyelids open. The hospital room came into blurry focus. She saw pale walls, monitors, and an IV stand beside her bed. And there, with his face lined with worry and exhaustion, sat Daniel.

For a moment, she thought she might still be dreaming. They had agreed to give each other space. Their last conversation had ended in tension and more unresolved questions. Yet here he was, clutching her hand as if it were a lifeline.

"Daniel?" Her voice emerged as a painful rasp, barely audible through the oxygen mask.

His head jerked up, relief washing over his features as their eyes met. "Sam. You're awake."

He reached for the call button, pressing it before returning his full attention to her. "Don't try to talk. The doctor said your throat will be irritated from the smoke."

A nurse appeared. She checked Samantha's vitals and adjusted her oxygen flow before writing notes on her chart. "It's so good to see you with us, Sam. We've all been worried about you. Dr. Lawson will be by shortly to check in on you." She cast an approving glance at Daniel before leaving them alone again.

Samantha reached up with trembling fingers and pulled the mask down slightly. "What are you doing here?" she whispered, each word scraping painfully against her raw throat.

Daniel leaned forward, gently replacing the mask. "Olivia called me after you were brought to the ER." His thumb stroked the back of her hand. "Anyway, where else would I be?"

The simple question held such tenderness that tears sprang into Samantha's eyes. She blinked them back, not wanting to appear weaker than she already was.

"The fire... " she managed, needing to know.

"Everyone got out," Daniel assured her. "There were some smoke inhalation cases, and some people sustained some minor burns, but there were no fatalities. The firefighters said it started in the electrical panel."

Relief flooded through her, temporarily overshadowing her physical discomfort. Her neighbors were safe, and that knowledge was worth every painful breath.

"Your apartment... " Daniel continued, his expression apologetic. "Your apartment sustained significant damage. According to what Olivia told me, it's mainly water and smoke damage."

Samantha nodded, having expected as much. But she was grateful for the news. Material possessions could be replaced. Lives could not.

Dr. Lawson appeared in the doorway, his presence a welcome interruption to the weighted silence that had fallen between them. He approached with a tablet in hand, reviewing her latest vitals.

"Sam, it's good to see you awake," he greeted, his tone professional but warm. "How's your breathing?"

Samantha gave a so-so gesture with her free hand, unwilling to remove the mask again.

"That's to be expected." Dr. Lawson checked her oxygen monitor. "Your oxygen saturation is at 91 percent now. That's better than when you came in, but it's still lower than what we'd like to see."

He placed his stethoscope against her chest, listening intently as she took several breaths at his direction. Although his expression was inscrutable, Samantha recognized the serious risks associated with smoke inhalation.

"We'll keep you on supplemental oxygen for at least the next twenty-four hours," Dr. Lawson explained, addressing both Samantha and Daniel. "Smoke inhalation damages the respiratory system in multiple ways. There's the heat damage to the mucous membranes, chemical irritation from the toxins released in the burning materials, and the direct cellular injury from carbon monoxide and hydrogen cyanide."

Daniel's grip on Samantha's hand tightened almost imperceptibly.

"The corticosteroids are helping to reduce the inflammation. But we need to monitor for delayed complications like pulmonary edema, pneumonia, and bronchitis. You know the drill, Sam."

She nodded, familiar with the treatment protocol from her own medical training.

"The good news is that your chest x-ray didn't show any significant damage to the lung tissue itself. With proper treatment and rest, I expect a full recovery." Dr. Lawson's expression softened slightly as he looked at Daniel. "She's lucky. Smoke inhalation is the leading cause of death in house fires, not the flames themselves."

Daniel's face grew ashen at this information, and Samantha gave his hand a reassuring squeeze.

"I've prescribed you some medication for the throat pain," Dr. Lawson added. "And I want you to be on complete voice rest for at least forty-eight hours. You need to let those airways heal."

Samantha made an 'OK' sign with her fingers, grateful for the directive that absolved her from attempting conversation.

"She's in good hands," Dr. Lawson assured Daniel. "The best thing you can do is help her to rest."

After the doctor left, silence settled over the room. The monitors beeped, marking time with electronic precision. Outside the window, the sky was a flat gray, promising more winter chill.

Exhaustion tugged at Samantha, her body demanding rest to heal the damage from the smoke. Yet she fought against closing her eyes, afraid Daniel might disappear if she succumbed to sleep—that his presence was merely a temporary reprieve from their unresolved conflict.

"Don't worry. I'm not going anywhere," he said softly, as if reading her thoughts. "You need to rest now. We'll talk when you're stronger."

There was something different in his voice. She could hear a gentle certainty that hadn't been there before. Samantha studied his face through heavy-lidded eyes, noting subtle changes she couldn't quite define. The hard edge of anger seemed softer somehow. And the shadows that had haunted his expression for so long appeared lightened, if not completely gone.

Too tired to make sense of it, she finally surrendered to sleep, comforted by the steady presence of his hand in hers.

The hospital room was hushed, and the afternoon light faded into early evening shadows. Daniel sat beside Samantha's bed, watching the gentle rise and fall of her chest as she slept. The oxygen mask fogged rhythmically with each breath, a visual confirmation that she was still with him and still fighting.

During the long hours of his vigil, nurses came and went, checking vitals and adjusting medications. Olivia returned briefly with a change of clothes for Samantha and a care package of necessities, then left again to coordinate with insurance companies and property managers. Willow, Anna, the Stewarts, and various friends had called, promising to visit the following day.

Through it all, Daniel remained, leaving Samantha's side only when the medical staff needed privacy for their examinations. He had called the school, arranging for a substitute teacher. He texted Stanley, explaining the situation. And he had prayed silent, stumbling prayers that grew more natural with each passing hour.

Now, as the room darkened, Daniel found himself reflecting on how different this hospital vigil felt from his last one. When Teresa died, he had raged against God, cursing the heavens for taking her. His grief had been a violent storm, leaving destruction in its wake.

But here, watching over Samantha, something else filled him. Concern, yes, and fear for her well-being. But Daniel was also grateful she was alive and that his premonition had been a warning rather than a prediction. And beneath it all was a growing sense of purpose. Perhaps their paths had crossed for reasons beyond simple chance.

"You've been there all day, haven't you?" Samantha's raspy voice startled him from his thoughts.

She had pushed the oxygen mask down slightly, her eyes clearer than earlier. The monitors showed improved vitals, her oxygen level now at 94 percent.

"Hey," he said softly, leaning forward. "You should keep that on."

"Let me leave it off, just for a minute," she whispered, her voice strained but determined. "Oh, Daniel. You look exhausted."

Daniel smiled despite himself. Even in her compromised state, she was more concerned with his comfort than she was with her own.

"I'm fine." He gently replaced the mask. "And I'm exactly where I need to be."

Samantha's eyes studied him, questions evident in their depths. The unresolved tension from their argument hung between them, acknowledged but temporarily set aside by the more pressing crisis of her health.

A nurse entered with Samantha's evening medications and a dinner tray. "It's good to see you awake," she said cheerfully. "Dr.

Lawson said you can try some clear liquids if you're feeling up to it." She helped Samantha into a more upright position, adjusting pillows behind her back.

"I'll step out while you eat," Daniel offered, rising from his chair.

Samantha caught his hand, her grip surprisingly strong. *Stay,* she mouthed through the mask.

The nurse smiled knowingly. "You can remove the mask briefly for eating, but don't forget to replace it between bites," she instructed before departing.

Left alone once more, Daniel helped arrange the tray and opened the container of broth. The steam carried a faint chicken aroma that made his own stomach growl, reminding him he hadn't eaten since morning.

"You should get something to eat, too," Samantha managed between cautious sips of the warm liquid.

"I will," he promised, though leaving was the furthest thing from his mind. "How's your throat feeling?"

"It feels like I swallowed pieces of broken glass," she admitted with a grimace. "But the medicine helps with the pain."

They fell into a companionable silence as Samantha worked through the meager meal of broth, apple juice, and lemon gelatin. Daniel supported her when needed, replacing the oxygen mask between bites. He felt unexpected contentment in these simple acts of care.

When she finished, he moved the tray aside and helped her settle back against the pillows. The strain of even this minor exertion showed in the pallor of her skin and the slight wheeze in her breathing.

"Daniel," she began, her voice barely audible even in the quiet room. "Thank you for coming. Even after..."

He shook his head, stopping her. "Don't. You need to rest your voice." He hesitated, then added, "Besides, we have a lot to talk about when you're stronger."

Curiosity flickered in her eyes, but fatigue was quickly overtaking her again. The medications, combined with her body's desperate need for healing, were pulling her back toward sleep.

"Tomorrow," he promised, squeezing her hand. "I have something important to tell you."

She nodded, eyes already closing as exhaustion claimed her once more.

Daniel settled back in his chair, watching as her breathing evened out into the rhythm of sleep. The silver feather lay in his pocket, a reminder of his encounter with Liam and the spiritual awakening that had followed.

Tomorrow, he planned to share everything. He would recount his experience in the park and his hesitant return to prayer. He would also explain the premonition that had prepared him for this crisis.

But for now, he was content to maintain his vigil, quietly grateful for second chances and the mysterious ways God seemed to be working in his life again.

Morning light filtered through the hospital blinds, painting stripes across Samantha's bed. She woke slowly. Her body was still heavy with fatigue, but her mind was clearer than the previous day. The painful rawness in her throat had subsided to a persistent ache, and breathing came easier, though still not without effort.

Daniel was asleep in the visitor's chair, his head tilted at an angle that would surely leave his neck stiff. He hadn't gone home. That much was evident from his rumpled clothes and the shadow of stubble on his jaw. His vulnerable state, so unlike his usual composed demeanor, touched a place deep in Samantha's heart.

She watched him for a moment, studying the faint lines around his eyes and the way his fingers curled loosely around the armrest. Even in sleep, there was a tension to him, as if part of him remained on alert.

Quietly, a nurse entered, checked Samantha's vitals, and noted them in the electronic chart. "Your oxygen levels are looking much better this morning," she whispered, mindful of Daniel. "It's now at 95 percent. Dr. Lawson will be so pleased."

Samantha nodded her thanks, relieved at the improvement. She gestured to her throat, then made a drinking motion.

The nurse poured water from the bedside pitcher into a plastic cup. "Take small sips only, and try not to talk too much. Your airways still need time to heal."

As the nurse left, Daniel stirred, blinking awake with momentary confusion before his eyes found Samantha. Relief washed over his features, followed quickly by concern.

"Hey," he said softly, sitting up straighter. "How are you feeling?"

Samantha briefly removed the oxygen mask. "Much better." Her voice was still rough but stronger than the day before. "I can't believe that you stayed all night."

It wasn't a question, but Daniel nodded anyway. "There was no way I was going to leave you."

The admission carried weight beyond the immediate circumstances. There was a softness in his expression and a clarity in his eyes that she hadn't seen before. Whatever had happened during their time apart had changed him in ways she couldn't yet define.

"Your breathing sounds better than it did yesterday." He reached for her hand with a naturalness that belied their recent estrangement.

Samantha nodded, replacing the mask. Though she was desperate to ask what was on his mind and what had prompted his promise of an important conversation, she remained silent. She respected the doctor's orders for voice rest.

Daniel seemed to understand her unspoken question. "I have so much to tell you." His thumb traced circles on the back of her hand. "Something extraordinary happened while we were apart. I can't explain, but it changed everything for me."

His words piqued her curiosity, but before she could respond, Dr. Lawson arrived for morning rounds. The next hour passed in a flurry of medical activity—examinations, medication adjustments, and discussions of her recovery timeline.

"Your lungs sound significantly clearer today." Dr. Lawson placed his stethoscope around his neck. "If your oxygen levels continue to improve, we may be able to switch you to a nasal cannula by this evening."

Samantha nodded, grateful for the progress. The mask was necessary but uncomfortable, making her face sweat and limiting her ability to communicate.

"I'm still concerned about the potential for a secondary infection," Dr. Lawson told Samantha and Daniel. "We'll continue the prophylactic antibiotics for the full course. And I want you to be on medical leave for at least four weeks, Sam. No arguments." He fixed her with a knowing look, familiar with her tendency to return to work whenever a need arises.

She made a reluctant gesture of agreement, already calculating how quickly she could reasonably resume at least partial duties.

"I'll make sure she rests," Daniel promised, surprising both Samantha and the doctor with his certainty.

"Good," Dr. Lawson nodded, his professional demeanor warming slightly. "She's going to need a lot of support during her recovery. Smoke inhalation effects can linger for weeks with shortness of breath, fatigue, and persistent coughing."

"She'll have it," Daniel assured him.

After the doctor left, Samantha turned questioning eyes to Daniel. His promise of care implied a future together that seemed at odds with where they had left things before the fire.

"I know," he said, correctly interpreting her expression. "We have a lot to figure out. But first, I need to tell you something important."

Daniel glanced toward the window, gathering his thoughts. When he looked back at Samantha, a vulnerability in his eyes made her heart constrict.

"On the night of the fire, I woke up around 2:30 in the morning with this strange feeling." His voice was quiet but intense. "I can't explain it. I had this overwhelming sense that you were in some sort of danger. It was so real and so specific that I almost called you, even though we had agreed to give each other space."

Samantha listened, her attention caught by the exact timing. The fire alarm had gone off in her building just after 2:30 a.m.

"At first, I tried to dismiss it as just my having anxiety over our relationship, or my having a bad nightmare. But it wouldn't go away. So, I did something I haven't done in years." His eyes held hers. "I prayed for you, Sam. And I asked God to keep you safe."

Emotion tightened her throat at his words, briefly making breathing more difficult. She had resigned herself to the possibility that Daniel might never find his way back to his faith. To hear him speak of prayer so openly seemed miraculous.

"But that's not all." Daniel reached into his pocket. "Something else happened the day before." He withdrew a small item and placed it on the bed beside her hand. It was a silver feather that seemed to glow with an inner light despite the harsh hospital fluorescents.

"I met someone," he continued. "I met an old man named Liam when I went to sit and think at Providence Park. I was sitting on a bench, thinking about us, and about my anger toward God, and he just appeared out of nowhere."

Daniel described the unsettling meeting, recalling the stranger's insightful observations, the pointed questions that revealed his spiritual estrangement, and the baffling vanishing that raised more questions than it answered.

"He said something that changed everything for me," Daniel explained, his voice thick with emotion. "He said, *'There's a difference between being abandoned by someone and choosing to walk away from them.'* And I realized then and there, when he said it, that he was right. God didn't leave me when Teresa died. I was the one who left Him."

Tears filled Samantha's eyes as Daniel continued his story. He described finding the silver feather on the bench where Liam had sat, his impulsive prayer on his knees in the park, and the subtle shift that had begun inside him.

"I wanted to call you right away and tell you everything. But I wanted to respect your need for space. I was going to text you the next morning, but then... " His voice caught. "Then Olivia called about the fire, and all I could think was that my premonition had been real. That somehow, God had prepared me for all of this."

Samantha reached for his hand, their fingers intertwining with perfect familiarity. Through the oxygen mask, she mouthed, *I believe you.*

"I don't understand all of it. And I don't know who Liam is, how I knew you were in danger, or why this is all happening now. But I do know this." He leaned closer, his gaze intense and certain. "I've been angry for so long. I've been blaming God for allowing Teresa to die, and I've been refusing to see the blessings that are still in my life. And that includes you, Sam. Especially you."

He lifted their joined hands, pressing a gentle kiss to her knuckles. "I can't promise that I've figured everything out. I still have lots of questions and doubts. But I'm trying to find my way back to relying on having faith in God. And I want to do it with you beside me... if you'll still have me."

Samantha's heart swelled at his words. She pulled the oxygen mask down, ignoring Dr. Lawson's strict instructions for once.

"I never gave up on you," she whispered, her voice rough but fervent. "And I never gave up on us."

Daniel's smile transformed his entire face, instantly erasing years of grief. "I know," he said softly. "Your faith in me, and in us, has been a light in this overwhelming darkness, even when I couldn't see clearly."

Samantha replaced the mask. With her eyes, she communicated what her words could not. She wanted him to see the depth of her feelings, the joy she felt witnessing his spiritual awakening, and the hope she held for their future together.

"I'm not going anywhere," Daniel promised, as if he knew what she was thinking. "Not today, not tomorrow, and not ever again, if I can help it. Whatever comes next, we'll face it together."

A peace settled over Samantha that surpassed her physical discomfort. Daniel had found his way back through smoke and fire, not just back to her, but back to the faith she had prayed he would rediscover. As her mother always said, God's timing was perfect, even when it arrived through unexpected trials.

Outside the hospital window, the winter sun broke through clouds, bathing the room in golden light. As it illuminated the silver feather beside their joined hands, Samantha couldn't help but see it as a divine affirmation and a tangible reminder that sometimes, love and faith emerge stronger through the refiner's fire.

Chapter 21

Daniel balanced the paper grocery bag in one arm as he knocked on Olivia's apartment door. Three sharp raps echoed through the hallway. Since Samantha's release from the hospital in the past week, a rhythm has been established in his visits. He came in the afternoons after school, and then again in the evenings. He gripped the grocery bag tighter, shifting his weight as he waited for an answer.

The door swung open to reveal Olivia's welcoming smile. "Daniel! You have perfect timing. Sam just finished doing her afternoon breathing exercises." Olivia stepped aside, ushering him in with the familiarity that had developed between them through their shared concern for Samantha.

"How's she doing today?" Daniel asked, his voice lowered as he followed Olivia into the cozy apartment.

"She's doing much better. The coughing fits are coming less frequently." Olivia took the grocery bag from his arms. "Oh, you brought the ingredients for her mother's chicken soup! She'll be thrilled."

"I hope I got everything right. I wrote it all down when she mentioned it in the hospital." Daniel removed his coat, hanging it on the rack by the door. The apartment was warm and fragrant with the scent of herbal tea and the faint medicinal smell of vapor rub.

"You can go on in. She's been waiting for you all day," Olivia said with a knowing smile. "I'll go ahead and start prepping these vegetables."

Daniel made his way to the guest bedroom, where Samantha had been staying since the fire destroyed most of her apartment and possessions. The door stood ajar, allowing him to see her before she noticed his presence. She sat propped against pillows with her mother's Bible open on her lap. Sunlight streamed through the window, casting a golden glow across her face. Despite the lingering pallor from her ordeal, she looked beautiful, strong, and serene. This made his heart ache with gratitude.

He knocked gently on the doorframe. "Hey, I just wanted to come and check in on you. Is this a bad time?"

Samantha looked up, her face brightening. "Daniel! Never. Please, come in." She closed the Bible, keeping her finger between the pages to mark her place.

He crossed the room and settled carefully on the edge of the bed, mindful not to jostle her. The doctors warned about her lungs still being sensitive from the smoke inhalation. "What were you reading?" he asked, nodding toward the Bible.

"I was reading Psalm 91." A slight raspiness remained in her voice. "It says, *'Whoever dwells in the shelter of the Most High will rest in the shadow of the Almighty.'*" Her fingers followed the words on the page. "My mother used to read this to me whenever I was sick, and it always brought me comfort."

Daniel reached for her free hand, entwining their fingers. Her skin was warm against his, a vital reminder that she was alive, healing, and present. He surprised himself by asking to hear more.

Samantha's eyes widened, then softened with understanding. She cleared her throat, reopened the Bible, and began reading:

"I will say of the Lord, He is my refuge and my fortress, my God, in whom I trust. Surely he will save you from the fowler's snare and from the deadly pestilence. He will cover you with his feathers, and under his wings you will find refuge."

As her voice filled the quiet room, Daniel closed his eyes, letting the ancient words wash over him. Just two weeks ago, he would have bristled at such overt expressions of faith. Now, he found himself drawing strength from them and the certainty in Samantha's voice as she read.

His mind flashed back to that terrifying night, the frantic drive to the hospital after Olivia's call, and the endless wait while doctors worked to clear Samantha's lungs. He also remembered the desperate prayers that poured from him after years of silence. Daniel had made promises that night while kneeling in the hospital chapel. He would no longer turn his back on God if only she would be spared.

And she had been. By grace, miracle, or skilled medical intervention. Perhaps all three. But Samantha had survived.

"You went somewhere just now. Where did you go?"

Daniel met her gaze. The honesty they established in their relationship compelled him to share his thoughts. "I was thinking about that night at the hospital and how scared I was of losing you." His voice grew hoarse. "For the first time since Teresa passed away, I found myself truly praying again."

"And God heard you," she said softly. It wasn't a question but a statement of faith.

"Yes, I think He did." The admission no longer felt like surrender but like coming home.

He reached into his pocket and pulled out a small velvet pouch. "I brought you something."

"Daniel, you don't need to keep bringing me gifts. You've already replaced half of my wardrobe." Her smile took any sting from the words.

"I know, but this is different." He placed the pouch in her palm. "Go ahead and open it."

Samantha loosened the drawstring and tipped the contents into her hand. A silver feather pendant on a delicate chain gleamed against her skin.

"Wow... this is so beautiful," she whispered, looking at him questioningly.

"Do you remember me telling you about meeting the *'mysterious'* Liam in the park? I met him the day before the fire at your apartment." He gently took the necklace from her hand. "After our conversation, he left behind a silver feather on the bench where we sat. I couldn't explain it then, and I still can't explain it now. All I can say is that I believe it was a sign that I wasn't alone, and that God was still reaching for me even when I'd turned away."

As he spoke, he undid the clasp of the necklace. Samantha leaned forward, allowing him to place it around her neck. His fingers brushed against her nape, the simple touch sending warmth through him.

"I had it made into a pendant for you," he continued as she touched the feather resting against her collarbone. "That conversation, and that moment, led me back to believing and led me back to faith. And that led me back to you, just in time for... " His voice caught, unable to finish the thought.

"Just in time for you to be there when I needed you most," Samantha completed for him, her eyes shimmering with unshed tears. "God's timing is perfect, even when we don't understand it."

He nodded, emotion clogging his throat. The silver feather caught the light as it rose and fell with her breathing. Just watching this movement was a tangible reminder of their journey and the divine intervention that brought them to this moment.

"I've been thinking," Daniel said after a moment, regaining his voice. "When you're feeling a bit stronger, how about coming to church with me? Would you go with me to New Hope Baptist?"

Samantha's face registered surprise before blooming into a smile that reached her eyes. "You want to go back to your former church?"

Daniel reached to touch the silver feather pendant around Samantha's neck.

"This was the first sign." His voice was thick with emotion. "Speaking to Liam and finding this feather was the first moment I realized that God hadn't abandoned me. I could hear Him speaking to me, even though I wasn't listening."

Samantha's breath caught as he continued.

"I want to take the next step. I spoke with Pastor Morrison about coming back to church." His voice steadied. "Will you stand beside me as I make these first steps?"

A tear slipped down her cheek, and she nodded. "I would be honored to stand beside you, Daniel."

Olivia interrupted their moment, appearing in the doorway with a tray of steaming tea. "Sorry to intrude, but the doctor stressed the importance of keeping Sam well-hydrated."

"No, you're not intruding, Olivia. In fact, you came at the perfect time." Samantha discreetly wiped away her tears. "Daniel was just telling me that he's thinking about returning to church."

Olivia's eyebrows rose, a smile spreading across her face. "That's wonderful news! When are you thinking of going back?"

"I'd like to do it this Sunday, if Sam's up to it," Daniel replied, accepting a cup of tea with a nod of thanks. "That will be almost a week from now. Hopefully, her breathing should be better by then."

"You can count on it," Samantha declared with determination. "There's nothing that could keep me away."

As Olivia excused herself to continue preparing the soup, Daniel reached into his backpack and retrieved a well-worn book. "I brought something else." He raised a copy of *To Kill a Mockingbird.* "I thought we could continue where we left off."

Samantha settled back against her pillows, a contented smile on her lips. "That sounds perfect."

Daniel opened the page they had marked before the fire, cleared his throat, and began to read. As Atticus Finch's wisdom filled the room, he felt a sense of rightness settle over him. They were healing together. Samantha from the physical trauma of the fire, and he from the spiritual wounds that had festered for too long.

Their journey was far from over, but for the first time in years, Daniel felt certain they were heading in the right direction, together.

Samantha tested her weight on shaky legs, gripping the bathroom counter for support. Her reflection in the mirror revealed the toll the past nine days had taken. Her face was thinner, and shadows were beneath her eyes that spoke of restless nights and her struggles during her healing process. Yet there was color in her cheeks again, and the persistent cough was finally beginning to subside.

The silver feather pendant Daniel had given her the day before caught the light as she straightened. Her fingers touched it reverently, and she was still moved by the significance of his gift. It wasn't just a pretty piece of jewelry. It was a symbol of his spiritual awakening and a reminder that God worked in mysterious ways, even through trauma and fire.

A soft knock sounded on the bathroom door. "Sam? Are you okay in there? Do you need any help?" Olivia's concerned voice called.

"I'm fine," Samantha assured her friend, opening the door with a wan smile. "I just needed to stand on my own for a bit. The doctor said short periods of activity would be good for my recovery."

Olivia studied her with a critical eye, as if she were the mother hen. "You look better today. I think you're looking almost human again."

"Thanks a lot," Samantha laughed, immediately regretting it as a small coughing fit overtook her. She pressed a tissue to her mouth until it passed.

"Come on, it's back to bed for you," Olivia insisted, taking her elbow to guide her. "You've done enough standing for one morning."

As they made their way slowly back to the guest room, Samantha's gaze lingered on the paperwork spread across Olivia's dining table. There were piles of insurance forms, inventory lists of lost possessions, and listings for vacant apartments. The aftermath of the fire had been overwhelming, but Olivia stepped in without hesitation, handling the calls with insurance adjusters and landlords while Samantha focused on healing.

"I don't know how I'll ever repay you for all of this," Samantha said as Olivia helped her back into bed.

"Don't be ridiculous," Olivia chided gently, adjusting the pillows behind Samantha's back. "This is what friends do. Besides, you'd do the same for me in a heartbeat."

Although Samantha acknowledged the truth, her deep gratitude was undeniable. "Still, I'm causing you so much trouble. I'm taking over your guest room, making you play nurse..."

"You stop that right now." Olivia perched on the edge of the bed. "First of all, this guest room was gathering dust before you came. Second, I'm not playing nurse. What I'm doing is supporting my best friend through a crisis. And third," her expression softened. "Having you here has been a blessing to me, and you're definitely not a burden."

Tears pricked Samantha's eyes. "I don't know what I'd do without you."

"Thankfully, you don't have to find out," Olivia teased, handing Samantha the water from her nightstand. "Now, drink. Doctor's orders."

Samantha obeyed, the cool water soothing her throat. After several sips, she asked, "Has there been any word from the insurance company?"

"They called this morning. The claim is being processed, and they've approved the temporary housing allowance." Olivia paused, looking hesitant. "There's something else we need to discuss, though."

Samantha tensed. "What is it?"

"Your apartment building owner is terminating all leases due to the extensive damage. Even the units that weren't directly affected by the fire have severe water and smoke damage." Olivia reached for a folder on the nightstand. "They're giving everyone sixty days to find new accommodations, but realistically, the building won't be habitable for months."

Samantha found the news deeply upsetting. She had known her apartment was damaged, but she had been clinging to the hope that she might eventually return to the home she had created. Now, that possibility was gone.

"I see." She tried to keep her voice steady.

Olivia opened a folder. "It's not all bad news. I've been looking at some options for you. There's a nice apartment complex that's only three blocks from the hospital. And there's another near my parents' house that just had a unit open up."

Samantha nodded mechanically, overwhelmed by the prospect of starting over. Not only had she lost most of her possessions, but now she was also losing her home.

Reading her expression, Olivia squeezed her hand. "Hey, I know it's a lot. But remember what Pastor Wilson always says? *'Sometimes God closes a door to open a better one.'*"

A memory surfaced. She remembered Daniel standing in her hospital room, his face alight with newfound faith, as he told her about his encounter with the mysterious Liam. He had prayed for her when he sensed danger, and he told her the fire had been the catalyst for his spiritual recommitment.

Samantha found strength in the recollection. "You're right. God has been faithful through all of this. He protected me from worse harm, He's provided me with the best friend anyone could ask for, and He's brought Daniel back to faith." She touched the silver feather pendant again. "If losing my apartment is part of His plan, then there must be something better ahead."

Olivia's face softened in approval. "Now that's the Samantha I know." She stood, smoothing her skirt. "Speaking of Daniel, he called while you were in the bathroom. He's coming by after school, and he's bringing his sister, Mandy. She wants to help you go through some of the clothing catalogs the insurance company sent."

Warmth spread through Samantha's chest at the mention of Daniel's name. Each day since the fire, his visits had become the bright spot she looked forward to. The way he read to her, prayed with her, and simply sat with her in companionable silence deepened their connection in ways she could never have anticipated.

"I'd like that." She was already imagining his presence and the gentle strength he exuded.

As Olivia left to prepare lunch, Samantha reached for her mother's Bible. It was one of the few possessions she was able to recover after the night of the fire. The familiar weight in her hands grounded her as she turned to Isaiah 43, finding comfort in the verses about passing through fire and water without being consumed. She read the passage to herself:

When you pass through the waters, I will be with you; and when you pass through the rivers, they will not sweep over you. When you walk through the fire, you will not be burned; the flames will not set you ablaze.

The words took on new meaning after her experience. She had quite literally walked through fire, and while she hadn't emerged unscathed, she had survived. Not only that, but a resilient and beautiful spirit was rising from the ashes. She was able to find joy in Daniel's renewed faith, their deepening relationship, and her own strengthened trust in God's providence.

She closed her eyes, offering a prayer of gratitude for life, for love, and for the mysterious ways God worked, even through seemingly insurmountable hardships. As she rested in that peaceful moment, a strong certainty filled her. She believed that this trial, just like many before it, was part of a larger plan that was unfolding exactly as it should.

Chapter 22

DANIEL STRAIGHTENED HIS TIE for the third time, studying his reflection in the mirror. Nerves made his fingers clumsy as he adjusted the knot, a task he had performed thousands of times throughout his teaching career. Today, however, was unlike other days. Today marked his return to New Hope Baptist Church since Teresa had passed away.

"Just church," he said to his image, aware that the truth was far more significant. This wasn't merely attending worship. It was a public declaration of his renewed faith and his decision to turn back toward the God he had abandoned in his grief.

His phone chimed with a text notification from Miranda: *We're leaving now. See you there. So proud of you, big brother.*

Daniel smiled at his sister's message. Miranda had been overwhelmed with joy when he told her about his decision to return to church. Her and Noah's support had been unwavering through his years of anger and doubt. Now, they would witness his home-coming.

He sent a quick response before pocketing his phone and keys: *Thanks, Mandy. See you soon.*

On his way out, he paused in his living room, his gaze falling on Teresa's photograph. For a moment, he simply looked at her smiling face, remembering.

"I think you'd approve," he said quietly. "I think you'd approve of Sam, and me finding my way back to Christ. Maybe you've been watching over me all along."

The thought no longer brought the crushing pain it once did. Instead, it carried a bittersweet comfort of acknowledging that love transcended death and that healing did not mean forgetting.

With a final nod to Teresa's image, Daniel left his house, locking the door behind him.

The drive to New Hope Baptist was familiar, muscle memory guiding him along the routes he had traveled weekly for the years before his grief-imposed exile. Yet, somehow, everything felt new, as if he were seeing the neighborhood with fresh eyes. The church's white steeple came into view, rising above the surrounding trees, a beacon against the clear blue sky.

Daniel parked in his old spot in the third row, about halfway down, and he couldn't help but smile at this small ritual he had maintained over the years. As he stepped out of his car, he spotted Samantha's silver sedan pulling in several spaces away. His heart lifted at the sight of her. This was the first time she had left Olivia's apartment since being released from the hospital. That she had chosen to use her limited energy to support him spoke volumes about her character and commitment to their relationship.

Rushing over, he reached her car as she was slowly exiting the passenger side. Olivia stood close, available to help if needed.

Daniel grasped Samantha's hand. "Hey, are you sure you're up for this? We can wait another week."

Though Samantha's eyes showed tiredness, her set jaw spoke of her resolve. "I wouldn't miss this for the world."

Daniel nodded, and offered his arm for support, which she accepted with a grateful smile. They began the slow walk toward the church entrance. Olivia followed a few steps behind, giving them space while remaining close enough to help if necessary.

"You look beautiful." Daniel admired her simple blue dress. She paired it with the silver feather necklace he had given her, the pendant catching the sunlight as they walked.

"Thank you," she replied, a hint of color warming her cheeks. "Your sister helped me pick it out. It's one of the few new things that have arrived so far."

As they approached the church steps, Daniel hesitated. The last time he had entered this building was for a funeral. It wasn't for Teresa's service. That had taken place at her family's church in Bristol Heights, their childhood home. On that day, he had come to mourn Mrs. Brown, a beloved member of the congregation. The sympathetic glances and well-meaning condolences had nearly suffocated him. He had quietly vowed never to return.

Now, standing at the threshold, he drew strength from Samantha's presence beside him. She squeezed his arm gently as if sensing his internal struggle.

"We're going to take this one step at a time," she murmured, her words carrying dual meaning.

Daniel nodded, taking a deep breath before ascending the first step, and each one that followed came easier. A peculiar lightness settled over him when they reached the top. It wasn't the absence of feeling but more like the release of a burden he had carried far too long.

Inside the foyer, familiar faces turned toward them. Daniel braced himself for the pitying looks he expected, but found genuine warmth and welcome instead. Mrs. Patterson, the church secretary who had sent him cards every holiday despite his absence, approached first.

"If it isn't Daniel Forrester," she said, her kind eyes misty. "It does my heart good to see you." She extended her hands to him, which he took within his own.

"It's good to be back, Mrs. Patterson." To his surprise, he meant it.

"And tell me, who is this lovely young lady at your side?" she asked, turning her attention to Samantha.

"This is my good friend Samantha Kelly." Pride was evident in his voice. "And this is her friend, Olivia Stewart."

"Welcome, welcome," Mrs. Patterson said warmly. "Any friends of Daniel's are friends of ours."

More greetings followed as members of the congregation recognized Daniel. There were handshakes and gentle embraces, but no one mentioned his long absence or Teresa's passing, for which he was grateful. Instead, they welcomed him home, as if he had never left.

Pastor Jameson Morrison, a dignified man with salt-and-pepper hair and compassionate eyes, approached last. "Daniel," he said, his deep voice resonant with emotion. "It has been far too long."

"Yes, sir, it has." Daniel clasped the pastor's outstretched hand.

"And you must be the Samantha I've heard so much about from Mandy," Pastor Morrison continued, turning to greet her. "It's wonderful to meet you, though I understand you're recovering from quite an ordeal."

"Yes, I am," Samantha confirmed with a small smile. "But nothing could have kept me away today."

The pastor nodded in understanding. "Well, we're honored to have you with us. Mandy mentioned you're a member of Cottonwood Faith Community Center?"

"Yes, and Pastor Wilson has been wonderful," Samantha replied. "But I've been considering transferring my membership."

Her words caught Daniel by surprise. They hadn't discussed church memberships yet, though he supposed it was a natural progression if their relationship continued to deepen.

Before he could reflect further, the organ began to play, signaling the start of the service. Miranda and Noah appeared at his side, their faces alight with joy.

"Are you ready?" Miranda asked, linking her arm through his free one.

"Ready as I'll ever be." Daniel smiled despite the butterflies in his stomach.

Together, they entered the sanctuary. Daniel paused just inside the doorway, overwhelmed by memories. The stained-glass windows cast kaleidoscopic patterns across the pews, and the polished wooden cross hung above the altar. He could never forget the familiar smell of old hymnals mixed with the lemon furniture polish used to shine the pews. Everything was exactly as he remembered, yet he was no longer the same man who had turned his back on this place.

They found seats in a pew about halfway down. It was close enough to feel a part of the congregation but not so close as to draw too much attention. As Daniel helped Samantha settle beside him, he noticed she was breathing a bit heavily from the exertion of the walk.

"Are you okay?" Concern creased his brow.

She nodded, squeezing his hand reassuringly. "I just need a minute. Don't worry, I'll be fine."

Daniel sat between Samantha and Miranda, with Noah and Olivia flanking them. The organ music swelled, and the congregation rose to sing the opening hymn. Finding the song in the hymnal, Daniel showed it to Samantha, even though he imagined she was already familiar with *I Need Thee Every Hour*.

His own voice was hesitant at first, the familiar lyrics feeling strange on his tongue after so long. But as the music continued, he felt himself begin to loosen. By the third verse, he sang fully, his voice joining the congregation in praise.

I need Thee every hour, In joy or pain; Come quickly and abide, Or life is vain!

The words resonated through him, no longer a hollow recitation but a truth he was beginning to reclaim. As the final notes faded, Daniel caught Samantha watching him, tears glistening in her eyes. She didn't speak, but her expression conveyed everything. Her eyes shone with pride, joy, and a deep understanding of how significant this moment was for him.

The service continued with more scripture readings and prayers. Daniel participated with growing confidence, and the rituals of worship became familiar once more, like rediscovering the steps of a long-forgotten dance. When Pastor Morrison began his sermon, *Coming Home*, Daniel felt as if the message had been prepared especially for him.

"The story of the prodigal son is often misunderstood," the pastor began, his gaze sweeping across the congregation. "We often-times like to focus on the wayward son's rebellion, his squandering of his inheritance, and his return home, which was motivated by hunger. But the heart of the story is about a father who never stopped watching the horizon, waiting for his child to return home."

Daniel listened intently as Pastor Morrison described the father's unconditional love and immediate acceptance. He ran to his son, defying the cultural norms that would have demanded that the son come crawling on his knees to him. The father restored his son's place in the family without any conditions or any probationary period.

Pastor Morrison's voice remained steady. "There are some of us who have wandered far from home. Maybe not in physical distance, but in the separation of our hearts from God. We've experienced pain, loss, and disappointment. We've questioned why a loving Father would allow such suffering. And we've turned away, convinced that God has abandoned us."

Daniel swallowed hard. He felt Samantha's hand slip into his, an anchor as the words struck close to home.

"But here's the truth that sets us free," the pastor declared. "God never stops watching the horizon for us. He never stops loving us. And when we take even one step in His direction, He runs to meet us on the road. Coming home isn't about making ourselves worthy of God's love again. It's about accepting that we never lost it in the first place."

Daniel let out a shaky breath. He had spent years punishing himself with his estrangement from God, and the love the Lord wanted to freely give to him. But the truth was much more straightforward. God had been waiting for Daniel to return home all along.

As the service concluded with a final hymn, Daniel felt a certainty settle over him. This was right. This was where he belonged, not just in this church, but in the community of the faith he had rejected. And more importantly, he needed to be in a relationship with the God who had never abandoned him, even when he had turned away.

After the benediction, the congregation began to disperse, and Pastor Morrison approached their pew. "Daniel, do you have a moment to talk in my office?"

"Of course," Daniel replied, glancing at Samantha.

"Go," she encouraged with a smile. "Olivia and I will wait for you in the fellowship hall with Mandy and Noah."

Daniel followed Pastor Morrison to his office, a warm space that was lined with bookshelves and family photographs. As they settled into chairs, the pastor regarded him with kind eyes.

"I can't tell you how much it means to see you here today. We've prayed for you continually since Teresa's passing."

"Thank you," Daniel said sincerely. "I wish I could say I felt those prayers, but the truth is, I was too angry to notice."

With a nod, Pastor Morrison showed he understood. "Grief affects us all differently. There's no right or wrong way to mourn, Daniel. God is big enough to handle our anger, our questions... even our temporary rejection."

Daniel let out a sigh. "It feels wrong to call it *temporary* when it lasted for over two years," he admitted.

"In the span of eternity, two years is less than a breath," the pastor replied gently. "The important thing is that you've found your way back. Mandy mentioned it had something to do with your friend Samantha's influence?"

Daniel smiled, thinking of her unwavering faith. "In part, it did. Sam showed me what living a life of faith looks like, even when I wasn't ready to embrace it myself. But there was also a strange encounter I had recently while I was in the park. I met a man named Liam. He seemed to appear out of nowhere and said exactly what I needed to hear."

Pastor Morrison leaned forward, his expression curious. "Sometimes God sends the right messenger at the right time. Would you mind telling me about it?"

Daniel recounted his conversation with Liam, including his perceptive questions, gentle challenges to his assumptions, and the mysterious silver feather that was left behind. As he spoke, Daniel realized how extraordinary the encounter had been, yet how natural it had felt while in the moment.

"I never saw him again, but I found myself praying that night for the first time in years. And the next day, when Sam was caught in the fire... " His voice caught at the memory.

"You felt as if God was already preparing you to face that trial," Pastor Morrison observed.

"Yes, I did," Daniel agreed. "And, I think that He was."

The pastor studied him for a moment. "Daniel, what are your thoughts about rejoining the church formally? There's no rush, of course. But whenever you're ready, I'd be honored to welcome you back into the membership."

The question caught Daniel off guard, though he realized it shouldn't have. His presence today was already a declaration of his intent. Still, the formal step of rejoining required further consideration.

"I think I'd like that, but I need a little more time. This is all still very new right now."

"Of course," Pastor Morrison assured him. "The door is open whenever you're ready to walk through it." He rose from his chair, extending his hand. "In the meantime, please know that you and your friends are always welcome here."

Daniel shook the pastor's hand, grateful for his understanding. As they walked together toward the fellowship hall, he felt a lightness in his step that had been absent for too long. The journey ahead would not be without challenges, but now, he felt more equipped to face them.

In the fellowship hall, he found Samantha seated at a table with Miranda, Noah, and Olivia. She was laughing at something Noah had said, her face animated despite the lingering fatigue. The sight of her there, integrated with his family, filled Daniel with a profound sense of rightness.

As he approached, Samantha looked up, her smile broadening. "There you are. We were just discussing some plans we might have for lunch."

He slid into the empty chair beside her, their hands connecting beneath the table. "Whatever you're feeling up to. I don't want to tire you out."

"I'm already out, so I might as well make the most of the day," Samantha declared with characteristic determination. "Mrs. Patterson mentioned a restaurant down the street that has an excellent Sunday brunch."

"She was talking about Sweet Tea Tavern," Miranda confirmed. "It's a church favorite for having a Sunday brunch."

As they gathered their belongings and prepared to leave, Daniel was filled with gratitude. He was grateful for this day, for these people, and for the second chance he had been given. And not just his second chance with Samantha, but with faith itself.

Outside, the sun beamed brightly in a clear blue sky. Samantha held his arm as they walked to the cars, her steps slow but steady.

"Thanks for coming," Daniel murmured. "I know it took a lot out of you."

"I wouldn't have missed it," she replied, gazing up at him affectionately. "Seeing you in church, singing those hymns... it was worth every bit of energy."

Daniel stopped walking and turned to face her fully. "Sam, I don't know where this journey is leading us, but I know I want to walk it with you. I want to be with you on a spiritual level, and every other level as well."

Samantha's eyes shimmered with unshed tears. "I want that too. I want it so much."

Behind them, Miranda cleared her throat. "How about we meet you two at the restaurant?" A knowing smile curved her lips as she ushered Noah and Olivia toward their cars.

Alone in the church parking lot, Daniel cupped Samantha's face, his thumbs gently brushing her cheeks. "I don't know if I could have found my way back to God without you," he confessed. "Your faith gave me something to hold on to when I couldn't believe in it for myself."

"God was working in you long before I came along," Samantha countered softly. "I was just privileged to witness the journey."

Her humility and refusal to take credit for his spiritual renewal only deepened his admiration. This was Samantha, always pointing to God's work rather than her own influence.

"Either way, I'm grateful. I'm grateful for your patience, for your unwavering faith, and for the way that you've helped me to heal."

He lowered his head, their eyes locking for just a fleeting moment. His lips met hers in a kiss that felt like a promise of a future destiny. Unlike their previous embraces, which had been tentative explorations, this kiss held the certainty of a shared future. His strong, protective arms encircled her waist, drawing her closer as if to shield her from the world around them. And all the while, he was gentle, mindful of her fragile strength as she continued her journey of recovery.

Samantha's hands moved slowly up his shoulders, then to the back of his neck, her fingers playing with his short locs. The gentle pressure of her touch sent electricity coursing through him, awakening sensations that had been long dormant. Her lips were soft and inviting, responding with equal passion and intensity.

The silver feather pendant pressed between them, serving as a physical reminder of their intertwined journeys. Daniel deepened the kiss, pouring into it all the emotions that his words failed to capture. He wanted to convey everything he couldn't adequately express—his gratitude, admiration, and the love blossoming between them. A love that felt both new and familiar, like returning to a long-lost home he hadn't known he had been searching for.

When they finally parted, both a little breathless, there was a moment of stillness. Samantha's face was flushed with more than just the exertion of the morning. Her tawny eyes mirrored the same wonder and desire he felt surging through his own heart.

"We should probably get to the restaurant," she said, her voice husky. "We need to get going before they send a search party."

Daniel nodded, reluctant to break the moment but aware of her limited stamina. "Are you sure you're up for brunch? I could take you back to Olivia's so that you can get some rest."

"I *am* tired," she admitted. "But I'm tired in the best possible way. And I want to celebrate this day with you."

Her sincerity touched him. Daniel felt the pieces of his life settling into a new configuration as they walked the remaining distance to their cars. The grief and anger that had defined him for so long were giving way to hope and renewal. His relationship with Samantha was deepening into a partnership that was precious and lasting. And his faith, once abandoned, was taking root once more.

They were healing together, physically, emotionally, and spiritually. And in that healing, they were finding a shared path forward, guided by the God who had never truly let either of them go.

Samantha settled into her seat at Sweet Tea Tavern, smiling at the server who placed a glass of water before her. The restaurant buzzed with post-church activity, with families and couples filling the surrounding tables. Despite her fatigue, she felt buoyed by the morning's experience. Seeing Daniel back at church was worth all the effort.

"So, what's good here on the brunch menu?" She glanced around the table.

"Everything," Noah replied enthusiastically. "But the chicken and waffles are legendary."

As they examined their menus, Miranda reached across the table to touch Samantha's hand. "I meant to tell you earlier... that dress looks beautiful on you. The color really brings out your eyes."

Samantha was moved by the compliment. "Thank you. And I appreciate your help with the shopping. It's been overwhelming trying to replace everything."

"Has there been any news on your apartment situation?" Miranda asked.

Samantha shook her head. "Not yet. The insurance adjuster is supposed to call tomorrow with more details about the settlement. But I'll definitely need to find a new place soon."

"There's no rush," Olivia assured her. "You're welcome to stay with me as long as you need."

"Just in case I forget to mention it later," Miranda began, exchanging a glance with Noah. "There's a lovely apartment opening up in our building next month. It has two bedrooms and a nice view of the park. If you moved there, that would make you neighbors with us."

Daniel looked up from his menu, his expression thoughtful. "That's actually not far from Greater Pines High School."

"Or the hospital," Noah added, a knowing smile playing on his lips.

Samantha caught the not-so-subtle matchmaking at work but found she didn't mind. "I'd love to see it, when I'm feeling stronger, if it's still available."

When their food arrived, the conversation flowed as they ate. Samantha marveled at how naturally she fit with Daniel's family. There was no awkwardness or sense of being an outsider. Instead, she felt welcomed, included, and valued.

Throughout the meal, she noticed small changes in Daniel. She saw how he bowed his head before eating, the ease with which he joined the conversation about upcoming church events, and a new light that had returned to his eyes. His spiritual reawakening was evident in these subtle shifts, confirming what she had sensed all along. His estrangement from God had been a response to grief rather than a true rejection of faith.

As brunch concluded, Samantha felt the day's exertions catching up with her. Though she tried to hide her fatigue, Daniel noticed immediately.

"You're worn out. Let's get you back to Olivia's." His voice betrayed his concern.

"I'm fine," she protested weakly, even as a yawn gave her away.

"You're amazing," Daniel corrected her gently. "But you're still recovering, and you've had a full morning."

Olivia nodded in agreement. "He's right, Sam. You've pushed yourself enough for one day."

Reluctantly, Samantha conceded. After goodbyes to Miranda and Noah, with promises to stay in touch about the apartment, Daniel and Olivia helped her to the car.

The drive back to Olivia's apartment was quiet, with Samantha fighting to keep her eyes open in the passenger seat. Daniel sat behind her, his presence comforting even as fatigue clouded her thoughts.

At Olivia's building, Daniel insisted on carrying Samantha from the car despite her protests that she could walk. Too tired to effectively argue, she found herself carefully cradled in his arms, her head resting against his shoulder as he followed Olivia into the house.

He laid her gently on the bed in the guest room, slipping off her shoes and covering her with a fleece blanket. Samantha fought against the pull of sleep, wanting to hold on to the day a little longer.

"I'll let you rest," Daniel whispered, brushing a strand of hair from her face.

"Stay," she murmured, catching his hand. "Just for a little while longer."

Daniel glanced toward the door, where Olivia gave a discreet nod before leaving them alone. He pulled a chair close to the bed, holding Samantha's hand as he settled beside her.

"Today was perfect." Her voice was heavy with approaching sleep. "Seeing you in church, watching you reconnect with your community... it was beautiful, Daniel."

"It was," he agreed, his thumb tracing circles on the back of her hand. "And it's just the beginning."

As sleep claimed her, Daniel gently pressed his lips against her forehead, a benediction more powerful than any formal prayer.

Her last conscious thought was wordless gratitude for this man and their journey. A journey of healing, faith, and love that was unfolding exactly as it should.

Daniel quietly closed the door to Samantha's room, finding Olivia preparing tea in the kitchen.

"Is she asleep?" Olivia asked, keeping her voice low.

"She was gone almost before I left the room. Today took a lot out of her." Daniel accepted the mug she offered.

"She wouldn't have missed it," Olivia said, gesturing for him to join her at the small kitchen table. "She's been talking about your return to church all week. It means everything to her to see your faith restoration."

Daniel nodded, warmed by this confirmation of what he had already suspected. "I'm still figuring everything out," he admitted. "But being in church today, and hearing Pastor Morrison's message felt right. It felt like I was coming home."

"Faith is rarely a straightforward path." Olivia took a sip of her tea. "What matters most is the direction that you're heading now."

They sat in comfortable silence for a moment. Daniel's thoughts drifted to the future, not just to his rekindled faith, but to what this meant for his relationship with Samantha.

"I'd like to speak with Pastor Wilson soon," he said suddenly. "I was thinking about officially joining Samantha's church. Or rather, her transferring her membership to New Hope, but only if that's what she wants."

Olivia peered at him over the top of her mug. "That's quite an important step."

"Yes, I know," Daniel acknowledged. "But after today, I can't imagine Sunday mornings without her beside me. I want us to be part of the same church so we can worship together."

"Have you discussed this with her?"

"We haven't talked about it specifically. But she mentioned she was considering transferring her membership to New Hope this morning while we were at church." Daniel traced the pattern on his mug, gathering his thoughts. "I want to do this right, Olivia. I know how important faith is to Sam, and I don't want to rush ahead of where I actually am spiritually just because I'm falling in—" He stopped abruptly, realizing what he had been about to confess.

Olivia's eyes widened slightly, but she simply said, "You don't want to rush because you care deeply for her."

"Yes," Daniel agreed, grateful for her discretion. "I don't want to promise more than I can deliver. But I also want her to know that my return to faith isn't just about her being caught in the fire or any type of momentary crisis. It's a genuine recommitment for me."

"Then you need to tell her that," Olivia advised. "Sam appreciates honesty above all else. She doesn't expect you to have everything figured out. She just wants to know what you're genuinely seeking."

Daniel nodded, taking in her counsel. "Thank you. For everything you've done for her. And for your acceptance of me, despite knowing about my struggles with faith."

"We're all works in progress," Olivia replied with a gentle smile. "The important thing is we don't have to do the work alone."

Their conversation turned to the practical matters of Samantha's recovery, her apartment search, and the challenges of replacing everything she had lost. The afternoon was waning when Daniel left, and golden light slanted across Olivia's neighborhood.

He drove home with a sense of purpose he hadn't felt in years. The day had not only marked his return to church but had clarified his vision for the future. A future that, he hoped, would include Samantha by his side, and their faith journeys intertwined just as their lives were becoming.

At home, Daniel moved through his evening routine with a new awareness. The house no longer felt empty or haunted by grief. Instead, it seemed to be waiting, holding space for possibilities yet to unfold.

He settled at his desk to prepare the week's lessons. Still, his thoughts kept returning to Samantha. Her courage in facing the fire's aftermath, her unwavering faith despite her loss, and how she supported his spiritual journey without pressure or judgment.

Today, seeing her integrated with his family and church community felt right, as if the final piece of a puzzle had fallen into place. He could envision a future where Sunday mornings meant sitting beside her in the sanctuary, her hand in his as they worshipped together.

Daniel opened his Bible, turning to the book of Psalms. The words of comfort and praise now resonated differently, no longer distant poetry but living truth. As he read, he offered silent prayers of gratitude. Prayers for Samantha's survival, his own spiritual awakening, and the grace that had been waiting for him all along.

Outside his window, stars appeared in the darkening sky, each a reminder of divine presence in the vastness of the universe. Daniel closed his Bible as peace settled over him. Whatever challenges lay ahead, he would face them with renewed faith, a community of believers around him, and, God willing, Samantha beside him.

They were healing together, finding their way back to wholeness, faith, and a love that promised to be stronger than any trial they might face.

Chapter 23

IT WAS ONE WEEK later, and Samantha stood at the edge of Lake Pleasant, watching the early morning mist rise from the water's surface. The late February air was crisp but not biting, and a hint of the approaching spring softened winter's edge. She took a deep breath, her lungs expanding without the painful catch that had plagued her since the fire.

"How does it feel to be outside?" Daniel asked from beside her, his hand warm against the small of her back.

"It feels good. The doctor was right. Breathing in this fresh air really does help."

It was their third morning of walking outdoors this week as part of her prescribed recovery regimen. Each day, they ventured a little farther along the lakeside path, building her stamina while enjoying quiet conversation away from the well-meaning, but sometimes overwhelming, attention of friends and family.

"Are you ready to keep going?" Daniel asked, offering his arm for support.

Samantha nodded, linking her arm through his as they continued at a leisurely pace. "I had a call from the insurance company yesterday. They've approved the full settlement for my personal belongings."

"That's great!" Daniel exclaimed. "Will it be enough to replace everything?"

"More than enough, actually. I've been thinking... " She hesitated, gathering her courage. "I might not replace everything right away. The fire made me realize just how little I really need."

Daniel glanced at her curiously. "What are you thinking?"

"I'm considering taking some of the settlement money and using it for something meaningful. Maybe I can donate some of it to the hospital's burn unit, or start a fund for some of the other fire victims."

The pride in Daniel's expression warmed her more than any physical heat could have. "That's a wonderful idea, Sam."

They walked in comfortable silence, the path curving around a bend where benches offered a view of the lake. By mutual agreement, they settled on one, close enough that their shoulders touched.

"How are you feeling about tomorrow?" Samantha knew Daniel was scheduled to meet with Pastor Morrison to discuss formally rejoining New Hope Baptist Church.

"Actually, I'm a little nervous," he admitted. "But in a good way. It's like I'm standing at the beginning of an important journey, and I'm ready for it to begin."

She squeezed his hand encouragingly. "I'm so proud of you."

"I wanted to talk to you about something related to that." Daniel shifted slightly to face her. "I've been thinking about our church situation."

"Our church situation?" Samantha echoed, curious.

"Yes. I know you're considering transferring your membership to New Hope, but I don't want you to feel pressured because of me. If you prefer to stay at Cottonwood Faith—"

"Daniel," she interrupted gently. "I've been praying about this decision since before the fire. It's not just about being where you are, though that's certainly part of it." With the lake in view, she collected her thoughts. "Being at New Hope feels right to me. The community has been so welcoming, and seeing you reconnect with your faith there... it feels like where we're meant to be. Together."

A sense of anticipation, ignited by the final word, lingered between them.

"Together," Daniel repeated softly. "I certainly like the sound of that."

He took both her hands in his. "Sam, these past weeks have changed everything for me. Watching you recover, seeing your faith despite all you've lost, has been humbling and inspiring."

Samantha felt her pulse quicken at the intensity of his gaze.

"I know we still have a lot to figure out. We have your housing situation, my ongoing faith journey... all of it. But I want you to know that whatever comes next, I want to face it with you."

"I want that too," she whispered, her voice catching with emotion.

Daniel lifted one hand to cup her cheek. "I'm falling in love with you, Samantha Kelly. And I think I've been falling since that first day in the grocery store when you rescued me from my salmon salad confusion."

A laugh bubbled up from her chest, joy mingling with tears. "And I'm falling in love with you, too, Daniel Forrester."

His smile was radiant as he leaned in, his lips meeting hers in a kiss that held all the promises of their shared declarations. Their previous kisses had been tentative brushes, dancing around the edges of their emotions and filled with overwhelming passion. This kiss was different. It held the weight of certainty and the culmination of a decision made with clear eyes and open hearts, finally free from any lingering doubts.

Daniel's hand slid from her cheek, his fingers threading through her hair with a gentle pressure that set her nerves alight. Samantha leaned into him, her palms finding their way to his strong shoulders, feeling the solid strength beneath the fabric of his jacket.

The kiss deepened, his lips moving against hers with a growing confidence that ignited something deep within her. Samantha felt herself responding with equal fervor, their connection transcending the physical to touch an inner sanctuary of the heart. It was as if their souls recognized one another, finding their counterparts after wandering through life alone.

When they finally parted, a shared glow enveloped them. Daniel rested his forehead against hers. "I've wanted to tell you that for so long," he confessed, his voice low and husky. "But I needed to be sure my faith was solid first. I couldn't ask you to build a life with someone whose foundation was shaky."

"And now?" Samantha asked softly, knowing they were on the cusp of building a beautiful beginning.

"Now I know that whatever happens, and whatever challenges we face, my faith is real." He took her hand, pressing it against his pounding heart. "Not only because of you, though I'm thankful that you helped me find my way back. But because I've reconnected with God directly, and I know that relationship will anchor everything else. Including what we're building together."

Tears of joy slipped down Samantha's cheeks. She had prayed for this—not just Daniel's return to faith, but his understanding that his faith must stand on its own, independent of their relationship.

"This is just the beginning." She touched the silver feather pendant at her throat. "It's the beginning for both of us."

Daniel nodded, his expression solemn yet joyful. "I know we have a journey ahead. We have your recovery, my continued spiritual growth, and trying to figure out where you'll live."

"And we'll do it all, one step at a time," Samantha reminded him, echoing the words they shared on the church steps.

"Together," Daniel added, sealing the promise with another gentle kiss.

As they continued their walk around the lake, hand in hand beneath the brightening sky, Samantha felt a sense of rightness settle over her. Their paths had converged in what some might call a coincidence. It all started with a chance meeting in a grocery store and a series of "accidental" encounters. But she recognized God's design in every seemingly unintentional happenstance.

They were healing together and finding strength in their shared faith and mutual support. Whatever challenges lay ahead, they would face them side by side, their love grounded in a foundation that could weather any storm, even one that came with fire and smoke.

The morning sun broke through the trees, casting diamonds of light across the lake's surface. Samantha squeezed Daniel's hand, feeling his answering pressure, a wordless communication of love, faith, and hope for all that was yet to come.

Chapter 24

Daniel looked in the mirror, readjusting his red tie a third time. The barely perceptible shaking of his fingers gave away his mounting anxiety. The small velvet box in his jacket pocket seemed to weigh a hundred pounds, though he had carried it for weeks, waiting for the perfect moment.

"It's time," he whispered, smoothing down his shirt one final time.

One year. One remarkable year since he had attended the Christmas Cantata with Samantha. The memory was vivid. He recalled his reluctance, her gentle patience, and the first spark of faith that was reignited in his heart amid the candlelight and carols. Now, twelve months later, he stood transformed. Not just by love, but by a spiritual awakening that deepened with each passing day.

Now fashioned into a small lapel pin, the silver feather caught the light as Daniel secured it to his jacket. It was a constant reminder of his encounter with Liam, the mysterious man in the park, and the divine intervention that pulled him back from his spiritual exile just in time for him to be there when Samantha needed him most.

Daniel's phone vibrated with a text from his sister: *Are you on your way? Everyone's starting to arrive!*

He typed a quick response before pocketing his phone. The ring box received one final check. Inside nestled the platinum band with its unique design of a small feather motif holding the diamond, crafted by a jeweler who listened patiently to the story behind the symbol.

As Daniel drove through the quiet streets of Brookside, Christmas lights twinkled from houses and storefronts alike. The radio played carols, and he hummed along, his heart full of contentment. This past year had been one of rebuilding, with Samantha's physical recovery from the fire, her relocation to a new apartment only fifteen minutes from his home, and their shared spiritual journey.

He remembered with particular clarity the Sunday three months ago when Samantha officially transferred her membership to New Hope Baptist Church. Pastor Wilson, from Cottonwood Faith Community Center, attended the service, giving his blessing as she took this step. He had said: *"Sometimes God moves us to new spiritual homes. Not because we're leaving something behind, but because He's guiding us toward the direction where we need to grow next."*

That day, standing beside Samantha as she was welcomed into his church family, Daniel knew with absolute certainty that she was the one God had chosen for him. The ring had been ordered the very next day.

The Stewarts' home came into view, its windows aglow with warm light. Olivia's parents decorated extensively for the holiday, with twinkling lights outlining the roof and windows and a grand wreath adorning the front door. Daniel parked behind several familiar cars, including Samantha's silver sedan.

Taking a deep breath, he offered a prayer that had become familiar over the past year. "Lord, thank You for Your perfect timing. Please, guide my words tonight."

The weight of the ring box against his chest reminded him of the journey ahead and the commitment he was about to make. It was a commitment not only to Samantha, but to a life of renewed faith.

Samantha carefully arranged the platter of Christmas cookies she had baked that morning, ensuring the stars and angels were displayed to their best advantage. The Stewart home buzzed with cheerful activity. Christmas music played from the speakers, mingling with conversation and laughter. The scent of pine from the fresh-cut tree blended with cinnamon and cloves from Mrs. Stewart's signature apple cider that was simmering on the stove.

"Those look almost too pretty to eat." Mrs. Stewart appeared at Samantha's side with a fresh bowl of punch. Her silver-streaked hair was styled elegantly, and her red sweater was festive with holiday embroidery.

"Almost," Samantha agreed with a smile. "But I won't be offended when they disappear."

"You've outdone yourself this year, dear," Mrs. Stewart said, her eyes warm with maternal affection. "I know I say this often, but your parents would be so proud of the woman you've become."

The comment deeply touched Samantha. Though it had been years since she had lost her parents, moments like these, especially during the holidays, still carried a bittersweet edge. The Stewarts filled that void as best they could, welcoming her into their family through their daughter Olivia's friendship.

"Thank you," Samantha replied softly. "That means more than you know."

Mrs. Stewart squeezed her hand before bustling off to greet newly arrived guests.

Samantha surveyed the living room, taking in the gathered friends and family. Near the fireplace, Olivia was engaged in a spirited conversation with Noah and Miranda. Along with several other church members, Jessica and Hanna arrived, their supportive friendship being instrumental in Samantha's recovery. Even Willow from Heavenly Delights had come, bearing a spectacular Christmas cake that had everyone sneaking admiring glances.

A year ago, Samantha could never have imagined this scene. She had been coming to terms with Daniel's spiritual estrangement, unsure whether their relationship could overcome such a fundamental gap. Now, she observed as these individuals from various corners of their lives mingled effortlessly, united by their shared faith and genuine care for one another.

The past year had been both challenging and beautiful. Her recovery from smoke inhalation had been slower than she had hoped, with lingering effects that took months to fully resolve. Weeks after she had left the hospital, she still felt winded from doing simple tasks like climbing stairs, her lungs protesting the exertion. Losing her apartment and possessions forced her to start over in many ways. But through it all, Daniel had been her constant, his renewed faith growing alongside her recovery.

She touched the silver feather necklace at her throat, a gift from Daniel after the fire, and she recalled how they had weathered each challenge together. Their Sunday mornings at New Hope Baptist had become the cornerstone of their week, with Bible study on Wednesday evenings and regular prayer flowing steadily through their relationship.

The doorbell chimed, and Samantha's heart quickened, knowing who it must be. She smoothed her emerald-green dress and adjusted the delicate gold bracelet Daniel had given her for her birthday two months ago. The dress had been carefully chosen. Its color was reminiscent of the Christmas season, but also a subtle nod to Daniel's comment weeks ago that green brought out the golden flecks in her eyes.

From across the room, Olivia caught her eye and smiled knowingly. There had been whispers and meaningful glances among their friends lately, but Samantha tried not to let her hopes run away with her. Christmas was special enough without having any specific expectations or demands.

When Daniel appeared in the doorway, his gaze immediately found hers across the crowded room. The look in his eyes, a mixture of love, certainty, and a touch of hallowed awe, made her breath catch. He strode purposefully towards her, exchanging brief greetings with those he encountered.

"You look beautiful," he said when he reached her, taking her hands.

"You're not so bad yourself." She noted how handsome he looked in his charcoal suit and crimson tie. The silver feather pin on his lapel matched her necklace. Their shared symbol was a reminder of divine intervention when they needed it most.

"Merry Christmas, Sam," Daniel said, his voice tender as he leaned in to kiss her cheek.

"Merry Christmas," she whispered back, sensing that this night might indeed hold something special beyond the usual holiday celebration.

Chapter 25

As the evening progressed, Daniel found himself growing increasingly anxious. The weight of the ring box seemed to grow heavier with each passing hour. He had planned to wait until after dinner, but now the timing felt wrong. He wanted this moment to be intimate, but also shared with those they loved.

While Samantha was in conversation with Willow and Olivia about baking techniques, Daniel slipped outside onto the Stewarts' back porch. The night was crisp but not bitter, and the stars were visible between scattered clouds. Christmas lights twinkled along the fence line, casting a magical glow across the backyard.

He leaned against the railing, closing his eyes as the cool air cleared his thoughts. Though the evening was going perfectly, a shadow of doubt unexpectedly crept in. It was not about his love for Samantha, which remained his surest truth. Rather, it was the old familiar question that plagued him during his estrangement from God. Was he worthy of such a blessing after turning his back on faith for so long?

The memory of his anger toward God resurfaced. He pondered those dark days when his grief had hardened into bitterness and when prayers felt like speaking into an empty void. He had rejected everything he once believed, convinced that God had abandoned him first.

"Lord," Daniel whispered into the night air. "Am I ready for this commitment? Have I truly returned to You fully enough to lead a godly home?"

The porch door opened behind him, and he turned to find Miranda stepping out, concern evident in her expression.

"Is everything all right?" she asked, joining him at the railing.

"I needed to get some fresh air." Daniel offered a strained smile.

Miranda studied him. "Are you having cold feet?"

"No... not exactly." He sighed, turning the lapel pin between his fingers. "It's more like I'm wondering if I've come far enough in my faith journey to be the spiritual leader that Sam deserves."

His sister's expression softened. "Daniel, do you remember what Pastor Morrison said at the men's retreat last month? *'Faith isn't measured by how far you've come, but by the direction you're heading.'*"

Daniel nodded. "Yes, I know. But sometimes I wonder if the years I spent angry at God have somehow left some sort of mark on me. Sometimes, I think that my old weakness might resurface in me when life gets hard again."

Miranda's voice was soft. "That's not faith talking. That's fear. And fear's not from God." She placed her hand over his. "The Daniel I've seen this past year isn't the same man who turned away from church after his spiritual crisis. You're stronger now precisely *because* you know what it's like to walk away and come back. That's a testimony, not a liability."

Her words pierced through the cloud of doubt that had briefly engulfed him. She was right. His journey away from faith and then back to it hadn't weakened his spiritual foundation. His journey had evolved from a testable theory into a lived reality.

"But what if I somehow fail her, Mandy?" he asked, voicing his deepest fear. "What if someday, when we face challenges, I'm not strong enough to be the spiritual rock she needs?"

"Then you'll lean on her strength in those moments," Miranda replied. "That's what marriage is. It's a covenant where you carry each other through the different seasons. Sometimes, you'll be the strong one, and sometimes she will. But, with God at the center, you'll be stronger together than either of you can ever be alone."

Daniel let her wisdom sink in, releasing the tension in his shoulders. "When did my little sister get so wise?"

"I've always been wise," Miranda quipped. "You were just too distracted to notice."

They shared a laugh that dispelled the last of his doubts.

"Thanks, Mandy. I needed to hear that." His smile was heartfelt.

"That's what sisters are for." She nudged his arm playfully. "Now, are you going to stand out here all night, or are you going to go back in there and propose to the woman you love?"

Daniel laughed, feeling the tension dissolve. "I'm going. But first... " He closed his eyes briefly, bowing his head.

Miranda stepped back, giving him space as she recognized the posture of prayer. This, too, had become natural again over the past year. Daniel had taken to the habit of speaking to God throughout his day, and not just in formal moments of worship or crisis.

"Father," Daniel prayed quietly. "Thank You for Your patience with me, for never giving up on me even when I walked away. Thank You for bringing Samantha into my life and for using her to help guide me back to You. I ask that you please bless our future and help me to be the man of faith she deserves. Amen."

Opening his eyes, Daniel found peace settling over him like a mantle. This was right. This was God's plan unfolding.

"Let's go back inside," he said to Miranda, his determination renewed. "I have an important question to ask."

The living room glowed warmly as Mr. Stewart led them in Christmas carols. Samantha sang along, her alto blending with the other voices as they filled the room with *Hark the Herald Angels Sing.* Her eyes continuously drifted to Daniel, who had returned from outside with fresh purpose in his stride and a newfound serenity in his expression.

Daniel caught her gaze again as the carol ended, and he moved toward her. The conversation in the room seemed to dim naturally, as if everyone sensed that a significant moment was approaching.

"Sam," Daniel said, taking her hand. "Would you join me for a moment?"

Curious, she allowed him to lead her toward the Christmas tree, which stood majestically in the corner, adorned with ornaments collected over decades of Stewart family Christmases. The lights twinkled, casting a kaleidoscope of colors across Daniel's face as he turned to face her.

Behind them, Samantha noticed a subtle shift. Guests rearranged themselves to witness what was about to happen. Olivia's camera discreetly appeared, and Mrs. Stewart pressed her hand to her heart.

"A year ago," Daniel began, his voice steady despite the emotion Samantha could see in his eyes, "I came to a Christmas service with you, fighting my own doubts and anger toward God. I was lost, Sam. Lost in ways I didn't even fully understand."

Samantha squeezed his hand encouragingly, her heart racing as she recognized the gravity in his tone.

"But God wasn't finished with me. Through a mysterious stranger in a park, through your unwavering faith, and through the near tragedy of the fire... He guided me back to Himself. And He led me straight to you."

Daniel reached into his pocket, and Samantha's breath caught as he withdrew a small velvet box.

"From the moment you saved me from the salmon salad dilemma in that grocery store, I knew God had a plan," he said with a smile that crinkled the corners of his eyes. "Every *'chance'* meeting, every conversation, every shared moment was part of His perfect plan."

He slowly lowered to one knee, and Samantha felt tears welling in her eyes. Around them, soft gasps and murmurs confirmed that this moment was indeed real, and not a dream spun from her deepest hopes.

Daniel opened a box to reveal a stunning ring. The platinum band held a diamond that caught the Christmas lights in prismatic splendor, and a small silver feather was worked into the setting. It was a perfect match to her necklace and his pin. "Samantha Marie Kelly. You've been God's instrument of healing in my life. Through you, I found my way back to faith. Will you continue this journey with me? Will you walk beside me in faith, sharing in ministry, and building a life centered on Christ?"

His voice grew husky with emotion as he completed his proposal. "Samantha, will you do me the extraordinary honor of becoming my wife?"

The room seemed to hold its collective breath as Samantha absorbed his words. Tears spilled onto her cheeks as years of prayers—for a godly husband, for a man who would share her faith journey, for love built on the solid foundation of shared beliefs—culminated in this perfect moment.

"Yes," she whispered, emotion making her voice tremble. Then, stronger. "Yes, Daniel, I will marry you!"

Joy erupted around them as Daniel rose to his feet, sliding the ring onto her finger. The perfect fit felt like another divine confirmation, as if even this detail had been orchestrated by heavenly design.

As he drew her into his arms, the room exploded with applause and cheers. Samantha was vaguely aware of Olivia's camera capturing the moment, Mrs. Stewart dabbing at her eyes, and Miranda and Noah embracing in shared joy.

But her focus remained on Daniel. She focused on the man who had journeyed from spiritual exile back to faith, who had stood by her through recovery and rebuilding, and who now promised to walk beside her for all their days to come.

"I love you," she murmured, her fingers curling into his lapels.

"And I love how God's fingerprints are all over our story," Daniel replied, his smile radiating a gentle warmth.

Their kiss was gentle yet profound, carrying promises that extended beyond the moment. Around them were their chosen family. They were all bound by love rather than blood, celebrating not just their engagement, but the miraculous journey that had brought them to this threshold.

Samantha stood on the Stewarts' back porch with Daniel's warm jacket around her shoulders as the celebration continued inside. The night had grown colder, but she barely noticed, too enraptured by the diamond glinting on her finger, a physical symbol of the commitment they had just made.

The ring felt at once foreign and utterly right on her hand. She twisted it, watching as the Christmas lights reflected in its facets. The small silver feather etched into the setting caught the light in an almost supernatural way, reminiscent of the mysterious feather that had changed everything for them.

"God, thank You." The whispered prayer rose unbidden from her heart. "Thank You for answering the prayers I've had since I was a girl, for bringing Daniel back to faith, and for healing the both of us through each other."

The past year had been a journey she could never have predicted. The fire that nearly took her life had become the catalyst for profound blessings. Her physical recovery had been difficult. There were months of breathing treatments, days when simple tasks left her exhausted, and the slow process of rebuilding her life from the ashes of her apartment. But through it all, Daniel had been steadfast, his renewed faith growing alongside her healing body.

The door opened behind her, and she turned to see Daniel stepping out to join her, two mugs of hot chocolate in his hands.

"I wondered where you had disappeared to." He offered her one of the steaming mugs. "Everyone's asking for the bride-to-be."

Bride-to-be. The words sent a thrill through her. "I just needed a moment to take it all in." She accepted the mug gratefully. The warmth seeped through her fingers as she cradled it. "To be honest, I'm a little overwhelmed, but in the best possible way."

Daniel settled beside her at the railing, their shoulders touching in comfortable closeness. "Are you happy?" he asked, his eyes seeking hers in the soft glow of the Christmas lights.

"I'm happy beyond words." Samantha leaned into his warmth. "The ring, the proposal. It's all perfect, Daniel. It's more than I ever dreamed."

She studied his face, memorizing every detail of this moment. She gazed upon the tenderness in his eyes, the relaxed set of his shoulders, and the confidence that had replaced the spiritual uncertainty that once shadowed him.

"Did you know this was coming tonight?" he asked, his expression curious.

Samantha laughed softly, the sound mingling with the distant music from inside. "I had my suspicions. Olivia has been practically bursting with secrets for weeks, and your sister couldn't look me in the eye without breaking into mysterious smiles." She touched his face gently. "But the timing with it being Christmas Eve and one year after the Cantata... that was a beautiful surprise."

"I wanted to honor where our journey truly began," Daniel explained. "That night changed everything for me. It was the first time I allowed myself to consider that maybe God was still there, still waiting for me to turn back."

Samantha nodded, understanding the significance. "I remember watching you that night, seeing something shift in your expression during *O Holy Night*. I prayed so hard that the music would reach places in your heart that my words couldn't."

"Your prayers were answered," Daniel assured her, covering her hand with his. "More than you know."

A comfortable silence fell between them, filled only with the distant sounds of celebration from inside and the soft carols still playing. Above them, stars pierced the darkness, reminding Samantha of another holy night long ago when heaven touched earth through the birth of a Savior.

"What are you thinking about now?" Daniel asked, watching her face with loving attention.

"Spring," Samantha replied, surprising herself with the answer. "A spring wedding would be beautiful. March, perhaps, when everything is blooming and new."

Daniel nodded in agreement, his smile broadening. "New beginnings in the season of renewal. That sounds perfect."

Samantha leaned her head against his shoulder, contentment filling every corner of her being. "I keep thinking about all the prayers my mother used to pray for me. She always asked God to send me a man of faith who would love the Lord first, and me second." Her fingers toyed with the silver feather at her throat. "For a while, I thought perhaps He hadn't heard that prayer."

Daniel gave her a reassuring smile. "He heard. His timing was just different from what we expected. God had to bring me the long way around, through doubt and back to faith."

Samantha closed her eyes for a moment, marveling at the reality of the ring on her finger. "And now, here we are."

Inside, someone began to play *Silent Night* on the piano. The melody drifted to them, the gentle notes carrying all the reverence of the holy night they celebrated. Samantha let the music wash over her, feeling Daniel's steady presence beside her.

"I used to wonder why God allowed me to lose so much," she confessed quietly. "My parents, my home in the fire... but now I see how each loss prepared me to recognize the true blessings when they came." She turned to face Daniel fully. "You're my greatest blessing, Daniel. Not just because I love you, but because watching God restore your faith has strengthened mine in ways nothing else could have."

Daniel's eyes glistened with emotion as he set down his mug to take both her hands in his. "You've been my light, Sam. When I was lost in the darkness, you kept shining and not demanding that I find my way. You helped to illuminate my path back to faith through your own."

Samantha felt tears gathering again, the joy of this moment almost too much to contain. "We should go back inside," she said, though she was reluctant to break the spell of their private celebration. "Everyone will be wondering where we've gone."

"Let them wonder," Daniel murmured, drawing her closer. "Just one more minute here, with just us and God."

As he leaned down to kiss her, Samantha rose on tiptoes to meet him, her heart so full it seemed it might overflow. His lips were warm against hers, the kiss tender yet infused with an unspoken promise of deeper passion waiting to unfold. She melted into him, feeling the perfect rightness of their union. They were two spirits perfectly aligned, not just with each other, but with divine purpose.

When they finally parted, Samantha kept her eyes closed, savoring the lingering warmth of his kiss and the intoxicating rush of emotions flooding her system.

"Mrs. Samantha Forrester," she whispered, testing the name on her lips for the first time. "I think I like the sound of that."

Daniel's smile was radiant in the Christmas lights. "I think I *love* the sound of that."

Hand in hand, they returned to the celebration inside, where their friends and family awaited to share in their joy. As they stepped through the doorway, Samantha knew with absolute certainty that this was exactly where God had been leading her all along. To this man, this moment, and this promise of a future built on the unshakable foundation of faith restored.

Epilogue

Four Months Later

Daniel's fingers traced the engraved surface of the Teacher of the Year plaque, its metal cool against his skin despite the late April sunshine streaming through the Greater Pines High School auditorium windows.

The irony of the moment wasn't lost on him. He had been adrift for two years—angry, disillusioned, and disconnected from his faith. Now, here he stood, surrounded by his students' eager, expectant faces, with his wife's radiant smile beckoning from the front row. The Lord's timing was nothing short of miraculous.

Samantha. His gaze found her instinctively. The sun seemed to conspire to make her even more beautiful, highlighting her copper skin and the playful curls cascading around her shoulders. He had given her delicate pearl earrings in Nassau. They shimmered softly, but the quiet pride in her eyes held a far greater allure. She wore that same expression when she walked down the aisle at New Hope Baptist weeks ago, though it had been mixed with joyful weeping.

The Teacher of the Year ceremony faded as his mind traveled back to their wedding day. Every detail remained vivid. He remembered how the church's stained-glass windows cast patterns across the sanctuary and how his hands shook as he recited the vows he had written. He also recalled the moment Pastor Morrison had pronounced them husband and wife. That sacred declaration sealed what God had clearly orchestrated from their very first meeting in the grocery store.

Their wedding had exceeded every dream, transforming the church into a sanctuary of joy and celebration. The Stewarts, Samantha's adoptive parents, had beamed from the front row as if she were their own flesh and blood. Olivia had dabbed at her tears with an embroidered handkerchief as she stood beside her best friend. His family had traveled from Bristol Heights, their presence a balm to wounds he hadn't realized still ached.

The Lakeside Hospital's nursing team and Dr. Brandon Lawson had joined his teaching colleagues in celebrating their union. The sight of them all together filled him with gratitude for the community that witnessed his descent into grief-stricken isolation and his gradual return to life and faith. Willow and Anna from Heavenly Delights insisted on contributing an elaborate bridal cake, its delicate sugar flowers a perfect reflection of the love that had blossomed between him and Samantha.

Memories of their Caribbean honeymoon flooded his mind. Not only the picture-perfect moments of snorkeling in crystal-clear waters or exploring the vibrant markets, but the tranquil, intimate ones that had knit their souls together.

Sunsets painted in palettes of orange and purple were enjoyed from their private balcony. Their laughter filled the tiny kitchen in St. Lucia as they attempted to make jerk chicken, and the aroma of coconut rice mingled with their bliss. The lighthouse canvas they discovered in St. Thomas now watched over their living room, a constant reminder of God's guiding light.

Back in the present moment, Daniel began his acceptance speech for his award. "First, I want to thank God." His voice was calm despite the emotion tightening his throat. The words carried a weight they hadn't held before, back when grief had hardened his heart against the notion of faith. "The Lord has guided me through some dark times, and revealed that His hope never fails."

"And I want to thank my amazing wife, Samantha." Their eyes met across the crowded auditorium. "She shows me daily what walking in faith and love truly means."

He watched her smile widen at his public acknowledgment, her hand resting over her heart. Their communion went beyond words. They had developed a language of glances and small movements that communicated more than lengthy conversations ever could. He had never expected to receive this gift again. He now had the gift of a bone-deep knowledge that goes along with sharing another person's heart.

"And to my family, who never stopped believing in me, regardless of my struggles. Your prayers and support mean more than words can express." His voice grew husky with emotion. "Mom, Dad, my brothers and sisters... your faith has been a light guiding me home, and I truly thank you all for that."

Daniel turned to his students, these young souls who had unknowingly been a part of God's plan to restore him. In the darkest days after Teresa's death, his classroom had been the one place where purpose still found him. His students' eager minds and genuine questions had anchored him to the present when grief threatened to drag him permanently into the past.

"And to each of you sitting here. You inspire me daily. Your hunger for knowledge, your determination to grow, and your beautiful spirit make every morning a gift. This award belongs to all of you who challenge me to be better."

Applause rippled through the auditorium. Coach Michaels flashed a proud thumbs-up, and Daniel spotted several seniors brushing away tears. He couldn't believe how far God had brought him from that bitter, closed-off man who had estranged himself from everyone who cared for him. Each face in the crowd represented another thread in the tapestry woven to bring him back to trust and purpose.

Samantha went to him after the ceremony. Weeks after their wedding, her sweet smile still made his heart race. She reached up to straighten his tie. It was a ritual of intimacy deeper than language. Her perfume's jasmine and vanilla scent encapsulated him, as familiar now as a prayer.

"I'm so proud of you for being awarded Teacher of the Year," she said, her voice filled with quiet pride. "Though I can't say that I'm surprised. The way you connect with those students is something really special."

Daniel felt warmth spread through his chest at her words. "Having you in the audience made it real," he admitted. "It feels good knowing I have someone to share it with."

"You have a whole roomful of someones." She gestured to where his colleagues still mingled with students and parents. "Look around and see how many lives you've touched, Daniel."

He followed her gaze, seeing the gathering through new eyes. He saw the football players whose lives extended beyond the field because of his mentorship, the shy students who found their voice in his literature discussions, and the faculty who welcomed him back after his season of grief with open arms.

"I never thought I'd be here again," he confessed quietly, only for her ears. "I never thought I would be able to find joy in teaching, in coaching, or in anything."

Samantha slipped her hand into his, their wedding bands touching. "God restores what was broken. And sometimes, He builds something even more beautiful from the pieces."

The truth of her words resonated deep within. These past four weeks of marriage had proven that daily. Their morning devotions, the way they prayed through decisions together, and the natural rhythm they found in serving their church community all testified to restoration beyond what he could have imagined.

Stanley approached, clapping a hand on Daniel's shoulder. "You deserve this, brother," he said, his voice gruff with emotion. "You're not just inspiring lives on the football field. You're motivating minds in the classroom, too." The words carried extra meaning from the man who had stood by him during his darkest days and never stopped praying for his return to faith.

Daniel felt a surge of gratitude for Stanley's steadfast friendship. Even when Daniel had rejected all expressions of faith, Stanley continued to show him God's love through his patient, nonjudgmental presence. He made a mental note to invite Stanley over for dinner soon. Their home had become a gathering place for friends and family, a reality Daniel would have deemed impossible during his years of isolation.

A cluster of nurses from Lakeside Hospital surrounded Samantha. Their excited chatter about an upcoming project Samantha was spearheading filled the air with infectious energy. Dr. Lawson remained at the edge of the group, his proud smile acknowledging how far they had all come. These individuals were more than colleagues. They were witnesses to God's provision in both of their lives.

Daniel watched his wife interact with her coworkers, struck by how her faith naturally infused everything she did. When she talked about her patients, it wasn't just about medical interventions but about providing comfort and dignity to those created in God's image. Her example continually challenged him to integrate his faith more fully into his teaching and coaching.

The spring breeze carried the sweet scent of honeysuckle across the parking lot as Daniel helped Samantha into the car. Before sliding into the driver's seat, he paused, gazing at the expansive blue sky. The sun glinted on his platinum band, and he swelled again with gratitude. Each gleam of light reminded him of promises fulfilled. Promises that appeared in the big moments and the quiet daily miracles of restored faith and renewed purpose.

"What are you thinking about?" Samantha asked, her smile holding that same warmth that had first drawn him from his isolation.

Daniel ran his thumb across his wedding band, a gesture that developed into his own form of prayer. "I'm thanking the Lord for His perfect timing. And for bringing you into my life when He did."

Samantha reached for his hand, their rings touching, physical reminders of spiritual truth. "He's not finished with us yet," she declared, her voice rich with anticipation. "This is just the beginning of our story."

Peace washed over Daniel. This was what it meant to live in hope. It wasn't only about pursuing hope, but embodying it daily with purpose and conviction. Samantha at his side, and their faith in Jesus Christ at their core, he felt they could conquer any challenge, their love flourishing through every season.

Their home flashed through Daniel's mind. It wasn't merely the physical space, but a sanctuary they built together. Scripture artwork speaking of promises adorned the walls alongside cherished photos marking their journey. The lighthouse painting above their fireplace reminded them of the Lord's guidance. But mostly, peace filled every corner since Samantha had brought her joy into his life.

Each morning, while he brewed coffee, Samantha would light a single candle, its flame representing divine presence. They would gather at the kitchen table with her mother's well-worn Bible, taking turns leading devotionals. This morning's reading from Ecclesiastes 4:9-10 still played on his mind: *Two are better than one, because they have a good return for their labor. If either of them falls, one can help the other up.*

Those words had become the foundation of their marriage, not just poetic sentiments but a truth lived daily. Each morning, they shared one gratitude or prayer request, hands clasped in a trust that grew stronger with each passing day. The simple act aligned them toward a purpose larger than themselves.

As they drove home under a sky painted with sunset colors, Daniel felt complete in a way he never thought possible after losing Teresa. But God's restoration exceeded his imagination, bringing him healing and abundant joy.

Their marriage stood as a testament to faithfulness. It was a living embodiment of the Almighty's power to restore and renew. Daniel understood with absolute certainty that he was exactly where God always intended him to be. He was surrounded by love, anchored in faith, and looking forward to the beautiful chapters yet to unfold in their story together.

THE END

I hope you enjoyed Renewing His Hope.
Please consider leaving your review.
Be sure to continue for an EXCERPT from my next book in the
Wings of Faith Series,
Soaring In Faith.

Excerpt from Soaring in Faith

Aaron Grant gripped the steering wheel of his white pick-up truck, knuckles tight as he pulled into a parking space at Greater Pines High School. The August sun beat down mercilessly through the windshield, forcing him to squint despite his dark sunglasses. The air conditioning labored against the Georgia heat, barely taking the edge off the suffocating warmth that had followed them from Bristol Heights.

He cut the engine and took a moment to collect himself. Drawing a long breath, he sent up a half-formed prayer, the kind he had grown reluctant to offer since his mother's diagnosis.

Lord, give me strength for this. The silence that followed felt as vast as the parking lot stretching before them.

"We're here, Naomi."

No response. His fourteen-year-old niece sat beside him, head-phones covering her ears, eyes locked on something in the middle distance. Her face, so much like his mother's, gave nothing away. Same cheekbones, same stubborn chin. Aaron tapped her shoulder, swallowing the frustration that seemed to live in his chest these days.

"Hey? It's time to head in."

She pulled the headphones down around her neck with obvious reluctance, eyes never meeting his. "Whatever."

Aaron bit back his first response. These past three months had tested every boundary he thought he had. Three months since the funeral. Three months since guardianship papers transformed him from a sporadic uncle who showed up on holidays into the man responsible for raising a teenager drowning in grief. Three months navigating a wilderness neither of them had chosen to enter.

"Principal Watkins is waiting for us." Aaron checked his watch. "We've got about thirty minutes before registration closes."

Naomi grabbed her backpack, climbed out of the truck, and slammed the door harder than necessary. The sharp sound made Aaron flinch. He let it go. Dr. Harrison had warned him about moments like this.

Pick your battles, Mr. Grant. Kids in grief fight for control wherever they can find it.

The school building loomed before them, red brick and glass gleaming in the late summer light. Students and parents streamed through the entrance, voices echoing across the parking lot in a chorus of greetings, laughter, and animated conversations. Aaron reached out to touch her shoulder, but she pulled away before contact.

"I can walk by myself," she mumbled, striding ahead.

Aaron followed, his work boots thudding on the pavement. Construction had been his life for nearly twenty years. He understood overseeing crews, interpreting blueprints, and calculating load-bearing requirements. The predictable nature of properly poured foundations and accurately measured beams were certainties he could grasp. But this? Two decades of building structures hadn't equipped him for the delicate work of rebuilding a traumatized teenage heart.

And nothing had prepared him for the silence that followed his prayers, either. Not after what happened with his mother. Not when every plea had gone unanswered.

Inside, the main office buzzed with back-to-school energy. A woman behind the front desk looked up, her silver-rimmed glasses resting low on her nose. Her voice carried the warmth of someone who had lived her whole life in Georgia.

"Can I help you?"

"Aaron Grant. We have an appointment with Principal Watkins." His words emerged clipped and efficient, the same tone he used with new subcontractors to establish authority and minimize small talk.

"Yes, Mr. Grant. I'm Mrs. Richardson. We've been expecting you and Naomi." She turned toward his niece with a warm smile. "Welcome to Greater Pines, sweetheart. We're glad to have you."

Naomi offered a barely perceptible nod but said nothing.

"Mr. Watkins will be right with you." Mrs. Richardson directed them to chairs near the principal's office. "Can I get either of you something cold to drink? It's blazing hot out there today."

"We're fine, thanks." Aaron settled into a chair that protested beneath his six-foot-three frame.

Naomi took out her phone and started scrolling through social media feeds. Aaron studied her profile, noting the shadows under her eyes that revealed sleepless nights. With the weight of guardianship, he found himself hyperaware of everything about her. He monitored her eating habits, sleep patterns, and how she withdrew further into herself each week.

"Are you nervous?" Aaron asked, attempting conversation.

She didn't look up. "About what?"

"New school, new town. It's a lot of change."

"It wasn't like I had a choice." Her voice remained flat, devoid of inflection.

Aaron stifled a sigh. Every conversation felt like navigating a minefield. One wrong step, and she would withdraw even deeper into the shell she had built around herself.

"I know this isn't perfect." He lowered his voice. "For either of us. But we'll find a way to make it work, Naomi."

She glanced up, skepticism written across her features. "How exactly? You work all day. I'll be at school. Then what? We just hang out in the same apartment and pretend we're a family?"

Her words stung. Before Aaron could formulate a response that didn't sound like an empty platitude, the office door opened and a tall man with warm brown skin and a neatly trimmed beard stepped out, hand extended.

"Mr. Grant? I'm Jeremy Watkins. Welcome to Greater Pines High."

Aaron stood, accepting the handshake with the firm grip his father had taught him was the mark of a man worth his word. "Thanks for meeting with us on such short notice."

"Not at all." Principal Watkins smiled at Naomi, his expression warm and welcoming rather than the usual condescension adults often showed teens. "And you must be Naomi. We're pleased to have you in our ninth-grade class."

Naomi offered another slight nod but nothing more.

"Please, come into my office. We have your transfer records, but I'd like to go over your class options before we finalize your schedule."

Aaron guided Naomi forward with a light touch between her shoulder blades, following Principal Watkins through the doorway. A blur of motion caught Aaron's attention as someone rushed past with arms full of papers.

The collision happened too suddenly to avoid. Aaron pivoted and struck another person with considerable force. Papers erupted into the air, falling like rectangular snowflakes. A surprised gasp echoed amid the chaos.

"Oh my goodness! I'm so sorry!" A rich, melodic voice spoke from somewhere beneath the shower of falling lesson plans.

Aaron crouched automatically, gathering scattered sheets. "That was on me. I wasn't watching where—"

The words died in his throat as he looked up.

The woman knelt across from him, hands moving quickly to collect the papers. Her dark, naturally curly hair was pinned in a loose bun, a few tendrils slipping free at the sides. Almond-shaped, dark brown eyes met his with a mixture of embarrassment and amusement. Her warm brown skin glowed with health. Aaron noticed her full lips curve into a polite smile, revealing dimples that transformed her entire face.

"You must be Mr. Grant. I'm Ms. Townsend. Meghan Townsend. I teach ninth-grade history." She gathered the last few sheets, straightening gracefully.

Aaron rose, nearly bumping heads with her as they both stood. Her presence filled the space around them. It wasn't her size, but an indefinable quality that capture his attention. She was about five feet seven, with a slender yet curvaceous figure, dressed in a deep blue wrap dress that complemented her warm complexion.

"Aaron Grant," he replied, extending his hand. "I'm registering my niece, Naomi."

When Meghan's hand met his, Aaron noted the contrast. His palm was rough and calloused from years of construction work, while hers was smooth but strong. The brief contact sent an unexpected current up his arm.

"I heard we'd have a new student today." Meghan turned toward Naomi with genuine interest. "I'm looking forward to having you in class."

For the first time since entering the building, Naomi looked directly at an adult. "Thank you."

"Ms. Townsend also coordinates our culinary arts program," Principal Watkins interjected, rejoining the conversation. "It's quite popular with our students."

"Cooking?" Naomi's voice carried the first hint of curiosity Aaron had heard all morning.

Meghan's smile widened. "We explore cultural history through food traditions. Last month we studied the Great Depression by making recipes families used in order to stretch ingredients. Next week, we're starting a unit on immigration patterns through Ellis Island, featuring dishes from different countries."

Aaron watched his niece's posture shift, the rigid defensive stance softening by degrees. This woman had accomplished more in thirty seconds than he had managed in three months.

"That sounds..." Naomi paused, as if afraid to show too much interest. "Different."

"I hope you'll consider joining us. We meet on Thursdays after school." Meghan's tone remained warm but not pushy. "And family members are always welcome to participate."

Aaron felt her gaze settle on him briefly, and something in her expression suggested the invitation wasn't merely polite protocol.

"We should probably finish up with registration," Principal Watkins said gently. "Ms. Townsend, thanks for helping with the paperwork rescue."

"My pleasure." She gathered her remaining papers, then looked back at Naomi. "I'll be seeing you. I'm in room 112."

As she walked away, Aaron found himself watching until she disappeared around the corner. When he turned back, he caught

Principal Watkins regarding him with barely concealed amusement.

"Ms. Townsend is one of our finest teachers," the principal said as they entered his office. "She's very dedicated to her students."

The next thirty minutes passed in a blur of forms, schedules, and policy explanations. Aaron signed documents while keeping one eye on Naomi, who had retreated back into silence. When they finally left the office, she walked ahead of him again, schedule clutched in her hand.

"That wasn't so bad," Aaron ventured as they headed toward the parking lot.

"I guess." She paused beside a bulletin board covered with college brochures and club announcements. "Uncle Aaron?"

The sound of his name in her voice—tentative, almost vulnerable—stopped him short. She hadn't called him anything but *"Aaron"* since the funeral.

"Yeah?"

"Do you think..." She looked down at her schedule again. "Do you think Grandma would have liked this place?"

The question hit him. His mother had agonized over every educational decision, researching programs and visiting schools even when money was tight. She had wanted the best for Naomi, always.

Aaron answered carefully. "I think, your grandma would have loved seeing you in that cooking program. She always said you had her gift for making people feel at home with good food."

Naomi's eyes filled, but she blinked quickly. "I miss her cooking."

"Me too, kiddo. Me too."

They stood there for a moment, surrounded by the noise and bustle of other families navigating their own first days. Then Naomi straightened her shoulders, a gesture so reminiscent of his mother that Aaron's chest tightened.

"We should probably go," she said. "You have that meeting with Mr. Donovan at four."

Aaron checked his watch, surprised she had remembered his schedule. "Right. Let's head home."

As they walked toward the truck, Naomi fell into step beside him instead of racing ahead. It was a small change, barely noticeable, but Aaron felt it like sunlight breaking through clouds.

In the truck, she buckled her seatbelt and pulled out her phone. But instead of immediately putting her headphones back on, she turned toward him.

"The cooking teacher," she said. "Ms. Townsend. She seemed nice."

Aaron started the engine, considering his response. "She did. And that program sounds like something you might enjoy."

"Maybe." Naomi was quiet for a moment, then added, "She looked at you funny."

Heat crept up Aaron's neck. "What do you mean?"

"I don't know. Just... different. Like she was really seeing you, not just being polite because you're a parent."

Out of the mouths of babes. Aaron pulled out of the parking space, uncertain how to respond to his niece's unexpected perceptiveness.

"Sometimes adults connect over shared concerns," he said finally. "We both want what's best for you."

"Mmm-hmm." Naomi's tone suggested she wasn't entirely convinced by his explanation, but she didn't press further.

As they drove toward home through the afternoon heat, Aaron's thoughts drifted back to those few moments in the hallway. Meghan Townsend had looked at him with genuine interest, not pity or obligation. For just an instant, he had felt like more than an overwhelmed guardian struggling to keep his head above water.

The light turned green, and they continued toward their new life, carrying between them the fragile hope that this beginning might actually lead somewhere better than where they had been.

Island of Hope
Honeymoon Novella

Want More of Daniel & Samantha's Story?

If you loved watching Daniel and Samantha fall in love, you won't want to miss what happens next!

Island of Hope: A Honeymoon Novella takes you to the sun-soaked shores of St. Lucia, where Daniel and Samantha:

- Establish morning devotionals as the foundation of their marriage

- Navigate humorous mishaps (including a disastrous jerk chicken attempt!)

- Dream about children and their future together

- Encounter strangers who become family in faith

- Discover that God speaks through snorkeling adventures and Caribbean sunsets

This Novella is available exclusively to newsletter subscribers as a FREE welcome gift.

Seven days in paradise. A lifetime of faith restored.

Some journeys lead you to paradise. Others lead you home.

About the Author

Barbara Jane Oliver is a faith and inspirational based author who lives in the beautiful state of Georgia with her loving husband and partner in all non-crimes, Ronald. She has been an avid reader from an early age, often hiding in her parents' closets to finish reading her books. Her love of reading nurtured her creative mind and sparked a passion for writing. She is also a U.S. Army Veteran and has been a registered nurse for over 20 years. Barbara and Ronald have a wonderful, blended family that includes two daughters, three grandsons, and two great-granddaughters.

I hope you enjoyed Renewing His Hope. If so, please visit my website for a list of my current and upcoming publications.

Author Web Page: https://barbarajaneoliver.com/
Instagram: https://www.instagram.com/barbarajaneoliver-author/
TikTok: https://www.tiktok.com/@bjoliver7

CLICK HERE to Free Novella and **SIGNUP** for my Newsletter.

Thank you so very much.
Barbara Jane Oliver

She thought love always left.
Until he chose to stay.

Some things are more beautiful
after they've been restored.

Also By Barbara Jane Oliver

ALTHOUGH THESE NOVELS ARE part of a series featuring inter-connected characters, the main romance centers on a unique story-line with its own arc and resolution. Each book can be enjoyed as a standalone novel, making it a pleasurable independent reading experience.

<u>WINGS OF FAITH SERIES</u>

- Before the Blessing: A Bristol Heights Novella (Colton & Nicole): Download FREE When You Subscribe to My Newsletter

- Renewing His Hope Book 1: Daniel & Samantha: Available Now

- Soaring in Faith Book 2: Aaron & Meghan: Available 23 February 2026

- Running with Grace Book 3: Brandon & Grace: Available 25 May 2026

<u>BRISTOL HEIGHTS SANCTUARY SERIES</u>

- Sanctuary in His Arms Book 1: Joshua & Simone: TBA

- Sanctuary of Truth Book 2: TBA

Visit Author Website For Additional Information

Thank You For Your Support

www.ingramcontent.com/pod-product-compliance
Lightning Source LLC
Chambersburg PA
CBHW070620300726
48975CB00006B/1868